## "WITH BEST WISHES . . ."

A commotion at the front door caused everyone, including me, to stop what we were doing and look in that direction. I saw Kathy come through the door, followed closely by the disheveled man from outside. The look on my friend's face was sheer panic. The man shoved her ahead of him, propelling her into a group of people who'd already had their books signed and were chatting. Then I saw what the man carried besides his canvas bag. It was a lethal-looking hunting knife with a very long blade.

"Sir," I said, "why don't you put down that knife and—"

"Shut up!"

I obeyed.

He slammed the canvas bag down on the table, sending copies of my books flying in all directions. The hand holding the knife began to shake as he reached inside the bag, withdrew a copy of my new book, and slapped it in front of me.

I know it sounds silly, but the only thing I could think of to say at that moment was, "Would you like me to sign that?"

# Panning for Murder

A *Murder, She Wrote* Mystery

## A NOVEL BY
## JESSICA FLETCHER & DONALD BAIN

Based on the Universal television series created by
Peter S. Fischer, Richard Levinson & William Link

AN OBSIDIAN MYSTERY

Obsidian
Published by New American Library, a division of
Penguin Group (USA) Inc., 375 Hudson Street, New York, New York 10014, USA
Penguin Group (Canada), 90 Eglinton Avenue East, Suite 700, Toronto,
Ontario M4P 2Y3, Canada (a division of Pearson Penguin Canada Inc.)
Penguin Books Ltd., 80 Strand, London WC2R 0RL, England
Penguin Ireland, 25 St. Stephen's Green, Dublin 2,
Ireland (a division of Penguin Books Ltd.)
Penguin Group (Australia), 250 Camberwell Road, Camberwell, Victoria 3124,
Australia (a division of Pearson Australia Group Pty. Ltd.)
Penguin Books India Pvt. Ltd., 11 Community Centre, Panchsheel Park,
New Delhi - 110 017, India
Penguin Group (NZ), 67 Apollo Drive, Rosedale, North Shore 0632,
New Zealand (a division of Pearson New Zealand Ltd.)
Penguin Books (South Africa) (Pty.) Ltd., 24 Sturdee Avenue,
Rosebank, Johannesburg 2196, South Africa

Penguin Books Ltd., Registered Offices:
80 Strand, London WC2R 0RL, England

Published by Obsidian, an imprint of New American Library, a division of
Penguin Group (USA) Inc. Previously published in an Obsidian hardcover
edition.

First Obsidian Mass Market Printing, September 2008
10   9   8   7   6   5   4   3

*For Herbert Schaus III*

# Authors' Note

This story is a melding of fact and fiction.

We've given the cruise ship on which much of the action takes place a fictitious name—the *Glacial Queen*. But everything that occurs on it reflects what happens on real ships that ply Alaska's Inner Passage.

The main characters are, of course, figments of our imagination. Any resemblance to living persons is purely coincidental.

However, Thelma Copeland, aka Dolly Arthur, was a very real and colorful person. Dolly was Alaska's most famous brothel keeper—her former "sporting house" in Ketchikan remains a prime tourist attraction to this day. Her boyfriend, "Lefty," was also real, although we've taken some liberties with how their relationship ended. Both are long dead.

All the Alaskan historical material in the book is accurate, as are the descriptions of the various cities and towns visited by the *Glacial Queen*.

Researching the book was a joy, and we urge everyone to make a visit to Alaska part of your future travel plans. It truly is a remarkable place.

Jessica Fletcher
Donald Bain
New York, 2007

# *Prologue*

*Weeks Earlier*

"You must be beside yourself with worry," I said.

"I haven't slept a wink since I received the call from the Alaska state police."

"She's disappeared? I mean, *really* disappeared?"

"Yes. At least that's what the police said. She left the ship in Ketchikan and never returned. They have a system for tracking people who get off the ship to enjoy shore time in the ports. They scan your passenger card when you leave the ship, and again when you return. Their computers show her leaving the *Glacial Queen* at nine thirty in the morning, but she was never scanned as having returned."

"Maybe their computers made a mistake," Seth Hazlitt said. My dear friend, and Cabot Cove's most popular physician, has an inherent mistrust of computers. Whenever he sends something via e-mail, he insists that the recipients confirm that they've gotten it. And to my knowledge he's never once used an ATM. "I prefer, thank you very much, to write checks," he proudly proclaims, "and to stand in line at the bank to cash them. Besides, you get to know the bank personnel that way. No sense in trying to get to know a machine."

We were gathered in my living room. It had been a particularly cold late spring, with some days when the temperature barely rose above freezing. I'd made a stew, whipped up a salad, and served a red wine recommended to me by my favorite Cabot Cove wine shop. After dinner, we retreated to my living room, where I had the fireplace going, and I served coffee and tea and a plate of cookies. With me were Seth; Sheriff Mort Metzger and his wife, Maureen; Charlene Sassi, owner of the town's favorite bakery and the source of the cookies; Michael Cunniff, one of Cabot Cove's leading attorneys; and Kathy Copeland, a dear friend of many years and the person relating this troublesome tale. She'd received the call about her sister five days earlier and had immediately flown to Alaska to confer with authorities there. She'd returned to Cabot Cove only yesterday.

"I spoke with that officer in Alaska," Mort said. "They seem like competent fellas."

"I'm sure they are," I agreed.

"Very nice and very professional," Kathy said. "And I appreciate you taking the time to speak with them, Mort."

"Least I could do," our sheriff replied.

"Kathy, I don't want to make light of your concern," I said, "but your sister, Wilimena, has been known in the past to—well, to disappear for periods of time."

Kathy sat back in her chair, rolled her eyes, and

sighed. "I know, I know," she said. "Willie has always been a free spirit. There have been times when I wasn't able to reach her for months at a stretch, but then she'd surface from wherever she'd gone and regale me with tales of her adventures. But this feels different."

She sat up straight and extended her hands as though to elicit our understanding and agreement with what she was about to say. "There's no reason for her to leave the ship and not come back. Sure, Willie would take off at the drop of a hat and follow some whim, but not this way. I just know something terrible has happened to her."

We fell silent as we contemplated what she'd said, and avoided further comment by each of us in turn taking much longer than necessary to choose a cookie from the platter. Mort broke the silence.

"You say you brought back some of her things," he said to Kathy.

"Yes. The cruise authorities sealed off her cabin and secured all of her personal belongings."

"Did the Alaskan police examine those things?" I asked.

"Some of them, Jessica. Willie always took along a large envelope in which to keep her receipts from a trip. The police photocopied them for me."

"Those receipts would give some indication of where she went and what she might have done in the various ports of call," I offered.

"Did you look through them yourself?" Michael Cunniff asked. He had been practicing law in Cabot Cove for as long as I'd lived there. He was in his late seventies but hadn't lost a step mentally. Physically, however, he was a mass of orthopedic maladies that necessitated his walking with a cane. With long, flowing silver hair and a penchant for colorful bow ties to accompany his many suits, he was an attorney right out of central casting—or maybe a U.S. senator of yesteryear.

"I must have gone over them a dozen times on the flight home," Kathy replied, referring to her sister's receipts. "They were all from the ports the ship had visited earlier, Juneau and Sitka. Ketchikan was the last stop in Alaska before returning to Seattle."

"And?" I asked.

Kathy shrugged. "They mean nothing to me. Just receipts from shops and restaurants Willie visited in those ports, and a bunch of shipboard receipts, too, from the various lounges and shops."

"I'd like to see them," Michael said. He'd been Kathy's attorney since she moved to Cabot Cove forty years ago.

"Of course," she said.

"Are the Alaskan police at all confident about finding Wilimena?" Seth asked.

"They said they would do all they could," Kathy answered, "but they also reminded me that Alaska is a very big place, especially . . ."

"Especially what?" I asked.

"Especially if Willie doesn't want to be found."

"Ironic, isn't it, Jess, that you'll soon be heading for Alaska?" Maureen said.

It was true. I'd visited our forty-ninth state years ago on a whirlwind book promotion tour, with Anchorage my only stop. It was one of those insane trips

in which you fly into a city in the morning, are met
by an energetic local PR person who runs you ragged
from one radio and TV station to the next, then lunch
with a local newspaper writer, book signings in the
afternoon, a talk at a library, and no time for dinner
because your plane leaves at six for the next stop. So
although I literally had visited Alaska, I'd never seen
it, and I had decided to rectify that by booking an In-
land Passage cruise—the same one Kathy's sister, Wilimena, had taken and from which she'd vanished, on
the *Glacial Queen*, a relatively new ship. I'd booked the
cruise months in advance, combining it with a long
weekend in Seattle prior to the ship's departure. I have
a favorite mystery bookstore there run by a marvelous
gentleman, Bill Farley, who always arranges for a book
signing whenever I'm within striking distance of his
store on Cherry Street.

My reason for choosing an Alaskan cruise, as op-
posed to visiting other places on the globe, was a nag-
ging need to get closer to nature. It had been building
in me all winter, and by the time January rolled around,
it had become almost an obsession. True, Maine teems
with wildlife, which is one of many reasons I love living here. But Alaska has a very different lure for those
of us enamored of nature and the remarkable array of
creatures with whom we share our planet. So many
of my friends have returned from up north filled with
lifelong memories of having sailed into the midst of a
pod of orca whales or having seen majestic bald eagles
in virtually every treetop. Witnessing nature up close
and personal has always helped me put things, includ-

ing myself, in perspective, affirming my place in this world.

"Maybe you could ask a few questions while you're there, Mrs. F.," Mort suggested. "You know, check in with the local police and see if they've made any progress in finding Wilimena."

"I'd be happy to do that," I said, "although I'm not sure they'd be anxious to share anything with me."

"But they would with me," Kathy said.

"Of course they would," said Mort. "You're the missing person's sister."

Kathy looked at me and said, "What I meant, Jessica, was . . . um . . . I was wondering whether you'd mind a traveling companion."

"A traveling companion?"

She nodded. "I don't mean to impose myself on you and your trip. Believe me, I know how much this trip means to you, and I wouldn't for a second intrude. But considering what's happened to Wilimena—and that you're taking the same cruise as she did, on the same ship—it just seemed to me that, well, that maybe retracing her steps would help me come to grips with her disappearance."

"I, ah . . ."

Truth was, I was looking forward to the Alaska cruise as a means of getting away from everything and anything and basking in a week of solitude, with whales, sea lions, otters, and eagles as traveling companions.

I looked over at Seth, who knew exactly what I was thinking, not only because he knows me so well but also because I'd spoken to him about my need to escape on a solo jaunt.

"Sounds like a good idea to me," Mike Cunniff said, running his hands through his hair. "Besides, Jessica, you seem to have a knack for getting to the bottom of things rather quickly, especially when it involves—"

He'd almost said "murder," and I was glad he hadn't.

"What a great idea," Maureen said to me. "You'd have company and—"

"Mo and I talked about taking that cruise with you, Mrs. F.," Mort said, "but it's a bad time of the year for me."

Startled, I turned to him. "I didn't know you'd been considering coming," I said.

"Will George be joining you?" Charlene Sassi asked, referring to George Sutherland, the Scotland Yard inspector with whom I'd become close.

"No," I answered. "Why would you think he would be?"

Charlene gave me a sly, knowing smile.

"It's probably not a good idea, me joining you," Kathy said.

"Oh, no, it's a—it's a good idea, Kathy. I just wasn't planning on traveling with anyone."

"I'd stay out of your hair, Jess," she said, "go my own way and try to find out what's happened to Willie." She laughed. "Chances are she met up with some handsome Mountie and decided to spend some time with him in Alaska."

"Or marry him?" Seth said.

Kathy sighed deeply.

"How many times has your sister been married?" Charlene asked.

"Let me see," Kathy said, counting on her fingers. "Four, I think. No—five!"

Everyone had an opinion and a comment to make about Wilimena's penchant for tying the knot, but we stifled the temptation to express them. Wilimena's multiple marriages obviously satisfied a need of hers, and who were we to judge?

"Lovely dinner, as usual, Jessica," Seth said as they prepared to leave.

"Simple," I said.

"Always the best kind," Seth opined.

I saw them to the door and waved good-bye as they got into their vehicles. I locked up behind them, then went to the kitchen and tidied up before undressing for bed and slipping into a fresh pair of pajamas, a robe, and slippers. I'd become sleepy during the latter part of the evening, but now found myself wide-awake. I added a log to the fireplace and sat in front of the yellow-orange flames, which cast pleasant shafts of light and shadow over the room. What consumed my thinking was, of course, Kathy Copeland's story about her sister's disappearance in Alaska. Had I been rude in not responding with enthusiasm to her suggestion that she accompany me on my Alaskan trip? I was certainly sympathetic to her worries and her determination to do what she could to find Wilimena.

I suppose a sense of urgency was lacking in my mind because of Wilimena's history. I'd met her on a number of occasions when she'd come to Cabot Cove to visit her sister. Wilimena was a bigger-than-life character, flamboyant and glamorous, so unlike Kathy, who was the salt of the earth and dressed and acted like it. My friend wore flannel shirts, jeans, and workman's boots most of the time. She was a master gardener and an excellent cook, and enjoyed the simple pleasures of a good book, a hike in the woods, or a fish fry down on the beach. She'd never married, which surprised me. Somewhere out there was a man who was missing out on a first-rate wife.

Wilimena, on the other hand, was flashy in a big-city sort of way, fond of glittery dresses that showed off her splendid figure, lots of jewelry, elaborate hair-dos of varying hues, and a heavy albeit effective use of makeup. Wilimena was, Kathy once told me, the younger of the sisters, but by only a few years. Despite Wilimena's over-the-top personality, which could quickly wear you down, she was personable and likable, which her numerous husbands had obviously recognized, too.

I was pondering the events of the evening when the phone rang.

"Hello?"

"Jessica? It's Kathy."

"Oh, I'm glad you're home safe."

"Seth's a careful driver. He was a dear to offer to bring me."

"He's a dear about so many things."

"That he is, Jessica. Listen, I'm calling because I feel terrible about having suggested I go with you to Alaska."

"Why would you feel terrible?" I asked. "It was a sound suggestion. It's just that—"

"It was pushy of me, Jessica, and I apologize."

"No apologies needed, Kathy. As a matter of fact—"

"Yes?"

"I was just sitting here thinking about that very thing."

"You were?"

"Yes, and I think an apology is due from my end, too."

"For heaven's sake, why, Jessica?"

"Because you're obviously in need of some answers to Wilimena's disappearance, and taking the same cruise that she took might provide them. And, as Mike Cunniff said, I do seem to have a knack for getting to the bottom of things. Besides, having company would be good for me. So, Kathy, I would be pleased to have you join me on the cruise."

"You would?"

"Yes, I would. I think you'd better call Susan Shevlin and see if she can get you space on the ship. It is, after all, very last-minute."

"I'll do it first thing in the morning. You're sure, Jessica?"

I laughed. "Yes, I'm sure, Kathy. Get a booking in the morning, and let's meet for lunch to discuss the trip."

"Wonderful! Thanks so much, Jessica."

"My pleasure, Kathy. Now, it's time for this lady to get to bed. See you tomorrow at Mara's. Twelve thirty okay?"

"I'll be there."

The conversation with Kathy, and the decision I'd

made, lifted the veil of ambivalence I'd been feeling, allowing fatigue once again to settle in. There's nothing like taking action when something unresolved is hanging over your head. I fell asleep quickly, a smile on my face.

# Chapter One

"I feel uncomfortable flying first class, Kathy, and you being in coach."

"Don't be silly, Jessica," she replied. "You've had your reservations for a long time. Mine are last-minute. Don't even think about it."

When I made my reservation to fly from Boston to Seattle, I'd used some of my accumulated frequent-flier miles to upgrade to a first-class seat. Kathy, who seldom travels, didn't have that luxury and was booked in the coach section of the aircraft. I'd suggested changing my reservation to coach so that we could sit together, but she'd adamantly insisted that I not. "I'd feel terrible," she said. "Besides, I've brought two good books with me. I wouldn't be a talkative seat companion, anyway."

I did, however, bring her as my guest into the airline's first-class lounge, and we spent the two hours before our flight enjoying the club's amenities.

"I can't believe I'm going back to Alaska so soon," she said as we sat by a window overlooking one of the airport's active runways, from which a succession of aircraft landed and took off. "I was just there," she added, "and me being such a coward when it comes to flying."

"A lot safer than riding in a car to the airport," I said. "Have you heard anything further from the Alaska police about your sister?"

"No. Well, they did call to report that they haven't made any headway in their search for her. I just hope—"

"Hope what?"

"That she isn't off on some jaunt and putting everyone to so much trouble, especially the police."

"Frankly," I said, "if that *is* what happened, you'll be greatly relieved. It would mean that she's alive and well."

"I know," she said, nodding earnestly, "and I pray Willie is all right. But it would be so embarrassing if she's off having fun and the police have been knocking themselves out trying to find her."

"Let's wait and see," I suggested. "More coffee or tea?"

I refilled our cups and returned to her.

"I did get a call," she said, "from one of Willie's ex-husbands."

"Oh? Which one?"

"The next to last." She laughed. "I used to joke with Willie that she should number her husbands, like baseball players. You know, like the old saying, you can't tell the players without a scorecard."

"Sounds like a sensible suggestion," I said, laughing along with her.

"Willie thought it was funny, too."

"What did this particular ex-husband have to say when he called?"

"He said he'd been trying to contact Willie without success. He wanted to know if I knew where she was."

"Did you tell him that she's missing?"

"Oh, sure. He was shocked, very concerned."

"Had you met him?"

"No. I never met him—his name is Howard—or the husband who came after, her most recent. Both were very short marriages. I don't think either one lasted a year."

I couldn't help but shake my head. "Your sister has cut quite a swath, hasn't she?"

"I'm afraid so, Jessica. Sometimes I'm embarrassed about how Willie has lived her life, but I always remind myself that it's her life, not mine, and that she's entitled to live it any way she chooses. Still—"

"They'll be boarding our flight soon," I said. "The airlines are closing the doors earlier these days to try and maintain a better on-time record."

"Then we should go."

We grabbed our carry-on bags and headed for the departure gate. A few minutes later, the call was made for first-class passengers to board. I gave Kathy a hug and said, "See you in Seattle."

As I stood and gathered my belongings to join others in the line, Kathy said absently, as though talking to no one in particular, "It must be the gold."

Her words caused me to stop and turn back to her. "What gold?"

"The gold Willie is convinced the brothel madam might have left us."

*"Brothel madam?"*

"All first-class passengers should be on board," the agent at the boarding desk announced, sounding as though she meant it.

"Go on, Jess," Kathy said.

*"Gold? Brothel madam?"* I muttered to myself as I went to the gate, showed my boarding pass, and entered the plane to be seated in first class. *"Gold?"* I repeated aloud. *"Brothel madam?"*

"Pardon?" a flight attendant said.

"What? Oh, sorry," I said. "Just talking to myself."

She gave me a strange look but managed a smile as I settled into the large, comfortable seat. *Gold? Brothel madam?* It was virtually all I could think of for the duration of the six-hour flight to Seattle.

The weather was clear as we approached the Seattle-Tacoma airport, affording those of us on one side of the plane a splendid view of Mount Rainier. The thought of spending a few days in the city prior to departing on the cruise wiped away any fatigue I might have been experiencing. Seattle is less than 150 years old, and it's known as the Emerald City, or Jewel of the Northwest, worthy of either label in my opinion. I've always enjoyed my time there: the easy mix of people and the spectacular views in virtually every direction are true spirit boosters.

First-class passengers were the first to deplane. I waited until Kathy eventually came through the door.

"Nice flight," she said. "I wasn't nervous, except for all those strange noises before we landed."

"All normal," I said. "Landing gear being lowered and locked into place, flaps extended, routine things like that."

"That's right," she said as we headed in the direction of baggage claim. "You know all about planes."

"I know very little," I said. "Just enough to get myself in potential trouble when I'm flying."

A cab whisked us to the downtown area, where we checked into the lovely Fairmont Olympic Hotel. I'd stayed there a few times before. This princely hotel, located on the southern edge of the retail center, has been operating since the 1920s and has been luxuriously restored to its former splendor, with all the expected amenities befitting a four-star property. Our rooms, each a small suite, were adjoining.

It was midafternoon, and after unpacking we met up for a walk. The sun shone brightly, and there was a slight breeze off the water that surrounds the city. Seattle's reputation for excessive, almost unrelenting rain, is a myth. Its annual rainfall is actually less than that of any major city on the East Coast. What fuels its wet reputation is a tendency for cloudy, misty weather— not rainfall, just a pervasive dampness. But there are plenty of fair days, too, and this was one of them.

"When is your book signing?" Kathy asked as we maintained a brisk pace to work out the kinks from having sat too long in the plane. Kathy is an inveterate walker, always seen around Cabot Cove in motion on her way someplace, arms swinging, legs moving in a regular rhythm, a determined expression on her face. She'd changed into a sweat suit and sturdy sneakers. Kathy is a short, chunky woman, perhaps a shade over five feet, two inches, with a full, round face, expressive blue eyes, and brunette hair worn simply. She often complains about being over-weight, although she isn't. She's simply one of those compact, physically fit people without an ounce of excess flesh.

"Tomorrow, at noon."

"Is it all right if I come?"

"Of course it is. I'd love to have you there."

"I always come to your signings in Cabot Cove, and I went to that one in Boston a few years ago," she said as we paused to window-shop.

"Seattle is different," I offered, setting off again. "Maybe it's because of the generally overcast weather, but Seattle probably has more bookstores than any other comparable city in the country, and more book buyers per capita than anywhere else. They devour books here, which is good for us writers. By the way, I've made a dinner reservation for us tonight at Canlis. Hope you don't mind my not conferring with you."

"Why would I mind?" she said. "You know Seattle. Besides, I trust your palate, Jessica."

"I think you'll enjoy Canlis," I said. "It's set in the hills with wonderful views of the city and beyond."

"Sounds yummy. I'm suddenly hungry."

Canlis might possibly be the most beautiful res-taurant in America. With stone columns soaring high above the dining room, and light and landscape flood-ing in through a translucent wall, the restaurant has an almost Zen-like atmosphere. We were seated at a prime table affording a fine view of the city as dusk began to settle. Because I'd raved about my last meal there, Kathy insisted that I order for us, which I did—Canlis chowder to start, rich with Dungeness crab, sea scallops, and prawns in a heavenly ginger-scented cream, and a sublime salad, followed by an entrée of wild Pacific king salmon with hazelnut-caper butter, and jumbo asparagus, all accompanied by a shared bottle of DeLille Cellars Chaleur Estate Blanc from Washington's Columbia Valley, recommended by our sommelier.

"Kathy," I said as we enjoyed our first sip of the wine, "you said at the airport that your sister's disappearance might have to do with gold and a brothel madam?"

"Just thinking out loud," she said.

"Thinking about gold and brothels?"

She nodded, laced her fingers around her glass, and stared down into it. "I'm embarrassed that I even brought it up."

"But now that you have, you can't keep me dangling like this. What gold? What brothel madam?"

She turned to look at me, exhaled loudly, and said, "Dolly Arthur."

"Who's she?"

"She's—well, she was the most famous madam in Alaska's history."

"I'll take your word for it, Kathy. But what does it have to do with Wilimena?"

"It's a very long story."

"We have all evening. Could it possibly have to do with Wilimena's disappearance?"

"Maybe. How do I begin?"

"At the beginning, Kathy. At the very beginning."

By the time our coffee and dessert had been served—peanut butter mousse with a chocolate cookie crust and caramelized banana—we were both sated and somewhat drowsy. But while the Canlis dining experience had taken center stage, the conversation was equally satisfying, and provocative. Kathy had spun a tale of gold and madams in detail for me, and quite a tale it was.

Kathy and Wilimena Copeland's mother was one of two sisters born to Kathy's grandparents. Kathy described her mother as a God-fearing Bible Belt woman, a staunch opponent of all things she considered sinful, including dancing, whiskey, gambling, reading anything except the scriptures, radio, newspapers, swearing, young couples being alone without an adult chaperone, and dozens of other perceived evils inherent in human beings.

"Sounds like a formidable lady," I said.

"I suppose you could say that, Jess. To be truthful—and I hate speaking ill of the dead—she was a very difficult woman."

"What about your father?" I asked.

"Dad was a quiet, meek man who didn't dare cross my mother, although he did leave us when we were young teenagers."

"That took courage on his part."

"I suppose he'd had enough and decided to be free of her iron hand." She paused, as though to summon the will to add to her story. "He ran off with a young woman who'd arrived in town with a traveling carnival."

"Oh, my."

"She was a contortionist," Kathy said. "She could twist herself into a human pretzel. That's how she was billed: Christiana, the Human Pretzel."

I couldn't keep from erupting into laughter. "I must say," I said, "your father seems to have gone to extremes when choosing a female companion."

"To say the least. Anyway, his departure left Willie and me to deal with Mom on our own. She was fond of playing us off against each other, good sister versus bad sister, who was most loyal to her and lived by her principles and who wasn't. Guess which one I was."

"Let me see," I said. "You were the good sister, at least as far as your mother was concerned."

"That's right," Kathy said. "Willie was—well, Willie became more rebellious with each passing year. She seemed to go out of her way to upset our mother, which I never agreed with. I'm afraid it set us at each other's throats."

"How unfortunate."

"But inevitable. Anyway, when Mom died, Willie and I forged a truce that has lasted to this day. It's not that we see things eye to eye. Far from it. But the love we have for each other and the common background we share have conquered whatever animosity we had earlier."

"Sibling rivalry resolved in an adult, mature way," I said.

"Yes, and I'm glad we were able to do it."

"What about your father?"

"I lost touch with him until he became ill. He'd married the pretzel and taken a job with the carnival as its bookkeeper. He came down with cancer. I knew it only because Willie told me. She'd sort of kept in touch with him, just a postcard now and then, which was more than I did. Anyway, I went to Kansas when he was dying in a hospice there and spent a few hours at his bedside."

"What about the—?" I couldn't help laughing again. "What about 'the pretzel'?"

"She'd left Dad a number of years before he became ill. I never did meet her, although Willie did once." Kathy started to giggle. "Willie said she looked more like a dying, tangled vine than a pretzel."

"A colorful description," I said. "Now, what about gold and this infamous madam you mentioned, Dolly Arthur?"

"Do you know, Jessica, that you are the only person in Cabot Cove I've ever told this to?"

"I'm flattered. Is it *that* sordid?"

"No, but I've always been embarrassed about my family."

"Well, you shouldn't be. We're not responsible for how our parents and other relatives behave, or how they choose to live their lives."

"I know." After a deep sigh, she said, "Dolly Arthur was my aunt."

"Arthur was her married name?"

"Her stage name."

"She was an actress before going into the brothel business?"

"I don't know. Maybe 'stage name' refers to her particular stage, her house of ill repute. Anyway, Dolly's real name was Thelma Copeland."

"Aha. The family connection. Did you have much contact with your aunt Dolly as you were growing up?"

"None! Absolutely none! My mother and her only sibling, Thelma, were as opposite as you could get."

"I'd call that an understatement, Kathy. What about the gold?"

"When Mom died in the early seventies, she didn't leave a will, and Willie took charge of settling the estate and disposing of Mom's personal possessions. I was happy she volunteered. I wasn't comfortable doing it. Willie claims she ran across some papers in Mom's house that indicated to her that Aunt Thelma, aka Dolly, might have become the owner of a sizable amount of gold panned during the Alaskan gold rush."

"Might have?" I repeated.

Kathy nodded and finished her coffee. "I never saw the papers to which Willie was referring because she lost them. Typical Wilimena, always losing things."

"Including husbands," I added as an editorial comment.

"Yes, them, too," she agreed ruefully.

"When did your aunt Dolly die?" I asked.

"Thelma died in 1975. She's buried in a cemetery in Ketchikan."

"Let's stick with her stage name, Dolly. It'll help me keep things straight in my mind."

"Okay."

"Willie was a young woman when she took on the task of settling your mother's estate," I said.

"Yes, she was."

"And she never found those papers again?"

"Never." She slowly shook her head and smiled. "In a sense, it didn't make any difference whether she found the papers or not. It made a good story, and—"

"And what?"

"I think that's how she's managed to attract so many husbands, Jessica. Here she is, beautiful and vivacious, and with the lure of an inheritance of gold from an Alaskan madam, who also happened to be her aunt. Is it cruel for me to think that?"

"Not at all. You may be right, but it doesn't matter. You think she might have taken her trip to Alaska to try and find the gold?"

"It's possible. With Wilimena, anything is possible."

"Had she made previous trips to Alaska in search of the gold?" I asked.

"Years ago. She told me she never had sufficient documentation to make any headway. But then she sent me this shortly before taking her most recent trip."

She pulled a note handwritten on perfumed pink stationery from her purse and handed it to me.

*Voilà! Kathy. I think we are both about to become rich! Love, Willie.*

"Intriguing," I said, motioning to the server for the check. "It sounds as though that absent documentation might have surfaced. Tell you what, Kathy. Let's pick

up tomorrow where we've left off. Right now, my cir-
cadian rhythms are about to crash."

Wide awake in my bed at the hotel, I tried desperately
not to think of a young woman, her body twisted into
a pretzel, her face somewhere in the tangle. In some of
my visions, she even had salt on her.

   Thankfully, fatigue won out and sleep finally
arrived.

# Chapter Two

The fair weather of the previous day in Seattle was only a memory when I awoke in my suite. A misty gray cloud had descended over the city, and the TV weatherman forecast more of the same for the next three days.

No matter. I've never been a traveler who complains about the weather, one of those people who consider a trip ruined if the sun doesn't shine every day. Weather changes, and so must we to accommodate it.

Kathy and I met for breakfast in the hotel's dining room. She carried a manila envelope.

"Sleep well?" I asked.

"I certainly did. I didn't think I would because of everything we talked about last night, but I fell right off. The book I was reading was still on my stomach when I woke up."

"I slept well, too," I said with a chuckle, "except I had trouble getting the pretzel woman out of my mind."

"I'm sorry."

"Speaking of pretzels, let's order."

After a hearty breakfast, I said, "Those receipts that Wilimena left in her stateroom—are any of them from Seattle?"

"Oh, sure. I separated them according to location." She opened the envelope she'd brought along. "Here," she said, handing me a batch of receipts neatly secured with a large red paper clip and placing others on the table. Receipts and notes from different cities were fastened with clips of varying colors. I went through the Seattle ones. According to the dates, Wilimena Copeland had spent two days in the city before catching her ship to Alaska. The top slip of paper caught my eye. It was from a shop specializing in items for personal security. Wilimena had purchased a stun gun for $79.95 and a Mace pepper spray device for $16.95.

"Looks like your sister was expecting trouble on her cruise," I said. "Had she been known to carry such things before?"

"Not to my knowledge," said Kathy.

"Maybe we should swing by this store and see if she might have said something about her trip, and why she thought she needed them. On second thought," I said, flipping through the remaining receipts, "maybe we should check out all of these."

After determining that the security shop was within walking distance of the hotel, we set out, eventually finding our destination in an industrial section of the city. The store windows were filled with exotic, state-of-the-art electronic gadgetry. The owner, a handsome, slender young man wearing a blue T-shirt, jeans, and a tan photojournalist's vest, had just opened the store and was busy turning on lights and removing dustcovers from display cases. "Good morning, ladies," he called out. "Be with you in a second."

His opening routine completed, he came to where we stood and offered an engaging smile. "Hi. My name's Bill. May I show you something specific? We just got in some new bags with hidden pockets. Very popular with women when they travel."

"Actually," I said, "we're not here to buy anything."

He adopted an exaggerated expression of disappointment. "Let's see," he said, "you're here to arrest me."

Kathy laughed. "Oh, no," she said. "You see—"

"Just kidding," he said. "You don't look like the police, anyway. So, I can't sell you anything. What *can* I do for you?"

I handed him the receipt. He perused it, then looked up and said, "You want to return one of the items. There's something wrong with it?"

"No," I said. "You see, my friend's sister bought these items on the date indicated. She's—well, she's disappeared and we're trying to find her."

"Disappeared? That sounds serious."

"Precisely," I said. "I just thought you might remember her and what she said about her plans when she was here in your store."

He handed the receipt back to me and shrugged. "I'm afraid I don't have any way to remember her from this receipt."

"Show him Willie's photo," I said to Kathy, who pulled it from her pocket.

"Her name is Wilimena," Kathy said, "but everyone calls her Willie."

"Oh," he said, his face brightening. "Her!"

"You remember her," Kathy said.

"I sure do. She's hard to forget. You don't meet many women named Willie. You say she's your sister?"

"Yes."

"And she disappeared in Alaska?"

"You knew about Alaska?" I said. "She told you she was going there?"

Bill laughed. "She told me lots of things. She's quite a talker."

It was Kathy's turn to laugh. "Willie is never at a loss for words," she said.

"Did she say why she felt a need to buy these self-protection devices?" I asked.

"As a matter of fact, she did," Bill replied. "She started kidding about how women can't be too careful these days with men hitting on them. I didn't argue with her. I mean, she was—is—a nice-looking woman who I imagine gets lots of male attention. Whether she needed a stun gun and Mace is another question. But if she felt more secure having those things with her, who was I to question it? She also said she was heading for Alaska to stake her claim in a gold mine."

"Gold mine?" I said.

"I think that's what she said. Maybe it wasn't a mine, but it had to do with gold."

I mentally dismissed Wilimena's claim that she needed the devices to stave off unwanted male attention and asked Bill to expand on what she might have said about the gold.

"All I recall," he said, "was that she claimed there was some distant relative in Alaska who came into a potful of gold and that she was on her way to claim it. Is it true?"

"I don't know," Kathy replied. "I'm hoping that we'll find out."

"Anything else you can remember, Bill, that might help us?" I asked.

He shook his head and smiled. "No offense," he said to Kathy, "but your sister is quite a flirt."

"I didn't know," Kathy said, not altogether successful in keeping amusement out of her voice.

"Yeah," Bill said. "She started coming on to me, even asked me to join her for a drink after I finished work. Ah—well, no offense, but she was a little old for me." He looked at us to judge how offended we were. "I mean," he quickly added, "she's a very attractive woman and all but—"

"No need to explain," I said. "And thank you for being so forthright. It's been a help."

He walked us to the door. "I hope you find her," he said. "If you do, swing back by here with her and I'll buy you *all* a drink."

"We may just do that," I said, silently adding to myself, *if we find her.*

Kathy and I stood outside the store and pondered our next move. Kathy had further arranged the receipts and notes left by Wilimena in order of their occurrence, with the earliest ones on top. Next in line was a receipt from an electronics store for a digital recorder and assorted add-ons.

"It's a shame we don't have it," I said. "When you picked up her things from the cruise line, no one mentioned a recorder?"

"No. Willie sometimes carried one with her to make notes about her various trips. I suppose she intended to do the same on the cruise."

"And probably did," I suggested. "Let's see what impression she left behind with this store owner."

The gentleman at the electronics store was in his late fifties or early sixties, dressed in a gray suit, white shirt, and red tie, markedly more formal than is the norm in Seattle, a pleasantly relaxed and informal city. He seemed sincerely upset when we told him that Wilimena had disappeared. "What dreadful news," he said. "I'm so sorry to hear it."

"We were hoping that something she said while in your store would provide a clue to her whereabouts," I said.

"I really can't believe that she would simply vanish like this," he said, wringing his hands and shaking his head. "A lovely woman. Truly lovely. So cultured and full of life. You don't think that . . . ?"

He'd obviously spent more time with her than simply as a salesman.

"We don't know what happened to her," Kathy said. "Did she say why she wanted the recorder and microphone?"

"Yes. She chose a top-of-the-line recorder and a small external microphone. I'll show you what she bought."

I was surprised at the small size of the recorder and microphone he withdrew from a display case. The minicassette recorder I always travel with seemed huge by comparison. I mentioned it.

"The technology has evolved so quickly," he explained. "No more tapes. It's all digital these days, memory chips."

"You could hide this recorder and microphone in a shirt pocket," I said, "and no one would ever know it was there."

"Precisely," the owner said. He glanced around the otherwise empty store as though to ensure our privacy, then leaned closer and said in a voice slightly above a whisper, "She told me that she wanted to record people without their knowing it. I suppose it was because so much gold was involved and—"

"She told *you* about the gold?" Kathy asked.

"Yes. It was such an exciting story. You say you're her sister. Is what she said true, that you have a distant relation who had all that gold?"

"I, ah—evidently," Kathy responded.

"You say there's no tape in this recorder," I said, turning the tiny device over in my hand.

"Exactly," he said. "No need for a tape." He stepped back and cocked his head. "You look familiar to me," he said.

"Oh?"

"I know. You're the writer, Jessica—Jessica— Jessica—" He started snapping his fingers.

"Fletcher," I provided.

"Of course. I've read some of your books. In fact, Wilimena mentioned at dinner that her sister lived in the same town in Maine as Jessica Fletcher."

"Dinner?"

"Why, yes. We enjoyed a wonderful evening together at Ray's Boathouse. It's a landmark restaurant in

Seattle." He chuckled. "They say that a visit to Seattle without visiting Ray's Boathouse is like going to Paris without seeing the Eiffel Tower. An overstatement, of course, but it is a very fine seafood house, with splendid views of Puget Sound."

"It is nice," I said. "I've eaten there a few times. What else did you talk about at dinner, Mr.—?"

"John Casale," he said, extending his hand. "A pleasure meeting you."

"Thank you. About dinner," I said.

"Oh, right. Let me see. We talked about many things. Willie—that's her nickname—Willie did most of the talking. I hung on every word. She's so worldly, been to so many fascinating places." He became somewhat conspiratorial again. "We made another date for dinner when she returns from Alaska. You don't think that—?"

"I'm sure everything will turn out just fine," I said, "and that you'll enjoy that second dinner together."

"I certainly hope so," he said. He handed us his business card. "Please keep me informed."

"Of course," Kathy said.

I couldn't help but laugh once we were outside the store. "Your sister is—well, your sister is quite an operator, Kathy."

"I always knew that, Jess, but I had no idea just how much of an operator she really is. No wonder she's had so many husbands. It seems that every man is fair game."

I grew pensive as we walked slowly in the direction of Pioneer Square, where my book signing at the Seattle Mystery Bookshop was scheduled for noon.

"What are you thinking?" Kathy asked.

"I'm thinking—no, more like I'm hoping that Willie's penchant for attracting men isn't at the root of her disappearance."

"You don't think—?"

"She seems willing to become involved with men she barely even knows. That sort of indiscretion can get a woman in trouble, especially with her compulsion to tell every man she meets that she's about to become a wealthy woman."

Kathy said nothing in response, but I knew she agreed with me.

The Seattle Mystery Bookshop used to be located below street level on Cherry Street, which cut down on foot traffic. But it had recently moved down the block to a more advantageous aboveground spot. I reminded myself as we approached it that Bill Farley was no longer the store's official owner. He'd written to tell me that he'd sold it to his longtime manager, J. B. Dickey, although he assured me he would remain active in the shop's daily activities. I was happy to hear that because Bill is a walking encyclopedia when it comes to murder mysteries.

Cherry Street is just off Pioneer Square, Seattle's oldest neighborhood. After World War II, the area fell into disrepair and disrepute, becoming home to cheap hotels, street drunks, and prostitution (the term "skid row" originated there; logs were skidded down the steep Yesler Way to the city's first lumber mill). But as often happens with such districts, the artistic community, in search of affordable living and studio space, began moving in and displacing the less desirable elements until Pioneer Square was restored to its previous glory. These days, the twenty-square-block historic district is home to myriad galleries, bookstores, quaint bars and restaurants, and assorted gift shops.

"Look, Jess, there's your picture," Kathy exclaimed as we stood in front of the store. A large poster with my photograph, the cover of my latest book, and information about the signing dominated one of the windows. I stepped closer to get a better look and peered past the poster into the store. A dozen people, mostly women, milled about, presumably waiting for the signing to begin.

"We'd better get inside," I said.

As I reached for the door handle, a man who'd been standing alone twenty feet away approached. "Jessica Fletcher," he said, sounding as though we were old friends.

"Yes?" I said, turning.

"I'm here for the signing," he said, extending a large hand.

I couldn't help but notice what he wore. His yellow and green sweater had seen better days and had numerous pulls and small holes, a few of which looked like cigarette burns. His khaki pants were in equally rough shape, badly wrinkled and stained. He wore black high-top sneakers and carried a large canvas bag that appeared to be filled to capacity.

"I've read every one of your books," he said. His voice was raspy and low, his eyes black and sunken in a long, gaunt face. He needed a shave.

"Well, I hope you enjoy the new one as much as you've liked the others," I said. "See you inside?"

Until that moment he'd had a semblance of a smile on his face. But my ending the conversation caused a change in his expression to what I read as anger.

As we entered the store, Bill Farley came from behind a small counter and warmly greeted us. I introduced Kathy to him. Two clerks whom I recognized from my previous signings there also came to us. I sighed. "I feel like I'm home," I said.

"We've set you up over there in your usual spot," Bill said, indicating a long table to our right. Multiple copies of most of my books were artfully laid out on it, dominated by my most recent hardcover. Behind the table stood a tall, narrow rack on which more copies were displayed.

"You're early," Bill said.

"I always try to be," I said. "I see I'm not the only one." I indicated the people perusing books in the shop's maze of narrow aisles.

Bill looked through the window to the man who'd approached me outside. "Ever seen him before?" he asked.

"No. Why?"

"He's a little strange, Jessica. He showed up yesterday thinking the signing was then. When I told him it was today, he became angry. Started swearing under his breath."

"I suppose he was inconvenienced by getting the date wrong. Is he a regular at the shop?"

"No. Never saw him before yesterday."

"He probably lives locally," I said, "since he's coming back again today. Either that or he's a tourist with plenty of time to spare."

His laugh was gentle. "Fans of murder mysteries come in all shapes and sizes," he mused. "I'm aware of that every time I attend Bouchercon."

Bill was referring to the annual Bouchercon gathering, the world's largest convention of mystery writers, editors, publishers, agents, and fans of the genre. It was named after the late beloved mystery writer, editor, critic, reviewer, and fan Anthony Boucher. I'd attended a few of the gatherings myself and enjoyed them.

"He's been here for at least an hour," Bill said. "In and out of the store. He already has your new novel. Must have bought it someplace else. Don't you just love people who buy a book at another store and come to this one to have it autographed?"

"Nothing new," I said, going to the table and settling in for the signing, which was scheduled to run for an hour and a half. Some of the customers already in the shop gravitated to me as others came through the door. I know writers who dread signings, but I'm not among them. I receive, and reply to, hundreds of e-mails each month, but I especially treasure the opportunity to actually meet the men and women who buy and read—and, I hope, enjoy—my books. They represent a diverse cross section of people, old and young (I especially like it that many teenagers write to tell me how much they enjoyed a particular book of mine), rich and not so rich, men and women (although women account for the largest percentage of book buyers, not only of mine but of books in general), gregarious and shy, talkative and quiet. Often their comments provide me insights into my works that I hadn't recognized when writing them. All in all, book signings provide an author the sort of direct feedback that is not only gratifying but helpful, too, when working on the next book.

I invited Kathy to sit next to me at the table and asked her to help me by gathering from each person the name of the individual to whom the book should be addressed and any special messages to be included— happy birthday to a family member or friend, or something else personal. Soon we were engaged in a spirited conversation with some of the women who'd approached, and I started the signing process. As I fulfilled my reason for being there, more people entered the shop, which pleased me. The only book signings I've not enjoyed were those when very few people showed up. I always feel bad for the store owners when that occurs.

The line of book buyers continued to grow, to my satisfaction, and I chatted with customers and signed copies of the book. Every once in a while I looked for the man whom I'd met outside the shop. He hadn't come inside as far as I could tell, and I wondered why. Had he decided not to bother having his book signed? That was a possibility, of course. Perhaps the number of people in line had discouraged him.

I excused myself and took a brief break to rest my hand, which had begun to cramp. Kathy and I went to the window and looked outside. No sign of the disgruntled gentleman.

"I'm going to get some air," Kathy said. "Can you do without me?"

"Of course."

She left the shop, and I resumed my seat at the table.

"Where do you get all your ideas?" a woman asked.

"I really don't know," I said. "Sometimes from something I've read in a newspaper or magazine. At other times, a plot just comes to me at odd hours. Usually, I play the 'What if?' game."

"What's that?" she asked.

"I ask myself that question. 'What if someone were to—?' "

A commotion at the front door caused everyone, including me, to stop what we were doing and look in that direction. I saw Kathy come through the door, followed closely by the disheveled man from outside. The look on my friend's face was sheer panic. The man shoved her ahead of him, propelling her into a group of people who'd already had their books signed and were chatting. Then I saw what the man carried besides his canvas bag. It was a lethal-looking hunting knife with a very long blade.

Someone else who also saw the weapon screamed. Bill Farley came around the counter and shouted, "What are you doing?"

"Shut up!" the man said, waving the knife above his head, which sent people scurrying down the aisles in search of a safe haven.

I didn't know what to do. I stood frozen in place. I saw that Kathy was all right. I considered trying to reach an aisle or ducking beneath the table. But before I could do anything, the man came to me, parting those who were still standing there with their books for me to sign. He held the knife in one hand, the canvas bag in the other. The blade was pointed straight at me.

"Sir," I said, "why don't you put down that knife and—"

"Shut up!"

I obeyed.

He slammed the canvas bag down on the table, sending copies of my books flying in all directions. The hand holding the knife began to shake as he reached inside the bag, withdrew a copy of my new book, and slapped it down in front of me.

I know it sounds silly, but the only thing I could think of to say at that moment was, "Would you like me to sign that?"

He seemed as surprised at what I'd said as I was. His eyes darted back and forth, and he started to say something, but no words emerged.

"Please, put down the knife," I said, taking advantage of the momentary emotional lull.

"You stole it," he managed to say.

"What?"

He pointed to my book. "You stole it from me."

"I'm sorry, but—"

"I gave you the idea for it," he said in a voice that sounded on the verge of breaking.

"I don't understand," I said.

"I sent you the idea," he said. "You stole it from me."

My mind raced. He was clearly demented. I searched my memory for having had some contact with him in the past, something to make sense out of what he'd just charged.

"The whole story was mine," he said. "I told you about it, and you said it was a good idea but that you were already writing something just like it."

"I'm sorry, but I don't remember anything like that. You must be mistaken."

The moment I said it, I was hit with a recollection of an e-mail exchange I'd had almost two years ago with someone who'd suggested an idea for one of my books. In the hundreds of e-mails I receive each month on my Web site, there is occasionally one that offers an idea for a plot or a setting. The people who send them mean well and are trying to be helpful and to interact with the writer's creative process. Every writer who receives such suggestions is aware, of course, of the possibility that one day a novel might parallel in some small way an idea put forward by a fan, and that that fan could decide that his or her idea was "stolen." It simply doesn't happen. Successful writers don't have any need or inclination to steal the ideas of others.

The man brandishing a knife in front of me obviously didn't believe that.

"California," the man said. "It was my idea to set the book in California."

My recollection of the e-mail exchange was clearer now. I'd received a message through my Web site from someone who thought that I should set one of my novels in California. Obviously, this was that person. As I recalled, he wasn't more specific than that. Just California. Had I replied to him? I was sure that I had. I personally answer every e-mail. What had I said in my reply? I'd undoubtedly thanked him for the suggestion and indicated that I was already at work on a book set in California.

"Could we sit down and discuss this?" I asked, trying to inject calm into my voice. "Without the knife?"

"You won't get away with it," was his nonresponsive reply.

"Please," I said. "I think we can work this out if only—"

The sound of sirens caused both of us to look out the window. Two marked police cars came to a screeching, haphazard halt in front of the shop, and uniformed officers jumped out and dashed to the front door. Thank heavens someone in the shop had called for help. The crazed man grabbed my arm across the table and pressed the weapon against my neck. I closed my eyes and waited for the thrust that would end my life. When it didn't happen, I opened my eyes and saw that everyone else in the shop was on their way out the door, Kathy, who'd been hiding in one of the aisles, emerged and took a few steps toward me.

"Go, Kathy, go," I said.

Her face reflected her conflict, but after a few moments she joined the others, leaving me and the man alone in the shop.

An amplified male voice said from just outside the door, "Let the lady go. The building is surrounded. Put down your weapon and come out with your hands up."

I suppose it was the appropriate thing for the officer with the bullhorn to say under the circumstances, but his words of warning seemed only to further agitate my captor. He lowered the knife from my neck and took a few steps away.

"We can talk about this," I said. "Your idea to set a book in California was a good one, but nothing will be accomplished this way. Please—I have no reason to want to hurt you, or to steal your ideas. I would never do that. This is just a misunderstanding that we can rectify—but only if you give me the knife."

I was pleased at how rational I was able to sound. My voice was steady. Inside, I was a mass of jangled nerves. I'd never encountered a situation like this in all my professional writing life. Yes, there had been a few fans who'd expressed their displeasure over the years at something I'd written, or took me to task for what they considered a lapse on my part. Some of my science-fiction-writer friends have told me about an occasional irate fan who threatened bodily harm for something they'd published, especially if they'd written a tie-in novel using familiar characters from a TV show or motion picture. Science-fiction fans are especially zealous and proprietary about beloved characters from those media. But I wasn't aware that it had ever happened to writers of murder mysteries. If I survived this, I'd have quite a tale to tell my fellow mystery writers.

The police continued to send amplified messages through the open door. At one point, I was afraid they were about to burst in, guns blazing, which was the last thing I wanted to have happen. My assailant seemed to have calmed down some; perhaps he'd become fatigued. He sat in the chair that Kathy had occupied and lowered the hand holding the knife to the table, the blade still pointed in my direction. I, too, sat, and continued to try to talk sense to him. His eyes were wet, and I wondered whether he would soon break into tears. Along with the abject fear I was experiencing, I also felt a parallel sense of pity for him. I wondered what his daily life was like. Was he delusional, hearing voices that told him to act irrationally? As best I could remember, his e-mail to me had been rational. I assumed he had a computer since he'd e-mailed me, but I also realized that he might be homeless and could have used a library computer.

I looked through the window to where a large crowd had gathered across the street and saw Bill Farley standing with others from the store. Kathy was with them.

"What's your name?" I asked.

"Walter."

"Well, Walter, you know who I am," I said. "Are you a writer?"

He nodded.

"What kind of things do you write?"

"Poems, mostly, but I want to write murder mysteries like you."

"Then I think you should. Do you have a story in mind?"

"I had one. You stole it."

"A story set in California," I said. "It's a wonderful setting for a murder mystery."

"Why did you do it?" he asked in a voice without energy.

"I don't think I did," I said. I didn't want to upset him any further by debating whether I'd set my most recent book in California because of his e-mail.

"Everybody always steals my ideas," he said flatly. "I have lots of them, but somebody takes them and makes all the money."

"That's terrible," I said. "Maybe we can figure out a way together to keep that from happening again."

My thoughts went back to when I was an English teacher before launching my writing career, and I felt as though I was sitting after school with a troubled student in need of guidance. The atmosphere in the bookshop was now calm. The police had obviously sensed that their best approach was to lay back and allow the scene inside to play out. They could see that we were simply talking and that the knife was no longer being bandied about in a threatening manner. All I hoped was that it would stay that way and that Walter would eventually succumb to reason.

Fifteen minutes later, it happened. It wasn't that he'd listened to what I'd said and agreed with me. He fell asleep sitting in the chair, his head lowered to his chest. I gingerly removed his hand from on top of the knife, placed the weapon behind a pile of my books, then silently stood and tiptoed away from the table to the door. Uniformed police rushed past me, yanked the man to a standing position, and cuffed his hands behind his back. *Don't hurt him*, I thought.

Kathy ran to me and wrapped me in a bear hug.

"Are you all right?" Bill Farley asked.

"Yes, I'm fine."

"A madman," one of Bill's clerks said.

"A pathetic soul," I said.

A photographer from the *Seattle Post-Intelligencer* snapped a series of photos of me and of the man as he was led from the shop to a waiting squad car. A reporter from that same newspaper asked me a series of rapid-fire questions, none of which I chose to answer.

"What did you say to him?" Kathy asked as we went back inside the bookshop.

"I have no idea," I said, "except that whatever it was, it was boring."

*"Boring?"* she and Bill asked in unison.

"I never realized how boring I can be," I said. "I put him to sleep."

"And saved your life," Bill said.

"That, too," I said. "Well, let's finish the signing. There are still some people who never had the chance to have their books autographed."

The remainder of our stay in Seattle was without incident, at least of the magnitude of the book signing. I gave a statement to the police and learned from them that Walter—his last name was Munro—was well-known to them as a vagrant who haunted local libraries. He'd been arrested a number of times for minor offenses, mostly of the public-nuisance variety, but had never done anything as serious as threatening someone's life. My dilemma was whether I wanted to press charges. I felt I had to, although I was not entirely comfortable with that decision. Had I the power to determine Mr. Munro's fate, I would have seen to it that he was committed to a mental institution where he would receive treatment. But the system had no place for my input. My experience led me to conclude that the man's mental illness had progressed beyond the "public nuisance" stage. Would his paranoia drive him to attack someone else? Obviously, that was a chance no one would want to take. I pressed charges after receiving assurance from the detective that he would do what he could to see that Mr. Munro received treatment.

My unwelcome confrontation made the front page of the *Post-Intelligencer* the next day, including one of the pictures snapped of me outside the shop. I effectively managed to hide from other members of the press who wanted interviews, and was anxious for Sunday, when our ship would set sail for Alaska, to arrive.

As for uncovering any further information about Wilimena's stay in Seattle, we hit a brick wall. Aside from the two shops we visited, none of the remaining receipts gave reason to follow up. The lack of receipts from restaurants, except for a couple of coffee shops, seemed to indicate that Willie had been successful in enticing others to pay for her meals.

We left the hotel at noon on Sunday to go to the pier from which the *Glacial Queen* would leave at four that afternoon.

"We haven't gotten very far in finding Willie," Kathy said as we rode in our hired car.

"We have a start," I said. "We now know that she bought a tiny device to record people when they didn't expect it, and two personal-security items. And, of course, we also know that she seldom, if ever, spent social time alone. I have the feeling that we won't be lacking men to interview who got to know your sister."

"I suppose you're right," Kathy said.

"And," I added, "we also know that gold was the reason for her trip. Up until meeting those two shopkeepers, you only surmised that. Now we know that it was very much on her mind."

"I just hope that . . ."

"Hope what, Kathy?" I asked as the driver pulled up to where the ship's passengers were arriving.

"I just hope that what almost happened to you at the book signing isn't an omen of what's going to happen on this cruise."

My laugh was forced. "That's behind us, Kathy," I said. "Besides, I don't believe in omens."

Maybe I should have.

# Chapter Three

After checking our luggage with a curbside agent, we entered a cavernous building where we joined hundreds of other passengers waiting to go through security and to be issued a photo ID for use on the ship. The *Glacial Queen* accommodates eighteen hundred passengers and eight hundred crew, which might seem like too many people with whom to spend a week in a confined space. But the ship is huge, and I knew from previous cruises that once aboard, people seem to disappear into a ship's recesses except when gathering for meals. Joining us in line were men and women of every age and size, sporting a wide array of attire, some looking as though they were ready for a fancy dinner party, some (most) casual in the extreme.

The line moved surprisingly quickly, and we were soon going up a long, slanted walkway to the ship, which sat majestically at the pier. Enthusiastic, smiling young crew members directed us to our staterooms, which were adjacent, thanks to some last-minute wheeling and dealing by Susan Shevlin, our crackerjack travel agent back in Cabot Cove. Each room was spacious and nicely appointed, and glass doors opened to a balcony with a small white table and two deck chairs.

While I waited for my luggage to be delivered, a voice came through a speaker informing all passengers that an emergency drill would be conducted within a half hour, with each block of cabins assigned to a specific deck. As instructed, in preparation for the drill, I pulled down an orange life preserver from a shelf in one of the closets, slipped into it, and was about to step out onto the balcony when there was a knock at my door.

I expected it to be Kathy. Instead, it was a young Asian man dressed in a starched white jacket and carrying a tray on which sat a metal champagne bucket holding a bottle of the bubbly and a bowl of fruit.

"Mrs. Fletcher, I'm Raymond, your cabin steward."

"Hello," I said.

"May I come in?"

"Of course."

"Compliments of the captain," he said, setting the tray on a coffee table in front of a small couch. He handed me an envelope.

"Thank you, Raymond."

"Please call on me if there's anything you need," he said, smiling. He gave me a direct number to dial. "Your luggage should be up shortly. Have a very pleasant cruise."

He left, and I opened the envelope. In it was an invitation to a five o'clock cocktail party hosted by Captain Rasmussen.

*How nice*, I thought, hoping that Kathy had received

one, too. I made sure I had my key before stepping into the narrow hallway and knocking on her door.

"Hi, Jessica," she said. "The room is lovely."

"It certainly is. Did you receive an invitation to a cocktail party this afternoon?"

"Yes, the room steward delivered it, along with fruit and champagne. I got this, too."

I read the typewritten note she handed me. It was from the ship's head of security, First Officer Kale.

Dear Ms. Copeland—
   I see from the passenger manifest that you will be joining us on this Alaskan cruise. Naturally, I was interested in why you'd chosen to be on the cruise after having been with us just a short time ago. As I promised you during your previous visit, we will keep you fully informed of any developments in the search for your sister. I assume that you've chosen to take this cruise to further investigate her unfortunate disappearance. I would like to meet with you at your earliest convenience to offer any continuing help, although as I've pointed out, it is now a police matter. But we stand ready to assist you in any way.

"I'm impressed that he picked up your name from the passenger manifest," I said. "You'll meet with him, of course."

"*We'll* meet with him," she said. "I'm afraid I wasn't very good at asking questions the last time I was with him."

"If you'd like," I said. "Ready for the emergency drill?"

"I suppose so. I've never been to one before."

"It's easy," I said. "We gather together in our assigned meeting spots near our lifeboats and are told what to do in case of an emergency."

"I hope we don't have to use that information."

I laughed. "I'm sure we won't, Kathy. Come on, put on your life vest. We don't want to be late."

After the emergency drill had been completed, and our luggage had been delivered to our rooms, the *Glacial Queen* left the Seattle pier and we were on our way to Alaska. I stood on my balcony and watched the busy waterfront slip by slowly and silently.

Kathy called First Officer Kale. He arrived at her cabin a few minutes later, and I joined them. Kale was a nice-looking young man in a nondescript sort of way. His blue uniform was tailored and pressed, his hair, carrot red, was close-cropped in true military style. At first, he was somewhat uncomfortable having me there, but Kathy explained who I was and why we were traveling together. While that seemed to mollify him, I had the impression from the outset that he would have been happier had neither of us been on the cruise.

"As I've told Ms. Copeland," he said to me after we'd taken seats around the coffee table, "there's really nothing further we can offer in the way of help regarding her sister's disappearance."

"I understand that," Kathy said, "but I couldn't just sit back at home without trying to do something to find her. I thought that by retracing Willie's steps, especially with Mrs. Fletcher, I might learn something that's helpful."

"Of course," Kale said, shifting in his chair. "It's just that—"

"It's just that having us onboard looking for someone who ended up missing from your ship might be unsettling to other passengers," I said.

He smiled at me and nodded.

"I assure you," I said, "that we'll be as discreet as possible."

"I don't doubt that for a minute," Kale responded, "and please don't misunderstand. We're delighted to have you as passengers. But, as you say, Mrs. Fletcher, we want to do everything possible to ensure that our other passengers are not inconvenienced."

"Then there's no misunderstanding," I said brightly. "As long as you're here, I do have a few questions."

"Go ahead."

"With so many passengers aboard, I imagine you can't know everyone on your cruise, but I was wondering if, when Kathy's sister was on the ship, you had an opportunity to observe her."

"Observe her?"

"Wilimena has a rather flamboyant personality. I'm assuming you must have seen her."

" 'Seen her'? Yes, of course. Over the eight days of the cruise, I get to interact with many of the passengers. Well, let me qualify that. I only come in direct contact with passengers who experience a security problem." Aware that he probably shouldn't have acknowledged that such things occurred on his ship, he quickly added, "Of course, those instances are rare, few and far between."

"I'm sure that's true," I said. "Was Wilimena one of those passengers—with security problems?"

He thought before replying. "Yes, she was."

"What sort of security problems did she have?"

Kale stretched his neck, ran an index finger inside his collar, and swallowed audibly. "Um, she, um, complained of being stalked by other passengers."

"Really?" Kathy said. "You didn't tell me that the last time we spoke."

"It never occurred to me," said Kale.

*Strange that it wouldn't occur to a security officer*, I thought.

"You said 'passengers.' Plural. Who were they?" I asked.

"There were accusations. Nothing was ever proven. I don't think it would be appropriate for me to reveal that."

"Even if it might help find Ms. Copeland?"

"I've shared what I know with the authorities, Mrs. Fletcher. It's their problem now." He placed his hands flat on his knees and prepared to rise, clearly ready to end this conversation.

"Please, Officer Kale," I said. "We won't keep you much longer."

He sank back into his seat, but his expression said he was not happy to continue.

"When you spoke with the authorities, did you share the names of those passengers, the ones Wilimena thought were stalking her?" I asked.

"No," he said, shaking his head, "I don't believe I did."

"May I ask why not?"

"Because it isn't my role to besmirch the reputations of our passengers," he said. "What Ms. Copeland was referring to was nothing more than harmless flirtations. Happens all the time on cruises."

"But women don't disappear 'all the time on cruises,' " I said, unsuccessful at masking my annoyance.

"I understand what you're saying, Mrs. Fletcher, but try to appreciate our position. We're in the business of providing a relaxing, fun-filled cruise to almost two thousand people every time we leave port. Unless something of a serious nature arises while a passenger is on board, we try to stay out of their lives. Ms. Copeland disappeared on a shore excursion. Our responsibility ends when passengers walk down the gangway, leave the ship, and set out on their own. Unless, of course, they're part of a planned shore excursion with one of our partners at the ports of call. We checked Ms. Copeland's itinerary, including those shore excursions she might have signed up for when booking the cruise. There were none."

"She was last seen getting off the ship in Ketchikan," Kathy said. "Maybe she signed up for a shore excursion after she left the ship."

"I suggested that possibility to the police," Kale said, obviously pleased to have something positive to offer. "They reported back that no one they questioned on the docks or in the travel kiosks remembered her."

Kathy sighed, turned from him, and rubbed her eyes. I felt for her. Our initial contact wasn't producing any useful information. We'd learned more from the shopkeepers in Seattle.

"Well, Officer Kale," I said, "I do understand your

position in all of this. But I'm also sure that you realize the seriousness of the situation. A woman who'd taken your ship to Alaska is missing."

"Yes, of course," he said, rising. This time he made it all the way out of his seat, and I knew our interview was concluding.

"Before you go—what was the outcome of Ms. Copeland's complaints about male passengers stalking her? Did you investigate?"

He shrugged and tugged at his cuffs. "I personally approached one of the men, a very nice gentleman traveling alone. When I told him of what Ms. Copeland had alleged, he was flabbergasted." Kale's eyes darted to Kathy's face and back to mine. "He said that *she'd* been making advances toward *him* ever since they met at the first night's captain's party."

Given what we'd heard from the Seattle shopkeepers, Kale's comment wasn't beyond the realm of possibility. I shouldered my bag and stood. Kathy did as well. As we escorted him to the door, Kale hesitated, then nodded sharply as if he'd just made a decision. "I don't wish to speak out of turn," he said, "but frankly, it was sometimes hard to assign much credibility to Ms. Copeland."

"Why was that?" Kathy asked.

Kale smiled kindly. "Your sister was—is—well, she is a woman with—how shall I say it?—with a vivid imagination."

"I'm not sure what you mean," she said.

He sighed. "Well, some of her dinner companions became weary of hearing her talk about the gold she was about to inherit."

"She spoke openly about that?" I asked, knowing the answer.

Another sigh. "She spoke about it—to everyone," he said. "Please call on me if I can be of any further help. But as I said earlier, it would be very much appreciated if you conduct your shipboard investigation quietly and without disturbing other passengers."

"We'll do our best," I said.

He'd already opened the door when I asked, "Were there any other 'security issues' involving Wilimena Copeland?"

He stepped into the corridor, saying nothing.

"Officer Kale?" I prompted.

"She claimed on two occasions that someone had broken into her cabin."

"And?"

"I could find no evidence of it."

"Thank you."

When he was gone, Kathy threw up her hands and said, "Maybe this wasn't such a good idea, Jess."

"Don't lose faith so quickly, Kathy. We've just started. From what Officer Kale said, Willie let the entire ship know about the gold."

"Yes, but all those people have gone home. We don't even know who they are. This is hopeless, Jessica."

"I don't think so," I said. "There have to be plenty of crew members who spoke with her during the cruise. They're still here. What we have to do is talk with as many of them as we can."

Kathy's glum expression didn't change.

"I know, I know," I said. "It's a lot to contemplate, but Willie's penchant for letting everyone she met in on the purpose of her trip might be behind her disappearance."

"It might have gotten her in trouble, you mean."

"Yes. It's possible someone could have followed her or even offered to accompany her in the hope of striking pay dirt himself. Or herself."

"How could she have been so foolish?" Kathy asked, tears filling her eyes.

"No sense in dwelling on that," I said. "Her indiscretions are in the past. We have to move forward." I took her arm. "How about taking a quick stroll around the ship before the captain's party? I like to acclimate myself to new surroundings, and I think we can use a little exercise. It helps to clear the mind."

Like all large, modern cruise ships, the *Glacial Queen* had numerous deck levels, eleven in all, with myriad function rooms spread throughout the ship. Our staterooms were on the navigation deck, four decks down from the topmost sports deck. We took the wide central staircase down five decks to the promenade deck, where we perused the shopping area, a few of the ship's bars, the Internet center where passengers could log on to the dozen available computers and receive computer instruction, the photo gallery where the photos taken of passengers as they boarded were displayed for sale, and the Upper Vista, one of two main dining rooms. We'd opted to dine at seven thirty, the later seating in the Upper Vista.

"It's a beautiful ship," Kathy said as we headed back up to the navigation deck to spruce up before the party. "And I've worked up an appetite from the walk."

"Me, too," I replied.

As we turned into the corridor where our cabins were located, we saw a man wearing white shorts, a white T-shirt, and sandals standing just outside Kathy's room. He wasn't aware of our presence until we were almost upon him.

"Good afternoon," I said.

He was clearly startled, as though he'd been caught at something he wasn't supposed to be doing. He mumbled a few words and hurried away.

"I wonder what he was doing here," Kathy said as we used our keys to open our doors.

"Probably has a cabin on this deck and wandered into the wrong hallway," I said. "It's easy to confuse them."

"I suppose."

"Meet up with you in fifteen minutes?"

Though I'd dismissed Kathy's suspicions about the man, I had found his behavior a tad peculiar. He didn't look familiar, yet I couldn't get his face out of my mind. I've developed a fairly keen sense over the years of remembering people's appearances, even after only momentary exposure to them. This gentleman was slender and no taller than five feet five inches. His face was extremely narrow, almost as though his head had been squeezed in a vise, causing his facial features to extend into sharp relief. His hair was thin, sandy and silky, worn almost shoulder length. I shook my head to erase his image. I needed to think about a change of clothes instead.

The cocktail party was held in the elegant Explorers' Lounge, toward the rear of the lower promenade deck. A harp encased in a cover testified to the sort

of music that would be played there later in the evening—classical and soothing.

"Ah, good evening," the ship's chief officer, Captain
Rasmussen, said as we reached him after proceeding
along a reception line of four uniformed officers. He
struck me as remarkably young to be in command of
such a large vessel, but I suppose I was operating from
a stereotype of what a ship's captain should look like—
silver-haired, and with a lined face from having stared
into the sun too long. Also, as I get older, I'm surprised
to find that everyone looks so young. It shouldn't be a
surprise, of course, but somehow it always is. Police
officers all look like rookies to me, even those who've
been on the force for years. Politicians are the age of
my nephew Grady. And I could swear those television
newscasters just graduated from journalism school.
Some of this may be our culture's obsession with youth
and looking young, but I have to admit it also may be
my advancing age. When I catch a glimpse of myself in
the mirror, I no longer see a young face, even though
inside I feel the same as when my late husband, Frank,
and I were courting. But the wrinkles and gray hairs
in my reflection remind me that that was many years
ago.

And here in front of me was another very young
man in a position of authority. Captain Rasmussen
took my hand in both of his and smiled warmly. "I
must say, Mrs. Fletcher, that we are extremely honored
to have such an important author on board." His voice
was low and well modulated, with the hint of a Dutch
accent.

I was flattered that he had heard of me. "I'm very

happy to be here," I said. I turned and indicated Kathy. "This is my good friend Kathy Copeland. We're traveling together."

"Of course," he said. "I had the pleasure of meeting with Ms. Copeland only last week. I didn't expect I'd be repeating the pleasure so soon."

"I didn't, either," Kathy said. "My decision to take this cruise was a very last-minute one."

"Well," Rasmussen said, "you're obviously traveling in good company. Enjoy some champagne and canapés. I'm sure we'll have a chance to chat more later."

We settled in two chairs in a corner of the room where a member of the ship's waitstaff brought us flutes of champagne and a tray of cold canapés.

"He's charming," I said.

"And handsome," Kathy said, biting into one of the hors d'oeuvres. "Yum. Delicious."

"I didn't realize you'd actually met with the captain when you were here last week," I said.

"I'd forgotten about it," she said. "I only saw him for a few minutes. He basically told me how sorry he was to have learned about Willie's disappearance."

"Did he indicate that he, too, knew about the gold?"

"No. At least he didn't mention it."

"Do you think he's married?" I said.

"Why? Are you interested in him, Jess?"

"No, of course not. I was just wondering whether Willie might have flirted with him."

Kathy shook her head, smiled, and sipped her champagne. "It's certainly possible," she said. "Why should he be any different?"

As she said it, Captain Rasmussen, who'd greeted his final guest at the door, came to us and took a chair next to Kathy.

"Well, Ms. Copeland," he said, "have the authorities given you any further news about your sister?"

"No, Captain. Nothing new at all."

"Pity. She was a very nice woman."

"Did you have a chance to get to know her?" I asked. "On a personal basis?"

His eyebrows went up. " 'Personal basis,' Mrs. Fletcher?" He laughed easily. "I'm afraid my duties as captain of this ship preclude me from getting personal with my passengers. Did I get to speak with her? Of course. She attended this reception just as you are doing this evening. We had a pleasant chat."

"Officer Kale said she'd complained of men making unwanted advances toward her," I said, "and of break-ins to her cabin."

"Yes. I received those reports from him. He assured me there was nothing to them."

"I'm sure my sister didn't make up those things," Kathy said, a modicum of pique in her voice.

"I'm not suggesting that she did, Ms. Copeland. But Officer Kale didn't find anything tangible to support her accusations. You must excuse me. I'm needed back on the bridge. Enjoy the rest of the party—and your cruise."

"Did Wilimena tell you about the gold?" I asked as he started to walk away.

He stopped, turned, and came back to us. "As a matter of fact, she did," he said. "To be perfectly honest with you, her constant reference to it all over the ship was not, in my opinion, a terribly prudent thing to do."

"Did you suggest that to her?" I asked.

"No. It was not my place. Good evening, ladies."

He gathered the other officers and they strode from the lounge.

Kathy finished her champagne and said, "I'm ready to go, Jess."

As we waited for an elevator to take us up to the navigation deck, she said, "I'm getting a little tired of people portraying Willie as some sort of kook, some unbalanced woman who imagines things."

"I understand," I said. "But—"

The doors slid open and we stepped inside.

"But she did act strange," Kathy said, finishing my sentence. "I acknowledge that. But it doesn't mean she's crazy."

"Of course it doesn't. The problem, Kathy, is that we're going to be speaking with a lot of people on the ship who might have that view of her. I'm afraid you'd better get used to it. What's important is that we find out what happened to her."

We had a little time left before our seating for dinner. Kathy retired to her cabin to do some reading, and I took a second tour around the *Glacial Queen*, taking in areas we'd not seen the first time. I ended up in the library, where a number of passengers had already settled in for some serious board games. My past experience suggested that they would be found there for the duration of the cruise, hunched over the boards, brows creased as they enjoyed their obsession. People on ships often gravitate to specific places, choosing one lounge over the others as their favorite or one pool they prefer, finding companions for their interests and returning each day to enjoy the experience.

I scanned books on a shelf and stopped at a slender, well-worn volume on the history of the Alaskan gold rush of the late 1800s. I pulled it down, sat in one of a pair of brown leather chairs separated by a small table, and started paging through it. I was reading about a fascinating woman known as Klondike Kate, a popular entertainer during the gold rush, when a short, slender woman in her seventies approached me, carrying a book. She had white hair, a deep tan, and blue eyes that sparkled radiantly.

"Would I be disturbing you if I sit here?" she asked, indicating the matching leather chair.

"No, of course not," I said. "Please do."

She took the chair, adjusted herself in it, and opened her book.

I went back to reading about Klondike Kate. After a few minutes, I glanced over at her. To my surprise, she was reading my latest novel. She sensed my interest, turned, and smiled sweetly. "I love your books, Mrs. Fletcher," she said.

"Thank you," I said, a little startled that she recognized me. Of course, my photograph on the back cover could explain that.

"I was told that you would be on board," she said demurely.

"You were?"

"Yes. My cabin steward always informs me of any famous people on the ship."

"You sound as though you take this cruise often," I said.

Her laugh was small and tinkling. "I would say so, Mrs. Fletcher. I live on the *Glacial Queen*."

At first, I thought she meant that she took a lot of cruises. On other ships, I've met people who pride themselves on how many cruises they've taken and how many ports they've visited. But then I realized that she meant what she'd said literally.

"How interesting. You *live* on board?" I said.

"Yes. I've been a resident for almost a year now. I lived on the *QE2* for almost two years. I loved that ship—so genteel and refined. But I decided it was time for a change—change is always good, don't you agree?—so I did a little investigating and decided on this ship."

I closed my book, shifted in my chair so that I faced her, and said, "I didn't realize that anyone lived on this ship."

"Oh, yes," she replied. "I'm the only one here, but I was one of three on the *QE2*—myself, another woman, and a lovely gentleman. I'm pleased to report that they are now married."

"Your two permanent shipmates?"

"Yes. I was her maid of honor."

My curiosity antennae were now fully extended. "Isn't it terribly expensive to live on a cruise ship?" I asked.

"I suppose it is, but not much more, if anything, than being in one of those homes for old people. And it's so much more pleasant than an institution. The meals are wonderful and so nicely presented. I have entertainment every night, and I get to see so many interesting places—Alaska, the Caribbean, Asia, Europe. Besides, there are always new and interesting people to meet. Like you."

"I see your point," I said.

"When Maynard told me you were on the passenger list, I asked him to run right out in Seattle and buy me your latest book. Maynard is my cabin steward, a dear, sweet young man." She lowered her voice to a conspiratorial level. "I always make sure to give him a large bonus at the end of each trip. The young people on the ship work so hard, you know, and send their money back home. They're all from other countries."

"You must know everything that goes on aboard the ship," I said.

"I imagine I do," she said. "By the way, my name is Gladys, Gladys Montgomery." She extended a bony hand with long fingers tipped by an expertly executed manicure.

"I'm Jessica," I said. "Do you mind if I ask you a question, Gladys? I assume you heard about the woman who disappeared from this ship a few weeks ago."

"Wilimena."

"That's right."

"Why do you ask? Are you going to write a book about her disappearance?"

"No. My interest is that—"

"Her sister is on this cruise, too."

"I know."

"You do? How did you find out?"

"She and I are good friends where we live, Cabot

Cove, Maine. I'm traveling with her. We're hoping that by retracing Wilimena's tracks, we might be able to find out what happened to her."

"My goodness, I really must scold Maynard. He missed that bit of information. He didn't tell me that you and Wilimena's sister were together."

I had to laugh. Along with the other benefits she mentioned of living aboard a luxury cruise ship, there was being in on the daily gossip.

"Did you get to know Wilimena?" I asked, confident that she had.

"Of course. I get to know almost everyone before a cruise ends."

"What was your impression of her?"

She sat back, laced her fingers together, and sighed. "That is a very difficult question to answer. I liked her, of course. Wilimena was—she called herself Willie, you know—Willie was charming in her own way. I admired her verve and spirit. She was so full of life and eager for adventure." She leaned closer. "She was about to become very wealthy, you know."

"From the gold."

"Yes. Poor thing. I don't consider myself a fortune-teller, mind you, but I have this feeling that it was the gold that brought about her demise."

"Her demise? You think she's dead?"

"I assume she is. Otherwise she wouldn't have disappeared like this. The way I see it, she was intercepted on her way to claim the gold by someone who knew about it and wanted it for himself. I suggested to her that she not talk about it so freely while on the ship, but she was giddy with anticipation. I suppose I can't blame her. I've never had to worry about money, thanks to my dear, departed husband, Joseph. He was quite successful on Wall Street."

"I'm glad he left you without worry," I said. "I understand Willie complained to the ship's security officer about men making unwanted advances toward her."

"Officer Kale. Yes, Willie was bothered by some of the more crass men on board, but to be perfectly honest, Jessica, I'm afraid she invited such attention. She dressed in what can only be described as provocative clothing." She wrinkled her nose and placed her fingers on my arm. "She was a little old for some of the outfits she chose."

I smiled. "She refused to acknowledge her age?"

"Exactly."

"Did you happen to get to know any of the men who were attracted to her? The ones who made nuisances of themselves?"

"Well, let me see," she said, an index finger to her lips. "There was Maurice."

"Maurice?"

"A Frenchman, but you knew that from the name. A shallow fellow, far too charming, in a Continental way, for my taste. He's been on the ship before, a few times, actually. He has some connection with the cruise line. I never bothered to find out more. What's the term I'm looking for? Smarmy. Yes, that's it. He was smarmy. Let me see. There was John Sims, too. A lovely man. Wilimena flirted quite openly with him, which is why I was surprised when I heard that she'd complained about his making unappreciated advances."

I wondered if John Sims was the "flabbergasted" gentleman to whom Officer Kale had referred.

"Do you know where Mr. Sims and Maurice came from? Where they live?"

She made a sour face. "Maurice? Heavens, no. I had no interest in learning anything about *him*. But John gave me his card at the end of the cruise. I have it here in my purse." She retrieved it and handed it to me. "John was a true gentleman, and I can assure you that he had nothing to do with Ms. Copeland's disappearance. My goodness, he's old enough to be her father—eighty if he's a day. I think he found it amusing that Ms. Copeland showed such interest in him. Flattered, I suppose, until she complained that *he* was making advances at *her*. He stayed clear of her for the duration of the cruise, avoided her as though she might have some communicable disease."

"I agree," I said, "that he's unlikely to know anything about where Wilimena has gone. Thank you, Gladys, for the information and for your insight."

"My pleasure, Jessica. By the way, we'll be dining together. I arranged for that once I learned that you would be sailing with us."

"How did you manage that?" I asked.

"They're so nice on the ship, so accommodating. Whenever someone interesting is booked, they allow me to join them for dinner. We have a table for six. I hope that's acceptable to you. I wouldn't want to intrude, but—"

"I'll consider it a privilege," I said. "Speaking of dinner, I'd better go to my cabin and get ready."

"Before you go, would you be so kind as to sign my book?"

I signed it, of course, thinking as I did of the crazed man at the Seattle Mystery Bookshop.

"How sweet," she said after reading what I'd written. "I'll treasure it."

I checked in on Kathy before going into my cabin, and told her of my encounter with Mrs. Montgomery and of the two men who'd spent time with Willie.

"She has the one man's address?"

"Yes. He gave her his card when the cruise was over."

"But we don't know any more about this Maurice character."

"Maybe we can find out through the ship's executive offices. They must have information about him. Give me fifteen minutes to spruce up."

The dining room's maître d' showed us to our assigned table. It was in a prime location, next to large windows at the ship's stern, affording us splendid views of the sea. The sun was setting, turning the ship's sizable wake into a panorama of golden ripples. Mrs. Montgomery, dressed in a stunning sequined lavender evening gown and sporting a dazzling array of jewelry that testified to just how well-off her husband had left her, was already seated. I introduced Kathy, and we took chairs on either side of her. Moments later, a middle-aged couple, Kimberly and David Johansen, were escorted to the table by the maître d'. After they'd been seated, the maître d' announced that a sixth person would be joining us. "He was somewhat unhappy with his assigned table and asked if it could be changed. Since you have an empty place, I hoped you wouldn't mind."

Gladys's expression said she wasn't particularly happy with the arrangement, but she said nothing. A minute later, the maître d' arrived with a handsome man whom I judged to be in his mid-fifties. He wore a blue blazer, gray slacks, a white button-down shirt, and a pale yellow tie.

"Thanks for rescuing me," he said immediately after taking the vacant chair across from Kathy. "My name's Bill."

After we'd introduced ourselves, he said, "I didn't think I'd end up at such a celebrity table. I know that you're Jessica Fletcher, the writer. And Mrs. Montgomery is known to all, or so I understand."

"You're traveling alone?" Gladys asked.

"Yes, ma'am. You might say this is a therapeutic cruise for me. My wife and I always planned on taking an Alaskan cruise, but unfortunately she died before we got around to it. I thought this would be a proper way to pay tribute to her."

"That's so nice," said Kathy.

"Where do you live, Mr.—? I didn't catch your last name," David Johansen said.

"Henderson. Bill Henderson. Seattle. Can you believe it? We lived right next door to where all the ships to Alaska leave from, but never booked a cruise." An expression of sadness crossed his square, tanned face, and he looked down at the table.

The Johansens didn't have much to say at first, but were eventually drawn into the conversation. They were celebrating their anniversary. He was a history professor at Wheaton College in Illinois; she was the editor of a weekly newspaper in their hometown. Talk at the table touched upon myriad topics, as is usually the case when strangers meet for the first time. David Johansen became animated when the subject turned to politics and world events, and he offered several strongly worded opinions on the day's most provocative news events. His wife, Kimberly, was particularly interested in education and what she perceived as the federal government's failure to promote it. There was, of course, interest in my books, particularly my working habits and how I came up with plots for my mysteries. Bill Henderson fit easily into the flow of things, demonstrating a keen interest in what everyone was saying and asking many questions. After I had explained how I try to develop three-dimensional characters in my books, he asked Kathy, "And what about you, Ms. Copeland? What occupies your time?"

Kathy smiled and shrugged. "I'm afraid my life isn't nearly as exciting as everyone else's," she said. "I'm pretty much a homebody."

"So am I," Henderson said. "And being a homebody can be just as exciting as you want it to be." His laugh was easy. "For me, there's nothing more exciting than when my lobster bisque turns out the way I want it to be."

Everyone laughed.

"No, I'm serious," he said.

"Kathy makes a wonderful lobster bisque," I said. "And she's quite a baker, too—usually takes one of the top prizes in our town's bake-off competitions."

He asked a series of questions about Cabot Cove, and Kathy enthusiastically answered them. I was pleased to see her in such good spirits. She'd fallen into moments of depression since we'd left on the trip, and I knew it was important for her to remain upbeat and optimistic. She undoubtedly did not hold out much hope that Wilimena would be found alive, and to be honest, neither did I. But maybe we were wrong. Until a definitive reason behind her disappearance was determined, we had to forge ahead and hope for the best.

Gladys Montgomery wasn't especially talkative. She sat ramrod straight at the table, a regal matriarch presiding over a family dinner. But she did offer an occasional comment. When David Johansen expressed a political opinion that revealed his conservative leanings, she said, "When one gets older, Mr. Johansen, one is expected to become more conservative, based upon the assumption that one has more to conserve. For me, the older I get, the more liberal I become, perhaps not so much politically but in accepting the human condition. We can only judge a society based upon the way it treats its less fortunate."

Johansen started to debate that with her, but she said it with such finality that he thought better of it and allowed the talk to change to less weighty topics.

"Well," Henderson said after we'd finished dessert and were about to leave the table, "I must say this has been my lucky night. You never know who you'll end up having dinner with on a cruise, and frankly—" He looked across the vast restaurant. "Frankly, I wasn't at all happy with the people they seated me with. Thanks for allowing the switch."

"It was our pleasure, Mr. Henderson," said Gladys, who'd obviously warmed to him as dinner progressed. We all had. He was a charming, pleasantly modest man, whose sincere interest in what others had to say made him the perfect dinner companion.

"Up for a little nightlife?" he asked as we gathered just outside the restaurant's entrance. The Johansens had headed off to catch the amateur talent show.

"I'll be doing what I usually do after dinner," Gladys announced. "Listening to the classical music concert in the Explorers' Lounge. You're free to join me."

"I just might do that," I said. "I assume we'll see each other at breakfast."

"Unless the good Lord has other plans," she said, and walked away.

"Might I take you ladies dancing?" Henderson asked. "I'm not much on my feet, but it's good exercise."

I laughed. "I'm afraid I prefer getting my exercise other ways, Bill. But you go ahead, Kathy. As they say, the night is young."

"Oh, I really don't think that—"

"Ah, come on," he said. "I promise I'll get you back to your cabin in time for a good night's beauty sleep."

Kathy looked at me for approval. I nodded. "Have fun," I said. "See you in the morning."

As I watched them walk away, I couldn't help but think that they made a nice-looking couple. Kathy, I knew, was fond of dancing and had taken ballroom lessons in Cabot Cove. She was also an ardent square dancer. How ironic if during this unpleasant journey in search of her missing sister, she found romance.

I considered joining Gladys in the Explorers' Lounge

but decided against it. The meal had been elaborate and filling. I needed to do something that involved more than sitting.

I wandered down to the lower promenade deck and followed the sound of slot machines to the casino, where the post-dinner gambling action was in full swing. I'm not a gambler, although I suppose that every time I devote many months to writing a book, I'm gambling that it will appeal to enough readers to make it worthwhile.

I have, however, been in casinos before and have even pulled an occasional slot machine lever, investing a couple of quarters for the experience. But what has always fascinated me is the craps table. Of all the games, that seems to be the one in which the players have the most fun, whooping and hollering, their fortunes rising and falling on the next roll of the dice.

A spirited game was in progress, and I sidled up to watch the action. I took in each player surrounding the green felt playing surface and smiled. Win or lose, they seemed to be enjoying themselves. As I observed the table, a man entered the casino, the same man we'd seen in our hallway earlier in the day. He came directly to the craps table and tossed a hundred-dollar bill on it. "Change," he told one of the young crew members, who shoved a pile of chips toward him. He wore the same clothes as when I'd first seen him: white shorts, T-shirt, and sandals. I wondered whether he'd worn that outfit to the dining room. While this first night at sea wasn't designated a formal night—tuxedo or suit and tie for men, evening wear for the women—I'd seen no one at dinner who wasn't dressed in what might be termed neat-casual, which didn't include shorts and sandals. Had he changed clothing after dinner before heading for the casino?

He hadn't noticed me, and I stood behind him, watching intently as the game continued. I had no idea what was going on. It seemed that when someone rolled a seven with the dice, it won money for the players at the table. But then someone else rolled a seven at a different time and it was a loser. Everyone was yelling and tossing chips on various sections of the table. How could anyone keep track of what was going on, especially the men and women in charge of the play?

A man standing next to the man in the white shorts muttered something about the dice going cold and left the table. A woman of approximately my age who'd been standing next to him motioned for me to take his place. I stepped up to the table, shook my head, and said, "I don't know how to play."

The man I'd been observing heard my voice and turned to face me. He grimaced, picked up what chips he had left on the railing in front of him, and left.

"Maybe another time," I told the woman.

"It's fun," she said. "This table is about to get hot. You'll miss the action."

I thanked her and looked for the man. He was gone. I peeked into the sports bar, where multiple TV sets featured replays of current sporting events. No luck. I walked through the nightclub, where a jolly bald man sat at a piano bar and sang tunes made familiar by Frank Sinatra, my kind of music. No white shorts there, either.

I retraced my steps to the dining room and went up

the circular staircase to the upper level where we'd had dinner. From reading material about the ship, I knew that the promenade deck was the only one that made a full circle—the exercise deck, three times around it and you've done a mile. I went to a door leading outside, stepped through it, and took in a deep breath of salty sea air. The full moon was now partially obscured by low clouds that seemed suspended like a gauzy gray shroud. There was a damp mist in the air; we were heading into less-pleasant weather than we'd experienced in Seattle. Still, it was good to be outdoors. Was I up to three turns around the deck? Probably not. That would wait until morning. But once around was appealing. The low-heeled red shoes with rubber soles that I'd worn to dinner would provide decent traction on the slippery deck.

As I started to walk, I thought about my unusual interest in the man dressed in white. I'm not an advocate of the "woman's intuition" theory. My experience has been that men have intuition every bit as keen as women's. Maybe my heightened interest in him was because I've devoted so much of my professional life to delving into crime, both literary and, unfortunately, real. I've spent considerable time with members of law enforcement; perhaps their natural curiosity and suspicious nature have rubbed off on me. Whatever the reason, there was something about the man that told me to be a little more observant.

An older couple coming from the opposite direction said hello as they passed. I was pleased to see them. There was something eerie about being out there alone, and I considered turning and following them, but I didn't. I kept walking in the direction of the bow, keeping my legs a little farther apart to compensate for the ship's motion through the water. There was more movement than there had been earlier in the evening. I stopped, went to the rail, and looked out over the sea. A pronounced swell had begun to build, a departure from the slick calmness that had prevailed when we set sail.

I continued on my nocturnal walk. The moisture-laden air was chilly, and I pulled the crimson jacket I'd worn to dinner a little closer around me as I neared the front of the ship. I glanced through windows into the public rooms, now populated with men and women enjoying their first night at sea. *Once around*, I told myself. *Pick up the pace, Jess.*

I walked faster until I reached the point where the deck curved to the left, bringing me to the bow. I stopped and drew a series of breaths as I looked ahead, seeing what the ship's crew was seeing from the bridge high above. A briny spray stung my cheeks and nose. I heard footsteps and turned. A power-walking young couple came into view.

"Good evening," I said.

"Hi. Getting stormy," the man said as they passed from my sight to the opposite side of the ship.

I was about to continue my walk when I heard more footsteps. I waited to see who they belonged to. They stopped just out of my line of vision. Maybe whoever it was decided to retrace his or her steps and not complete the circuit. But I didn't hear the sound of feet fading away.

I took steps back in the direction from which I'd

come. As I rounded the bend, I came face-to-face with the man in the white shorts. He obviously hadn't expected to be confronted by me, judging from the look of confusion on his thin face. He stared at me for a moment with eyes that were almost yellow in the diffused light of the moon, before hurrying away, almost at a run.

"Excuse me," I called after him.

He turned his head but never broke stride.

I started after him but thought better of it. Instead, I completed my one turn around the deck, ducked inside, and went to my cabin. After donning an extra jacket to ward off the chill, I went out onto my balcony and gazed out over the expanse of black water.

Who was this man who I was now certain had a special interest in me, and possibly in Kathy?

I would not let another day go by without finding out.

# Chapter Four

Gladys Montgomery was already at the table when Kathy and I walked into the dining room the following morning. The *Glacial Queen*'s grande dame, in a stylish aqua pantsuit, was adorned by only slightly less jewelry than she had worn the night before. I thought back to her comment at dinner about judging societies by how they treat their less fortunate, a philosophy not often associated with wealthy older women. No doubt about it, this was a formidable human being, as secure in her views as she was financially.

When Kathy had picked me up to go down for breakfast, I immediately noticed something different about her. She seldom wore much makeup, and always applied it with a light touch. This morning, however, she'd applied a deep red lipstick, eye shadow, and mascara, and had painted her cheeks a glowing pink. Or were the pink cheeks natural, generated by an inner liveliness?

"You look ready to attack the day," I commented.

"Nothing like a good night's sleep," Kathy replied with a wide smile.

"Did you enjoy the concert last night?" I asked Gladys after we'd taken our seats at the table.

"Very much. They played Vivaldi. It's said that Vivaldi wrote four hundred concertos. I prefer to think that he wrote one concerto four hundred times. Still, it was pleasant, although the violinist's intonation was slightly off."

"I don't know much about classical music," Kathy said. "My tastes run to bluegrass, and country and western."

If my friend's musical tastes failed to please Gladys, the older woman didn't state it. She merely smiled and consulted her menu.

After we'd ordered, I asked Kathy how her evening had gone.

"It was fun," she said. "Bill is a very good dancer."

Gladys looked at us over half-glasses. "You're speaking of Mr. Henderson?" she asked.

"Yes," said Kathy.

"A very pleasant man," Gladys said, now turning her attention to that morning's shipboard notice of activities, accompanied by a description of Glacier Bay, our first stop after a day and night at sea. Actually, we wouldn't be stopping there in the usual sense of getting off the ship to explore the area. Glacier Bay was a body of water surrounded by some of Alaska's most spectacular glaciers. According to the flyer, we would arrive at eleven, and after passing Reid and Lamplugh glaciers, the ship would hold its position for much of the day just off such spectacular sights as the Grand Pacific and Margerie glaciers. My level of anticipation was high. I'd read about glaciers before leaving home and was eager to see just how far they'd retreated in this age of global warming. I'm no scientist, but it seems to me that *something* is happening that isn't good for this planet we inhabit.

I'd walked slowly when entering the dining room that morning, taking in each table in search of the man who was wearing white shorts and a T-shirt last night. He wasn't there.

"Gladys," I said, "you seem to know everyone on the ship. Did you notice a small, wiry man with a thin face yesterday? He was wearing white shorts and a white shirt."

She made a disgusted face. "He doesn't sound like someone I would pay particular attention to. Why do you ask?"

"Just curious," I said.

"The man we saw in the hallway?" Kathy asked.

I nodded as our breakfast was served.

As we were about to depart, the Johansens arrived. "Slept in a little," he said.

"That's a nice thing to do once in a while," I said. "How was the talent show?"

Kimberly laughed. "It was so funny," she said, "but amateur talent shows always are. I suppose that's why the TV show *American Idol* is so popular."

"I consider it cruel to make fun of well-meaning people," Gladys intoned.

"They're having fun," David Johansen said defensively.

"Perhaps," said Gladys.

"Excuse us," I said, pushing back my chair. "Time to get the day moving."

Kathy and I left the dining room and found two vacant overstuffed chairs alongside a window.

"Nasty weather," Kathy remarked. The rain was coming down hard, a stiff wind splattering drops against the pane.

"I hope it clears a little before we reach Glacier Bay," I said. "So, tell me about last night."

Kathy laughed. "What's to tell? We went to one of the clubs where they were playing old-fashioned swing music—you know, like Benny Goodman and Glenn Miller."

"Sounds nice."

"It was. He's a very interesting man, Jess. He was a jet pilot in the air force before becoming a financial advisor."

"Quite the combination," I said, "flying military jets and advising people on their financial futures."

"He has so many interests. Cooking. Gardening. He volunteers at a Seattle soup kitchen, too."

"Sounds like you have a lot in common. He missed breakfast."

"He said he was going to meet someone for breakfast in the Lido."

Like most cruise ships, the *Glacial Queen* has a buffet restaurant for those who don't wish to have meals in the main dining rooms. In this case, it's the Lido Café.

"I'm glad it was such a pleasant evening," I said. "Now, let's plan what we're going to do today. I want to see whether we can find out more about that passenger, Maurice. And the dining room staff that served at Willie's table during her cruise might have something to offer."

"All right," Kathy said.

"But let's leave time later today to enjoy the glaciers."

"Absolutely. Jess, about that man we saw in our hallway. Why are you interested in him?"

I told her about my run-in with him on the deck the previous night.

"You think he's following you?"

"It appears that way. Of course, it could just be coincidence. And I have to admit that I was the one doing the following in the casino."

She turned to peer out the window. Everything was gray outside, sea and sky. I saw her reflection in the pane. Her expression, so ebullient earlier, was now serious.

"Kathy?"

"What? Oh, sorry, Jess. I was thinking about that man. Do you think he might have known Willie?"

"I have no idea, Kathy, but I intend to find out who he is. Tell you what. I'll head down to the administrative offices and see if they'll tell me anything about this Maurice character. Why don't you see if you can find out which table Willie sat at in the dining room. We'll meet up in the library in an hour."

The ship's administrative offices, more commonly called the front office, was amidships on the main deck. There was a line of passengers waiting to transact business with the staff behind the counter, and I joined them. I was almost to the desk when I spotted First Officer Kale passing through the area.

"Officer Kale?" I called as he neared me.

"Good morning, Mrs. Fletcher. Have a pleasant breakfast?"

"Oh, yes. Very pleasant." I led him away from the others. "I was wondering if you would do me a large favor."

"If I'm able."

"One of the men that Wilimena Copeland complained about was a French gentleman named Maurice."

I knew from his expression that he was aware of the man to whom I referred.

"I'd like to know his last name and where he can be reached."

Now his expression said I'd asked for the impossible. "That would be inappropriate," he said, verbally supporting the stern look on his face.

"I understand the restrictions you feel you're under," I said, "but I'm also certain you can appreciate that this is a highly unusual situation."

"Of course. But—"

"I assure you that no one will ever know where I got my information. Please. There's a woman missing, and her sister has come all the way from Maine in hopes of finding out what happened to her. Surely you can break a rule or two to help her. Help *us*."

He sighed. "All right," he said. "I'll be back."

He returned a few minutes later with a computer printout containing the information I wanted. My eyebrows went up. "He *lives* in Alaska?" I said.

Kale nodded. "I'm trusting you, Mrs. Fletcher, to be discreet with what you choose to do with this information. Mr. Quarlé is a very good customer. He's a frequent passenger on our Alaskan cruises."

"I won't betray your trust," I said. "Thank you."

I left the area and went up to the Ocean Bar. I was the

only passenger there at that hour. I sat at a small table next to a window and studied more closely what Kale had given me. Maurice Quarlé's address was listed in Juneau, Alaska. We were scheduled to arrive there at seven the following morning. The printout indicated that he was unmarried and owned a travel agency in Alaska's capital. That would explain his status as a frequent guest on cruise ships like the *Glacial Queen*. My friend Susan Shevlin, who owns Cabot Cove's leading travel agency, always seems to be off on some familiarization trip hosted by a resort, airline, or steamship company. I've even had the good fortune to accompany her when her husband, Jim, Cabot Cove's mayor, was unable to find the time.

Had this Maurice Quarlé pursued Wilimena Copeland to the extent that she'd complained to the ship's security officer? It was hard to come up with a definitive answer to that question, knowing as I did her reputation as an inveterate flirt. But there was a bigger question to be answered. According to everything we'd learned to date, Willie had confided in everyone she met about inheriting gold from her aunt, Dolly Arthur. It was only natural to assume that she'd done the same with Mr. Quarlé.

Gladys Montgomery didn't have much use for him, even termed him "smarmy." Did she use the word to indicate a lack of morals and ethics, or was it purely her read of his personality? If it was the former, he was the wrong sort of person for Wilimena to have confided in about her pending gold strike. I made him number one on my priority list of things to do when we reached Juneau.

A waiter approached and I ordered a cup of tea. As I waited for it, David Johansen passed by. "Enjoying a little solitude?" he asked.

"Yes. You can usually find quiet time in a bar in the morning," I said.

"Mind if I join you?"

"Not at all."

My tea was delivered, and Johansen ordered coffee.

"I hope you don't mind my asking," he said, "but I hear through the grapevine that you're on a mission."

"Mission? How so?"

"To find a missing woman. Someone told me that Ms. Copeland is her sister."

I couldn't help but laugh. "The ubiquitous grapevine at work," I said. "Even on a ship hundreds of miles from shore."

"Especially on a ship," he said. "We're a captive audience. Have you made any progress in finding Kathy's sister?"

"No," I said, "but we've just started. Tell me, David, what does the grapevine have to say about it? Maybe there's something in the rumor mill that would be helpful."

"Well, from what I've heard, she was on her way to Alaska to claim gold left to her by her aunt, a famous brothel madam named Dolly Arthur."

"I'm impressed," I said. "The grapevine has it right so far."

"Dolly Arthur's real name was Thelma Copeland."

My eyebrows went up. "How do you know that?" I asked.

"The Alaskan gold rush is of particular interest to

me. I teach it as part of a course back at the college.
I've done a lot of reading about Dolly Arthur and others like her. Women who came to Alaska during that
period were a hardy breed, tough as nails. They had to
be to survive."

I sat back and nodded. "How coincidental," I said,
"that you would end up at our table."

"I've been thinking the same thing. Know what I'd
like to do?"

"Tell me."

"I'd like to interview Kathy. I'm sure she can add to
what I already know about her aunt Dolly."

"It's more likely that she'll learn from you, David.
But I think getting the two of you together is a splendid
idea."

He finished his coffee and stood. "I promised to
meet Kimberly in the shops. Always presents to buy
for the folks back home. Enjoy the rest of the day, Jessica. The glaciers are breathtaking." He pointed out the
window. "Looks like the rain is stopping. As long as it
stays overcast, we're in luck. The incredible blue colors
within the glaciers are best seen in overcast conditions.
Catch up with you later."

Kathy was already in the library when I arrived.

"Any luck?" she asked.

"I'd say so," I said, handing her the printout about
Maurice Quarlé.

"How did you get this, Jess?"

"First Officer Kale. He did me a favor."

"I'm glad he cooperated," Kathy said. "I was beginning to think that no one involved with the ship
would."

"How about you?" I asked. "Did you come up with anyone in the dining room who remembers serving Willie?"

"I sure did," she said proudly.

"Good for you."

"I spoke with a maître d' who remembered Willie. The lead waiter, too."

"Great! What did they have to say?"

She looked at me sheepishly. "I didn't ask them much, Jess. I thought you'd be better at that."

"All right. Who are they?"

She'd written their names on a slip of paper.

"They'll be too busy at lunch to talk with us," I said. "Maybe they have a break between lunch and dinner when we can corral them. Have you seen your Bill Henderson?"

"Yes, I bumped into him on my way here from the dining room. He said he'd be joining us for lunch."

"Good. I think what we might do next is—"

I saw *him* out of the corner of my eye, standing at the door to the library.

"Excuse me," I said.

I got up and headed for the door. The man with the thin face and flaxen hair—he'd changed into blue shorts and a pale yellow T-shirt—saw me coming and took off. I walked faster until I reached the hallway, where I saw him disappear around a corner. I went after him, walking fast at first and picking up the pace as he began to run.

"Hello," I called in a voice just below a shout. "Excuse me!"

He took a left turn, which brought him to a bank of

elevators and the center staircase. He went down the stairs two at a time.

"I want to talk to you!" I shouted and started down after him. But I tripped on the carpeted top step. Fortunately, I grabbed the brass banister before starting my descent and was able to keep myself from falling headfirst. But the force of my body hurtling forward and spinning around wrenched my arm and shoulder. I came to rest a few steps below where I'd started, on my rear end.

"Mrs. Fletcher! Are you all right?"

It was Bill Henderson, who was on his way up the stairs. He reached down and offered his hand to me.

"I think I'd better sit here a minute," I said, wincing against the stabbing pain in my shoulder.

"Of course. I'll get a doctor."

"No, no, please," I said. "That's not necessary. I'll be fine. Did you see that man?"

"What man?"

"The man running down the stairs. In the blue shorts and yellow T-shirt."

"No, I didn't. I saw you start to fall and—"

"That's all right," I said, taking his outstretched hand and slowly pulling myself to my feet.

"Did the man do something to you?" he asked as I leaned against the railing.

"No. It's just that—I think he's been following me."

"Following you? Why?"

"That's what I intend to ask him."

"Do you know who he is?"

I shook my head. "That's question number two. Thank you for your help, Bill. I feel like a clumsy fool."

"These stairs can be tricky," he said. "And with the ship's movement, taking a misstep is easy. I've done it myself."

"You make me feel less oafish," I said.

"Good. Come on. Let's find a quiet place for you to sit down."

"I left Kathy in the library."

"Then we'll go there."

Before we could take a step, Kathy appeared. "Are you all right, Jess?" she asked.

"I think so. Just a little sore."

"Why did you rush out of the library like that?"

"I saw the man who'd been following me."

"You did? Where is he?"

"I don't know. When he saw me, he bolted down these stairs."

"Strange behavior," Henderson said.

"Yes, I'd say so," I replied.

"We should report him to the ship's security people," Kathy said. "The man might be dangerous."

"Probably just some weirdo," Henderson said. "There's always a couple of them on a cruise. My suggestion? I think you should go to your cabin and rest. Taking a tumble like that can put a real strain on your entire body."

"You're probably right," I said. "But I want to be able to enjoy the glaciers." I checked my watch. "We should almost be to Glacier Bay."

"Won't be long," Henderson said. To Kathy, he said, "Take Mrs. Fletcher back to her cabin. I'll stroll around the ship and see if I can spot this character. He was wearing—?"

"Blue shorts and a yellow T-shirt."

"Right. If I spot him, I'll let you know."

"Thank you, Bill."

"My pleasure. Look forward to seeing you at lunch, provided you're feeling up to it."

He walked away, and Kathy and I headed for our cabins.

"You're in pain," she said, noticing the way I was walking and the grimace on my face.

"It could have been worse," I said. "If I hadn't had my hand around the banister, I would have gone all the way down."

"You shouldn't have chased him," she said.

"Too late for that advice."

Once inside my cabin, I decided not to lie down on the bed. I was afraid I wouldn't wake up for a long time, and that would mean missing Glacier Bay. Instead, I went out onto the balcony, sat in a chair, with a blanket wrapped around me to ward off the chilly air, and watched as the ship slowly made its way into the bay and toward the major glaciers that would provide our sightseeing for the day.

I thought of many things while sitting there. Who was the man I'd so foolishly chased? There was no doubt any longer that he was showing a particular interest in me. If not, why would he have run away like that? I had to find out who he was and whether there was some connection between him and Wilimena's disappearance.

I also thought of Bill Henderson. He could not have been more solicitous when coming to my aid. In the parlance of the man-woman mating game, he was undoubtedly a "catch." Thinking that there was the possibility that he might continue to show a sincere interest in Kathy brought a smile to my lips. How wonderful it would be if they became a couple and married one day. My smile broadened further as I reminded myself that I was terribly premature in conjuring such scenarios. I was behaving like Dolly Levi, the matchmaker in *Hello, Dolly!*

I extended my arm and was pleased that the pain had subsided somewhat. I got up, went to the railing, and looked down into the cold bay. Pieces of ice, large and small, floated by. A person wouldn't last more than a few minutes in that frigid water before hypothermia set in. Just the thought of it sent additional chills through me. I leaned over the railing a little to see ahead of the ship. In the distance was a gigantic wall of ice, its top obscured by lingering, low-hanging clouds. Even from that far away I could see the blue tint emanating from the ice. David Johansen had been right. The overcast skies would provide the perfect viewing situation, and I couldn't wait to get closer.

Kathy knocked on my door a few minutes before noon to see if I wanted to join her for lunch. I was feeling considerably better and readily agreed. "Let's make it a quick one," I suggested.

Our waiter told us that Mrs. Montgomery had decided to have lunch served in her cabin. The Johansens weren't there, either. That left Kathy, Bill Henderson, and me to enjoy a fast soup-and-salad meal.

"I didn't have any luck finding the guy in the blue shorts and yellow shirt," Bill said. "Sorry."

"I'm sure he'll turn up," I said. "The only time I ever

see him is when he's following me. Other than that, he seems to vanish into the ether."

Bill laughed. "Maybe he's a demented fan of your books, Jessica."

Kathy joined in the laughter. "We've already encountered one of those," she said. "Tell him, Jess, about the book signing in Seattle."

I recounted the tale for him, and he listened intently, responding appropriately at times and asking an occasional question. When I finished, he shook his head and said, "It's a miracle you lived to tell about it."

"Actually," I said, "I felt sorry for him. He was a poor soul with a very mixed-up mind."

"Time to go glacier watching," Kathy said.

"Join us, Bill?" I asked.

"I might drop by later. I have something else to tend to. I understand the captain will position the ship with one side facing the glaciers for about an hour, then turn it so passengers on the opposite side get a good view."

"A sensible approach," I said as we left the dining room.

Bill went off, leaving Kathy and me to decide on a vantage point from which to view the glaciers. We considered going to the Vista Lounge at the bow of the ship, a large, two-story area that accommodates hundreds of passengers. But it was bound to be crowded. Besides, it appeared that the ship was positioning itself to afford our side the first prolonged view. What better place than on one of our own balconies?

We chose mine. I ordered up tea and cookies—my shoulder, although less painful, still ached, and I know of no better salve than freshly baked cookies. We slipped into jackets and hats and stepped outside. The ship had now reached its anchoring position, maybe five hundred feet from the largest of the glaciers, and was turned so that we could feast our eyes on it. I looked down the length of the ship and saw that there were people on every balcony. I could hear them, too, laughing and expressing wonder at the scene. I'd left the door to the balcony slightly open in order to hear when room service arrived. When it did, we poured tea and took our cups and the cookie platter back outside.

"I feel so at peace," Kathy said as the majesty of the glacier dominated everything.

"I know what you mean," I said. "Just imagine, that incredible mountain of ice is nothing but ages of snowfall that never melted. I read that the annual snowfall here every winter would cover a six-story building."

"But the glaciers are getting smaller, aren't they?" Kathy said. "Global warming."

"They are getting smaller. No debate about that. But they're still huge."

The bay in which we were anchored had once been covered by the glaciers. Today, due to the receding of the ice masses, the bay was now more than sixty miles long, and growing longer each year. Scientists predicted that as much as another fifty cubic miles of icebergs could disappear over the next half century.

Below us, the floe of ice that had calved from the face of the iceberg was considerably thicker than when we'd entered the mouth of Glacier Bay. Huge hunks of it floated by, and I wondered aloud whether there was a chance that one of the larger ones might damage the ship's hull. I knew the answer: We wouldn't be there in this multimillion-dollar ship if that were a possibility.

The sparkling blue-white face of the glacier was like an enormous gem shimmering in the diffused light of the ashen sky above. Kathy and I stood silently and allowed the majesty of the sight to sweep over us and render speech unnecessary. It was one of those moments when one's place on the planet was put into perspective. Two humpback whales surfaced a few hundred feet away and disappeared again beneath the water. Dozens of harbor seals resting on bergs at the base of the glacier seemed oblivious to the hunks of ice that occasionally fell from the two-hundred-foot front wall and crashed into the bay, creating waves that reached the *Glacial Queen* and gently rocked the huge ship. There was one particularly large hunk of ice that broke loose, preceded by a loud crackling sound as thousands of air bubbles, trapped in the glacier during the high pressure that helped in its formation, were released. Then the chunk let loose and came crashing into the water, sending spray a hundred feet into the air and even gaining the attention of the otherwise blasé seals.

I'm not big on taking photographs when I travel, but Kathy was snapping pictures throughout this dazzling show of nature. Our tea had gotten cold, but I sipped some anyway and nibbled on a few cookies. Eventually, the captain came on the PA system and announced that he was now turning the ship to give passengers on the other side a good view.

"I'm freezing," Kathy said, slapping her upper arms.

"Go inside. The show is over."

She paused at the door. "You?"

"I'm going to stay out a bit longer. Actually, I'm relatively comfortable."

I remained on the balcony and observed as the ship made a slow, deliberate turn in the water. The bow pointed directly at the glacier, and then the mass of ice went out of my sight line. Losing visual contact with it snapped me out of my contented reverie, and I started to feel the cold. I thought of my tumble on the stairs, and of the slight, pinched-face man in shorts and a T-shirt.

I looked through the glass doors. Kathy was sprawled on the bed; the TV was on.

I took what I intended to be one final look at Glacier Bay before calling it quits, directing my attention to the solid chunks of ice in the water below. I almost missed it at first. I'd turned away and started to go inside, but returned to the railing and peered down again. "Can it be?" I asked myself, a brisk breeze carrying my words up into the air. "Oh, no!"

I pulled open the door and called, "Kathy, quick, come here!"

"What?"

I motioned for her to join me. She tossed on her jacket and came to where I stood.

"Look," I said, pointing down.

"What am I looking for?" she asked.

"There," I said. "On that piece of ice."

She followed my finger. "It looks like—"

"It is," I said.

"Is that the—?"

I nodded.

Although it was in the distance, there was no mistaking its form. It was a man lying facedown on a sizable piece of ice that had calved from the giant glacier.

Nor was there any mistaking who he was.

He wore blue shorts and a yellow T-shirt.

# Chapter Five

I dialed the number that Officer Kale, the ship's security officer, had given Kathy but received a busy signal. No surprise. Surely others had spotted the body, too, and had called to report it.

We returned to the balcony and looked down to the deck where we'd received our emergency instructions during the predeparture drill. Large, covered, orange motorized lifeboats were suspended from formidable winches. Members of the *Glacial Queen*'s crew, most wearing coveralls, scurried about, and it was obvious that they were in the process of getting ready to lower one of the boats into the bay. It was a complicated procedure, and I was impressed at how expertly and smoothly they seemed to be going about the task.

"He must have fallen overboard," Kathy said, stating the obvious.

"No debate about that," I said.

"What a horrible way to die," she said.

"It certainly is."

"Are you sure he's the man who's been following you, Jess?"

"Yes, I'm sure, unless another passenger decided to wear blue shorts and a yellow shirt. That's possible, but—"

"What will they do?"

"I suppose they'll bring him aboard and secure him in the morgue until we reach Juneau."

"There's a morgue on the ship?"

"All cruise ships have morgues," I replied. "I learned that when I was researching one of my novels, *Murder on the* QE2. The cruise lines don't like to advertise it, but every ship has a place in which to store bodies. Cruise passengers tend to be older, and there are bound to be deaths." I paused. "From natural causes," I added. "Heart attacks, strokes."

"Or people falling overboard."

"I doubt whether most people who fall overboard are ever found, at least by the ship they were on. They probably aren't even missed until the ship is many miles away. But in this case we're at anchor. It's fortunate that he ended up on that slab of ice. Otherwise, we might have left Glacier Bay and never known that he'd gone overboard."

There was a banging on my door. Kathy went to answer it, and I watched her greet Bill Henderson.

"You've heard, of course," he said.

"Yes."

"That's all anyone is talking about. Can you see him from here?"

I pointed.

"Oh, boy," he said. "How could something like that have happened?"

"Hopefully," I said, "they'll figure it out once an autopsy is done."

"Autopsy?" Bill said.

"To see whether he was drunk, or using drugs. I have a suspicion that alcohol is involved in most cases of passengers' falling off ships."

"He'd have to be pretty drunk to do that," Bill said. He put his arm around Kathy. "You okay?" he asked.

"I'm fine. Jessica says it's the same man who's been following her."

Wide-eyed, Henderson looked back at me. "Is that true?"

I nodded. "At least it appears to be," I said.

The three of us stood at the railing and observed the process taking place a few decks below. Half a dozen crew members entered the lifeboat, and the winch slowly lowered it to the water, inch by inch, foot by foot, the wind causing it to sway back and forth, until it reached the bay and bobbed up and down on swells emanating from the calving of ice from the glacier. The roar of the engine reached us as the boat pushed through the water and the ice floe in the direction of the dead man. The piece of ice that he was on also moved in the current, necessitating skillful piloting of the lifeboat to intercept it. The boat finally moved into position, and a member of the crew scrambled up through a hatch, crawled across the covered bow, and extended a long pole attached to a hook of some sort. I noted that he was careful to keep the hook from touching the body itself. Instead, he grabbed hold of a jagged edge of the ice and maneuvered it around to the side of the boat, where two men leaned through the open doorway and used similar devices to bring it closer. Once it was alongside, hands replaced the hooks, and the body was pulled into the lifeboat.

"You have no idea who he is?" Bill asked me.

"None whatsoever," I responded. "But I have a feeling that I'll know soon enough."

"What can I do?" Bill asked.

"Just having you here is comforting," Kathy said. "Let's go inside. Looks like there's nothing more to see out here."

We sat around my cabin for a few minutes before our collective curiosity got the better of us.

"Maybe we should go to one of the public rooms and see what others know about it," Kathy suggested. "We'll never learn anything staying here."

I agreed.

"I doubt if any of the crew will know anything," Bill said. "Even if they do, it's not likely that they'll talk about it."

"True," I said, "but there's nothing wrong with trying. Officer Kale proved helpful this morning. Maybe he will be again."

We decided to start down on the main deck, where the ship's offices were located. We weren't the only ones who'd made that decision. That section of the ship was chockablock with people. A small bar in the center was three-deep with customers, and countless others milled about. The topic of conversation was, of course, the body found floating in Glacier Bay.

"Mrs. Fletcher," Kimberly Johansen said as she saw us arrive.

"Hello," I said.

"You've heard, of course."

"Yes."

"Can you believe it?" she said. "A murder right here in our midst."

"Whoa," I said. "A murder? Who said that?"

"It's going around the ship," she replied. "Someone pushed a man to his death."

A woman who'd been eavesdropping came closer. "You're Jessica Fletcher, the mystery writer," she said. "I knew you were on board." Before I could respond, she asked, "Who do you think did it?"

"Who do I think—?"

"Like a plot from one of your books."

"No one can possibly determine so soon how and why he went overboard," I said.

"How else could it have happened?" she retorted.

"Well, yes," I said, "but—"

A man and a woman joined us. "Do you think it was one of the crew?" the man asked.

"Was he with a woman?" asked his wife. "Maybe they had a fight and—"

"A woman disappears off this ship, and now *this*! Maybe the ship is jinxed."

"What woman?" someone asked.

"On this cruise?"

"Did she go overboard, too?"

"Excuse me," I said, and led Kathy and Bill away to a more secluded corner. "I can't believe I'm hearing this," I told them.

"No one wants to believe he just fell," Bill commented. "Everyone loves a good soap opera."

"Soap operas are fictitious," I said. "This is v-e-r-y real. I want to see if Officer Kale is available."

"Come with you?" Bill asked.

"No. He might be more willing to talk to me alone. Why don't you two go up to one of the lounges? I'll meet you there."

"The Crow's Nest?" Bill suggested. "On the observation deck? It should be fairly quiet up there."

We agreed to meet in that bar on the ship's uppermost deck.

I knocked on the door that I'd seen Kale go through when he went to fetch information about Maurice Quarlé. A woman in uniform answered.

"Is Officer Kale here?" I asked.

"Yes, he is, but he's terribly busy."

"I imagine he is. Would you be good enough to tell him that Jessica Fletcher would like a word with him?"

"All right, but I'm sure he won't be able to."

She went through another door and returned a minute later. "He said he can see you, Mrs. Fletcher, but only for a few minutes."

"I promise not to take more of his time than that. Thank you."

Kale was in shirtsleeves when I was escorted to his office. He was behind his desk, talking on the phone. He waved me in and pointed to a vacant chair. He concluded his conversation, leaned forward, elbows on the desk, and said, "I hope you're not here to talk about Ms. Copeland's disappearance, Mrs. Fletcher.

You may have heard that we have another problem on our hands."

"That's why I'm here, Officer Kale. I just thought you should know that a rumor that the man found in Glacier Bay was murdered is consuming the passengers."

He looked shocked. "Where did they hear *that*?" he asked.

"I don't think anyone heard anything," I said. "But vivid imaginations don't allow facts to get in the way. My point is, some people are even questioning whether the *Glacial Queen* is jinxed."

"Jinxed?"

"Because other passengers have learned that Kathy Copeland and I are on this cruise because of Kathy's sister's disappearance. I assure you we didn't inform them of that."

Kale sat back and slowly shook his head. "A passenger falls overboard, and all of a sudden it's murder. Sounds like one of your mystery novels."

"I won't take any more of your time," I said. "I just thought you'd want to know."

"And I appreciate you telling me, Mrs. Fletcher. Any suggestions?"

"I think a carefully worded announcement over the PA from Captain Rasmussen might go a long way in calming nerves."

"I'll suggest it."

"I'm sure he'll appreciate the suggestion. Before I leave, I'd be interested in knowing the identity of the man who died."

"I'm not at liberty to reveal that."

"I understand your reticence. But you should know

that the man in question had been following me ever since we boarded."

His expression exuded skepticism.

"I know what you're thinking, Officer Kale, but I'm not claiming that he was stalking me as a woman in whom he was interested. He had another, less sanguine reason, and it wasn't romantic. I'm determined to know what it was."

"I wish I could help."

"You can. Surely you know his name and where he's from. That's all I need to know, and I promise that I will be the only passenger with that information."

"Including your friend Ms. Copeland?"

"Yes, including her—unless it turns out that he had something to do with her sister's disappearance."

He nodded. "Okay," he said. "I trust you. Maybe you can do something for me in return."

"If I possibly can, I will."

"What if you write and deliver that reassuring speech you suggested the captain make? You're a famous writer. I've heard people talking about you being on the ship. Maybe a soothing message from you would do the trick."

"I'm willing," I said.

"Good. I'll tell Captain Rasmussen what I've asked you to do. I'm sure he'll agree. Now, about the unfortunate incident today. The only identification the man had on his person was his shipboard ID card."

"That's it? Not even a wallet?"

"Nothing other than the card. His name is John Smith."

"You aren't being serious."

"Oh, I'm very serious, Mrs. Fletcher. I checked the records. He boarded using a driver's license. His name and photo on that card matched up with who he claimed to be."

"Where was his cabin?"

"K-one-one-two-three, our lowest-priced accommodation, an inside cabin on the main deck, near the stern."

"Had you had any interaction with him?" I asked.

"No, none at all. I saw him once up at the Lido buffet and recall thinking he was acting strange—nervous, ill at ease."

"Are you aware of any contact he might have had with other passengers?"

"No. I checked with the dining room maître d', who informed me that Mr. Smith had not come to his assigned table once since leaving Seattle. Evidently he preferred to take his meals in the Lido."

"That's unusual, isn't it?"

"Yes, but not unheard-of. There are always a few passengers who avoid group dining and would rather eat alone. The Lido gives them the opportunity to do that."

"Where was he from?" I asked.

"New York City."

"That's a long way to come to take a cruise to Alaska in the least expensive cabin and to not enjoy shipboard meals served in the dining room."

Kale managed a pained smile. "I'm paid to ensure security on the ship, Mrs. Fletcher, not to psychoanalyze passengers."

"Is there a next of kin?"

"None listed."

"What's the process with the body once we reach Juneau?"

"Authorities there have been alerted. They'll take possession of the deceased, perform an autopsy, and do whatever else is legally appropriate."

"I suppose I'd be overstepping my bounds by asking to see his cabin."

"I'm afraid you're right. It's been sealed and will remain that way until the authorities in Juneau have conducted their investigation."

"I understand. You've been most helpful, Officer Kale. I appreciate it."

"About that message?"

"Yes, of course. I'll write up something immediately and give it to you for your approval."

"Good. Now, I really must get back to what I was doing."

"You've been more than generous with your time."

I got up to leave, but paused at the door. "Can you think of any reason why this Mr. John Smith, from New York City, would want to follow me?" I asked Kale.

He shook his head. "Haven't a clue," he said.

Bill Henderson had chosen a good place for us to rendezvous. The Crow's Nest was virtually empty. Bill and Kathy had ordered drinks, and he offered to get me one, which I declined.

"Did you have any luck with Officer Kale?" Kathy asked.

"Yes, but I'd rather wait to fill you in. Right now I have to write a message to broadcast over the ship's PA system."

Their expressions asked the obvious question, and I explained what I'd agreed to do.

"Tell you what," I said. "I'd do better writing this message back in the cabin. I could also use a nap after I deliver it to Officer Kale. Let's separate and meet for dinner."

I left the bar and went to my cabin, where I wrote what I thought would allay the fears of my fellow passengers. But before I delivered it to Kale, I used the phone in the cabin to call Cabot Cove.

"Mort," I said when he answered, "it's Jessica."

"Hey, Mrs. F. How are things in sunny Alaska?"

"Cold," I said, "in more ways than one."

"Any progress in finding Kathy's sister?"

"Afraid not. At least not yet. Mort, you spoke with a police officer in Alaska on Kathy's behalf, didn't you?"

"Sure did. Spoke with two of them."

"Can you give me their names?"

"Sure. They're both with the Alaska State Troopers. As I understand it, only the biggest towns have their own police force—Anchorage, Fairbanks, places like that. The troopers take care of most serious crime. Let me see. Okay. I spoke with a Detective Flowers. Nice guy, was real helpful. Seems like he handles missing-person cases up there. But then I called a buddy of mine—well, not really a buddy, but I got to know him pretty well at a couple of law enforcement conferences. Joe McQuesten. Joe's family goes way back in Alaska. Seems like his grandfather ran a store during the gold rush. Pretty important guy."

"Is he involved in investigating Wilimena's disappearance, too?"

"Not officially, but he said he'd keep tabs on it. He works pretty close with Flowers."

"That's good information, Mort. Thanks."

"Anytime. Anything exciting happening on your cruise?"

I thought of the dead man in Glacier Bay, but decided not to get into it with Cabot Cove's sheriff. "No, Mort," I said, "nothing exciting. I'll stay in touch."

"Okay, Mrs. F. Oh, by the way, I was speaking with Doc Hazlitt today. He said that if I heard from you, I should remind you to be careful walking around on the decks. They get slippery, he says, and he wouldn't want you to fall overboard." He laughed. "That's typical Doc, always worrying about you."

"Tell him I'll be careful, Mort. He needn't worry. People don't go falling off ships. Love to all."

# Chapter Six

"Ladies and gentlemen, this is Captain Rasmussen speaking from the bridge. Many of you know that noted mystery writer Jessica Fletcher is a passenger on this cruise. She has something of interest to say regarding the incident that occurred this afternoon. Mrs. Fletcher?"

I'd been escorted to the bridge after Officer Kale and Captain Rasmussen had approved what I'd written. Being on the bridge was a thrill for me. I'd enjoyed that privilege only once before. That was during a transatlantic voyage on the QE2. It's a remarkable experience to stand up there and observe the smooth, seamless work of the young officers under the watchful eye of their captain. Of course, security is always tight; the door to a narrow staircase up to the bridge isn't marked, and a uniformed security guard stands just inside it. A steamship's bridge is akin to an airliner's cockpit. In neither case would having an unwanted visitor be prudent.

Rasmussen handed me the microphone. I cleared my throat and looked down at the paper in my hand. I hadn't expected him to introduce me, so I had to make an adjustment in my opening line.

"Thank you, Captain Rasmussen. Yes, this is Jessica Fletcher, a passenger on this wonderful Alaska cruise. Many of you were witnesses to an unfortunate accident this afternoon. Naturally, such a tragic event is upsetting for everyone. But some of you have allowed your imaginations and creative instincts to overrule reality." I chuckled for effect. "That's my job as a mystery writer. The fact is that no one knows what led to the accident that took the life of one of our fellow passengers, and we won't know until the authorities in Juneau have conducted a proper investigation. Until that time, I think it would behoove all of us to avoid speculating. Until that investigation has been completed, we should all consider it an unfortunate accident— and nothing more. Let's continue to enjoy this lovely cruise. Thank you."

I handed over the mike.

"That was very nicely done, Mrs. Fletcher," Rasmussen said after signing off.

"I hope it accomplishes what it's intended to accomplish," I said. "And thank you for allowing me up here on the bridge. What spectacular views you have from this vantage point."

"I never tire of it."

He motioned for me to join him away from the other officers. "Mrs. Fletcher, I understand from Officer Kale that you believe the gentleman who fell from the ship this afternoon had been following you."

"That's right."

"Why?"

"I don't have the answer to that, Captain Rasmussen, but I'm working on it."

"Are you sure those creative instincts you spoke of aren't at play here, too?"

"I think not, Captain. I'm sure I'll be better able to answer that question once we learn more about the victim. Thank you again."

"No, thank *you*, Mrs. Fletcher. I'm certain you've calmed any anxious passengers. Enjoy the rest of the cruise."

One of the junior officers led me down from the bridge and wished me a good afternoon. I decided against a nap. Instead, I went to see whether the ship's Greenhouse Spa and Salon had a last-minute opening. I was in luck. Someone had canceled and I was able to be served without a reservation. It was a beautiful shipboard spa; I felt more relaxed the moment I walked through the doors.

"I am glad you made that announcement," the receptionist said after I'd given my name. "Passengers have been coming in here convinced there's a madman killer loose on the ship."

"I hope it helps," I said.

"The incident is probably good for the spa's business," she quipped. "Nervous passengers look for ways to relax."

"I'm not a nervous passenger," I said, "but I wouldn't mind an hour of relaxation."

I perused the menu of therapies offered and asked for her recommendation.

"How about an Aroma Spa Ocean Wrap? We apply a heated seaweed mask that has pine and rosemary oils in it and then wrap your body in a special foil. Guaranteed to make the world go away. And we follow up with a massage, full or half body."

"We'll have to make it a half massage," I said. "I don't have that much time."

Ninety minutes later, I emerged feeling blissfully relaxed yet invigorated at the same time.

"That was heavenly," I said as I was leaving.

"Glad you're happy," the spa manager said. "Do you know which passenger went overboard, Mrs. Fletcher?"

"No," I said, not about to breach Officer Kale's confidence in me.

"Someone said it was a man wearing blue shorts and a yellow shirt."

"I heard that, too. Did you know him?"

"No, but I'd seen him. He was hanging around outside the spa, looking in all the time. Very nervous. I had the feeling he was hoping to catch a look at a half-naked woman. I'm probably wrong about that, but he gave me the creeps."

"Well," I said, "it sounds as though it might be the same person, but we can't be sure. Thanks again for a much-needed respite."

*Is she right, that he was a seaborne Peeping Tom?*

*Or was he looking for me, assuming I would use the spa at some point?*

*Was his name really John Smith?*

*Was he really from New York?*

*And why was he so interested in me?*

Bill Henderson had joked that he might be a demented fan.

I was sure that he wasn't.

Which left only one logical conclusion.

He had something to do with Wilimena Copeland's disappearance.

It had to do with the gold!

# Chapter Seven

I met up with Kathy again and we went to the Upper Vista dining room. The staff was setting up for dinner when we entered. Kathy pointed to a maître d' as the one who'd said he remembered Wilimena.

"Excuse me," I said. "My friend says that you remember her sister from a previous cruise."

"Oh, yes, of course. Ms. Copeland." He grinned. "She told me to call her Willie." The grin turned to laughter. "She was a funny lady. That is a funny name for a lady."

"Yes, it is," I said. "Would you be able to find a few minutes to speak with us?"

"Of course."

We sat at a table that was still to be set up for the evening meal.

"You do know," I said, "that Willie has disappeared."

"Yes, I have been told that. I pray that she is all right."

"Did she say anything to you during her cruise that might help us learn what happened to her?"

His brow creased, and he licked his lips as he thought. "I'm afraid that I can think of nothing that would be helpful to you."

"Did she mention what she planned to do onshore during your regular stops?"

He shook his head. "No, nothing—except to find the gold that was left to her by a family member."

"She told you about that?" I said.

"Oh, yes. She was such a generous woman, so happy. She took my address and said she would send me a gift when she had her gold. Her waiters, too. Everyone would receive a gift."

I glanced at Kathy, who sighed.

"Was there someone who was especially friendly with Ms. Copeland? With Willie?"

"Pardon?"

"Someone on the cruise who spent a lot of time with her? A man perhaps?"

He shrugged. "She was a very beautiful lady," he said. "Many men—how shall I say it?—many men wanted to be with her."

"What about Maurice?" I asked.

"Monsieur Quarlé? He is a very good customer on this ship."

"So I've heard. Did you see him spending much time with Willie?"

He shook his head, but not convincingly.

"We've been told that he and Willie became good friends during the cruise."

His verbal denial was even less genuine. "I saw nothing like that," he said. "No, I never see them together. Maybe once, twice, you know, to talk like friends. But you sound like you think that maybe they had romance on their minds. Maybe, maybe not."

"Thank you for taking the time to speak with us," I said, having decided that there wasn't anything to be gained by prolonging the conversation. Maybe one of the waiters who'd served Wilimena would be more helpful. I asked for permission to speak with them, which the maître d' reluctantly granted, making much of how busy they were getting ready for the dinner crowd.

The two waiters who'd served Willie during her cruise were young and eager to please. They smiled constantly and did a lot of head nodding. But their English wasn't good enough to deal in the sort of subtleties I was seeking, and Kathy and I left the dining room frustrated.

"They did agree that she promised to send them gifts," Kathy said, looking for something positive to have come out of our inquiries.

"It sounds like she promised gifts to everyone she met," I said. "Willie must have an insatiable need to be loved."

"She's always been that way," Kathy said. "Even as a little girl. She was always playing the princess. She knew that she was the pretty one in the family, and everyone reinforced that."

She said it with an unmistakable hint of regret in her voice, and I felt for her. Obviously, her sister had used her good looks and outgoing personality throughout her life to capture the limelight. It's been my experience that people like that, particularly women, seldom find lasting happiness, as they are always seeking someone or something new to feed their need for approval. But Kathy, who is one of the most grounded and inwardly contented people I've ever known, had undoubtedly envied her sister growing up, and obviously still did to some extent. Amazing how siblings coming from the same parentage and household can be so different.

At dinner, the conversation at each table was, of course, about the death of John Smith. I'd kept Officer Kale's confidence about the dead man's identity, but everyone seemed to know it by the time we gathered in the Vista dining room. Rumor mills are powerful engines, especially within the confines of a cruise ship. Of course, I received many compliments on my PA announcement, but whether it did any good in minimizing speculation that a murder had taken place was pure conjecture. Some passengers said it had, but judging from the buzz at the table next to us, I had my doubts.

"How can someone just fall off a ship like this?" a man asked his tablemates. "He had to have been pushed."

"Mrs. Fletcher says we should wait until all the facts are in," replied his wife.

A couple from a nearby table came to where I sat with Kathy, Gladys Montgomery, the Johansens, and Bill Henderson. "I have a theory about what happened today," the man said, leaning close to my ear.

I listened patiently. His thesis was that John Smith had insulted a married woman and the husband had taken his revenge.

"Interesting," I said, "but what do you base it on?"

"Common sense," he replied haughtily, and re-

counted for us just such a situation that he'd read
about years ago. I didn't bother to suggest that what
had happened on a ship years ago didn't have any
bearing on today's unfortunate event. He and his wife
eventually left us, he with a satisfied expression on his
broad, craggy face.

As had become our habit, we left the dining room
together but then went our separate ways. Kathy and
Bill said they were going to catch the second night of
the passenger talent show, which the Johansens said
at dinner had been hysterically funny. David Johansen
had asked Kathy if she would sit down at some point
the following day for an interview. She readily agreed,
although she pointed out that we'd be arriving in Juneau at seven in the morning and she and I planned
to spend the day in Alaska's capital. They arranged to
meet at six the next evening in the Crow's Nest, where
a cocktail hour would be under way. According to the
daily program delivered to each cabin in the morning,
the gangway would be raised at seven thirty and we
would be on our way overnight to Sitka.

I elected to join Gladys Montgomery in the Explorers' Lounge for the classical music concert, which featured harp and flute in a lovely rendition of Mozart's
Concerto for Flute and Harp, followed by a Beethoven
piece I'd not heard before. The music was soothing, and
I noticed that Gladys almost nodded off a few times,
although she never allowed her eyes to fully close.
There weren't many people in the audience, perhaps
two dozen, but they were obviously lovers of classical
music. Their attention to the musicians and their im-
mersion in the music were total.

Following the concert, Gladys announced that she was heading for bed. I wished her a good night's sleep and went up one level to the promenade deck, where the library was located. I found the book about the gold rush that I'd started perusing the previous day and settled in a quiet corner to continue reading. I hadn't noticed the first time that there was an entire chapter dedicated to Kathy's aunt, Thelma Copeland, better known as the infamous Dolly Arthur.

According to the book, Dolly had worked as a waitress in Vancouver, B.C., before heading for Alaska. She realized by the time she was eighteen that there was more money to be made from entertaining men than waiting tables, so she came to Alaska to seek her fortune. I found it interesting that she did not consider herself a prostitute. She preferred to call herself a "sporting woman" and said she had no use for "whores," describing them as crass and uncouth.

During her first year in Ketchikan, she worked at Black Mary's Star dance hall. But she soon branched out on her own and opened what quickly became one of the town's most popular bordellos.

There were three photographs of Dolly in various poses. She appeared to be a big woman with a full figure and a hint of mischief in her smile. Accompanying text claimed that she had a vicious, hair-trigger temper and used four-letter words at the drop of a hat. But she was well liked by everyone in town, her reputation enhanced by a penchant for tipping lavishly.

This brief story of her life read like a novel. I was particularly fascinated with material concerning those men in her life who were more to her than paying customers. One in particular, a longshoreman named Lefty, especially caught my eye. According to the author, Lefty and Dolly enjoyed a relationship that lasted more than twenty years. Not that they were together constantly during that period. Lefty had a reputation as a ladies' man, and he often left Dolly for long stretches at a time. But he always returned. Dolly was quoted as saying, "Lefty went away sometimes, but he always came back to me."

It was the final paragraph about Dolly's relationship with Lefty that had special meaning for me. According to legend, Lefty struck it rich in a creek north of town and gave the gold he panned to Dolly for safekeeping. Shortly after that, Lefty left town for a few days, promising that he would be back within a week. He didn't return. Rumor had it that he'd been killed by another miner in a dispute over the ownership of the stake Lefty had claimed. His body was never discovered. That left Dolly with riches far beyond whatever money she made by running her house of ill repute. The few people who knew of the gold Lefty had given her assumed she would shut down her business and move to a less harsh place in which to live out her final years. But that didn't happen. She continued to run the brothel until legal prostitution was finally ended in 1954, and she lived there until her death in July 1975.

I closed the book, sat back, and tried to envision what life must have been like during those rough-and-tumble days in Ketchikan. It was a wide-open town, with its legal red-light district along Creek Street and with an equally thriving industry in rum running to get around Alaska's Bone Dry Law, which preceded

America's Prohibition act by three years. Dolly Arthur, and other women like her, must have been a special breed to have ventured into the wilds of Alaska, a rugged, lawless frontier.

I replaced the book on the shelf and chose another, a history of the various towns and cities we would be visiting on the cruise. I was on my way out of the library when Officer Kale stopped me.

"Enjoying your evening, Mrs. Fletcher?" he asked.

"Very much," I replied. "The classical music concert was lovely. I've been doing some reading and thought I would take a book back to my cabin."

"I understand you've been questioning some of the crew about Ms. Copeland's disappearance."

"That's right," I said. "Ms. Copeland's sister and I spoke with some of the staff in the dining room."

"So I've been told," he said. "I thought we had an understanding that you wouldn't interfere in shipboard activities."

"I hardly consider the few minutes we spent with them to constitute interfering in anything," I said.

"Don't misunderstand," he said. "As I told you and Ms. Copeland, I stand ready to help you in any way I can. I'm well aware of how upsetting the disappearance of Ms. Copeland's sister must be, and I share your desire to come to some conclusion and achieve closure. At the same time, I have an obligation to the other passengers on the ship."

"I think we understand each other perfectly," I said.

"Yes, I'm sure we do. As long as we're discussing this, would you mind telling me what the dining room staff had to say?"

"Not at all. They tried to be helpful but really had little to offer. It does seem that Wilimena Copeland openly discussed the purpose of her trip with everyone, including your dining room staff."

"You're talking about the gold she claimed was hers."

"Yes. It wasn't very prudent of her."

"My sentiments exactly."

"Well," I said, "Ms. Copeland and I appreciate your concern, Officer Kale. If you'll excuse me."

"Enjoy the rest of your evening, Mrs. Fletcher."

As I watched him walk away, I experienced an unexpected negative reaction. While he was certainly pleasant enough, and seemed to carry out his duties professionally, there was something unsettling about him. I couldn't put my finger on it, and I quietly reminded myself that I was probably reacting to something that had nothing to do with him. Still, I've learned over the years to put some credence in such vague feelings and not to summarily dismiss them.

I was filled with a torrent of thoughts as I slowly made my way in the direction of my cabin. Naturally, I thought of the man—allegedly John Smith—who'd met such a cold, cruel death in the icy waters of Glacier Bay. Where on the ship had he gone over the side? Had he slipped? Had he deliberately flung himself over the rail? Or had someone helped him end his life?

I thought of Kathy, too, who was off enjoying the evening with Bill Henderson. It was good that she was finding some happiness during the cruise. Traveling all this way in search of a missing sister, and anticipating an unhappy ending, must be weighing heavily on her.

The one hope for optimism had to do with Willie's personality and past behavior. Disappearing for months at a time was not unusual for her, according to Kathy, and the hope was that this was simply another one of those whimsical flights from reality.

I took a detour and went down to the main deck, where Officer Kale had said John Smith's cabin was located. I passed by the front office and shore excursion areas and proceeded toward the stern of the ship. There was no doubt which cabin had been his. Crime scene tape, red instead of the usual yellow, was draped across the door, and a young man in uniform stood watch.

"Good evening," I said.

"Good evening, ma'am."

"There must be something unusually interesting in that cabin," I said, adding a large smile to mitigate my obvious curiosity.

"Yes, ma'am," he said, the stern expression never leaving his youthful face.

"Mind if I ask what's in there?" I said.

"I'm not at liberty to say, ma'am," he said, maintaining his erect posture.

"Now you really have me wondering," I said pleasantly.

He said nothing.

"Well," I said, "I was just passing by and was curious. Have a nice evening."

No one was at the small circular bar in the atrium portion of the deck, and I sat at one of the stools. "I'd like just a taste of brandy," I told the bartender. After I'd been served, I looked down into the snifter and had

the fanciful notion that the answer to Wilimena's disappearance might be seen in the shimmering amber
liquid, like a fortune-teller seeking wisdom and insight
in tea leaves. I smiled at the thought. All I saw in the
brandy was the reflection of the overhead lights.

"Excuse me," I said to the bartender. "I was wondering whether you remember a woman who was on a
previous Alaskan cruise."

"I don't know," he responded. "Who was she?"

"Her name was Wilimena Copeland."

I started to describe her, but the bartender's easy
laugh made that unnecessary. "Willie, you mean," he
said, his laugh louder now. "Everyone remembers her.
She was—"

"A bit of a character," I provided.

"If you say so, ma'am."

"Did you serve her at this bar?" I asked.

"Oh, yes. I believe this was her favorite spot to end
each evening."

"I didn't know that," I said, tasting the brandy. "Did
she usually come here with the same people?"

"Not really," he said, polishing glassware as he
spoke to me. "Well, she and Mr. Quarlé showed up together a few times."

"I'm sure they did," I said. "I know that Maurice
was quite fond of her."

"You know Maurice?"

"Oh, yes, I certainly do. Did Willie and Maurice say
what they planned to do when they went ashore?"

He shook his head. "Not that I remember," he said,
laughing again. "Maybe look for the gold together."

"Ah, yes, the gold," I said.

"She said she would send me a gift after she found it," the bartender said.

"I'm sure she did," I said, taking a last sip of brandy. "I think I'll call it a night. Thank you."

I signed the check using my cabin number and got up to leave.

"Do you know what happened to her?" the bartender asked, not laughing this time. Word of her disappearance had obviously gotten around.

"No, I don't, but if I find out I'll let you know."

I had a sinking feeling as I walked away that if I did find out what happened to Wilimena Copeland, any news that I might convey to this bartender would not be happy.

# Chapter Eight

I realized something was different the moment I opened my eyes the following morning. It took me a few seconds to figure out exactly what it was. We were no longer moving.

I opened the drapes and looked down over the town of Juneau. I checked the small travel alarm I always bring with me on trips; it was a few minutes past seven. We must have just arrived.

I quickly showered and dressed for the day. I didn't know what the weather would be like in Juneau, or how changeable it might be, so I chose clothing that could be layered and put on my most comfortable walking shoes. I was going to call Kathy's cabin, but her knock on my door beat me to it. We decided to have breakfast at the Lido buffet instead of the dining room because it would be faster. I was anxious to get ashore and start the process of tracing Willie Copeland's movements in Juneau.

After leaving the buffet line with our breakfast trays, we found a vacant table by a window.

"Did you bring Willie's receipts from Juneau?" I asked.

"I have them right here," she said and handed them to me.

I went through them and saw that, as with the receipts from Seattle, she had arranged them in chronological order. I put them in the pocket of my windbreaker and took a bite of my Western omelet. "When you went through Willie's papers, Kathy, did you come across addresses of various staff members?"

"No. Why?"

"I just wonder where they might have gone. The staff in the dining room said she had promised to send them gifts and had collected their home addresses."

"That's right," she said. "Someone must have taken them."

"I would like to know who," I replied. "How was the talent show last night?"

"Very, very funny, Jess. Some people are amazing in how they'll get up in front of hundreds of strangers and think they can sing."

"They probably sound wonderful at home in the shower. What's Bill up to this morning?"

"He said he wanted to use the gym, and he's entered in a Scrabble tournament. I made a date to meet him at noon at that kiosk back on the pier." A sheepish grin came over her face. "I really like him, Jess. I really, really like him."

"That's wonderful. I'm looking forward to getting to know him better."

We finished breakfast and headed to a lower deck, where passengers disembarked from the *Glacial Queen*. After having our ID cards scanned into a computer, we were allowed to leave the ship down a long gangway that brought us to the Juneau dock. Tourists were everywhere. I looked in both directions and saw that we weren't the only cruise ship docked there that morning. Three other huge liners flanked the *Glacial Queen*, their passengers joining ours to create shoulder-to-shoulder people everywhere you looked.

"I can't believe how crowded everything is," Kathy said.

"The tourist season is in full swing," I said. "The shopkeepers must love to see the ships come in. They have only this short season to make a profit."

"Where to first?" Kathy asked as we made our way through knots of people in the direction of the main street.

"Number one on the agenda is to find Maurice Quarlé. I went through every guidebook I could find for Juneau, but there's no mention of him or his travel agency."

"Do you think Susan Shevlin back home might be helpful?" Kathy asked.

"Good suggestion. If we fail to locate him, I'll call Susan and see if he's listed as a registered travel agent. I suppose the best thing we can do now is to ask around town for him. Juneau isn't very big. Surely he'll be known to other businesspeople. In the meantime, we have Willie's Juneau receipts. We'll follow whatever trail they lead us on. Maybe we'll get lucky."

"What about the man who went overboard?" she asked.

"That's something else I want to follow up on. I have the names of two Alaska State Troopers. Mort Metzger gave them to me. One is—"

"Detective Flowers is the one I spoke with when I was here," Kathy said.

"That's right. I forgot you'd been in contact with the police."

"He handles missing persons, I think," Kathy said.

"Yes, that's what Mort said. He also has a friend he's met through law enforcement conferences, a trooper named McQuesten, Joseph McQuesten. Mort says he and Flowers work closely together. We'll try to reach both of them today. Let's follow the receipt trail, although I suppose we'll have to wait until the shops open."

I was mistaken in assuming that shops in Juneau wouldn't open until later in the morning. Obviously, shopkeepers set their hours according to the arrival times of the cruise ships. Every door was open, and the stores were filled with browsers and potential buyers.

"Look!" Kathy said excitedly, pointing to soaring evergreens behind the row of stores along the main drag. I immediately saw the object of her excitement. At the top of one of the trees was a magnificent bald eagle.

"There's another," she said, pointing to an adjacent tree.

I laughed. While my purpose in inviting Kathy to accompany me to Alaska was to find out what had happened to her sister, my original intention in taking the cruise had been to see as much wildlife as possible. We were off to a good start in that regard.

We waited until a Native American officer in a yellow rain slicker stopped traffic and motioned for us to cross the broad avenue, which placed us on a sidewalk teeming with other visitors. I pulled the slips of paper from my pocket and looked at the first one. "Over there," I said, pointing to a large building with a sign in front that said: TAKU. "It's a fish store and smokehouse," I said. "The receipt says that Kathy ordered smoked salmon to be sent to New York. Is that where she last lived?"

"I think so, although it was always difficult to know where she was living at any given time. But yes, she'd called me from New York on several occasions just before she left for Alaska."

"Let's see if they remember her placing that order."

Many yards from Taku, the aroma of smoked fish assaulted our nostrils, a not unpleasant experience. I enjoy smoked fish of every variety and often visit a smokehouse in Cabot Cove to buy thinly sliced salmon for parties. Taku was a large store with a retail counter. To the left were windows through which the smokehouse operations could be viewed. A pleasant middle-aged man wearing a large white apron greeted us.

"What a lovely shop," I said, taking in a wide variety of fish beautifully displayed in glass cases filled with crushed ice.

"Thank you," he said. "What can I do for you ladies?"

"The salmon looks wonderful," I said.

"Only the best. We feature wild salmon, sockeye salmon. That's our state fish."

"We have pretty good salmon back home in Maine," Kathy said.

"I know you do," the shop's owner said, "but we like to think that Alaska has the best in the world. Would you like to send some back to your friends in Maine? When you get home, you can do a taste comparison."

"I believe we just might do that," I said. "But we have another reason for visiting you this morning."

"Oh? What might that be?"

I handed him Willie Copeland's receipt. He studied it, shrugged, and handed it back.

"It's my sister," Kathy said. "As you can see from the date on the receipt, she was here not very long ago."

"Was she unhappy with her purchase?"

"We don't know," Kathy replied.

He looked puzzled.

"You see," I said, "the woman who made this purchase has disappeared. She got to Ketchikan but hasn't been seen since."

"That's terrible."

Kathy handed him Wilimena's photo.

He smiled. "Her! I remember her very well. Lovely lady, very classy."

"Did she come in alone?" I asked.

He pursed his lips and narrowed his eyes. "No, she didn't."

"Do you know who she was with?"

"Sure I do. It was Maurice."

"Maurice Quarlé?"

"You know Maurice?"

"Sort of," Kathy said.

"Did they say what they would be doing while in Juneau?" I asked.

He shook his head.

"Where is Maurice's travel agency?" I asked.

"He really doesn't have one," was the reply. "I mean, the way I understand it, he's sort of a one-man consultant to the steamship companies. He's always off on some cruise or another. I think he teaches French on some of the cruises, and he books tour groups."

"Do you know where he lives in Juneau?"

"No. As I say, he's not home very much. Wait a minute. One of my smokehouse workers might know."

He disappeared into the smokehouse and had a conversation with a young man dressed all in white. He returned and said, "Maurice rents a room in a house at the top of Mount Roberts where the tram goes up to the observatory. He doesn't know the name of the street or house number, but he says there's a sign in front of the house—Serenity House. People like to name their houses around here."

"I'm sure we'll find it," I said. "Now, let me order some of the world's best salmon to send back to our friends in Maine who think *they* have the best salmon."

We both laughed, and the order was written up.

There were four other receipts to follow up on. We visited those shops without learning much about Wilimena's plans. The four additional shops all featured jewelry. I'd never seen so many jewelry stores in one small area in my life. There were dozens of them, some focusing on Native American crafts, but most offering the sort of pedestrian jewelry found in any store in the Lower Forty-eight.

In only one of them did we find a salesperson who remembered Wilimena. The woman said she recalled her because they had a long conversation about the price of gold and whether stores like hers purchased unprocessed ore from individuals. "Ms. Copeland told me that she would soon come into possession of a large amount of raw gold and would be seeking an outlet for it. I invited her to come in to talk about it again, and she said she would." It was more of a snicker than a laugh. "We occasionally have people stop in who claim they have gold for sale, but frankly, we never pay much attention to them. But I will say that Ms. Copeland seemed sincere. Did she ever get her gold?"

"We're hoping to find out," Kathy said. "Thank you for your time."

Having exhausted places to check out based upon the receipts Wilimena had left behind, we decided to go into a small coffee shop and make some calls from there. I got the number of the Alaska State Trooper barracks in Juneau and dialed it. The officer who answered informed me that Detective Flowers was out of the office but Trooper McQuesten was there. I introduced myself when he came on the line and mentioned that I was a friend of Sheriff Metzger's.

"A pleasure speaking with a friend of the good sheriff back in Maine," he said. "How is Mort?"

"Just fine, Trooper McQuesten. He sends his best. I'm here in Juneau with the sister of Wilimena Copeland. Mort told me that you were friendly with the detective working on her case, Detective Flowers."

"That's right," he said. "I promised Mort that I would keep tabs on it. As far as I know, there hasn't been any progress. Mort tells me that you're quite a famous writer of murder mystery novels."

"Well, I do write murder mystery novels. Whether I'm especially famous or not is another question. Wilimena Copeland's sister, Kathy, and I are hoping that by retracing her steps, we might help resolve what happened to her."

"Have you had any luck so far?"

"Afraid not. I'm sure you've heard about the unfortunate incident yesterday on the *Glacial Queen*."

"Of course."

"I admit to having a special interest in the man who went overboard in Glacier Bay."

"Why is that?"

I explained my suspicion that the man, whose name was allegedly John Smith, had been following me ever since we boarded the *Glacial Queen*. I also indicated that I had the feeling that this John Smith might have had something to do with the disappearance of Wilimena Copeland.

"That's very interesting, Mrs. Fletcher. Mort told me that you've helped him solve some pretty difficult cases."

"I'm afraid Mort has overstated it," I said with a chuckle. "But I have had the misfortune of being involved in my share of real crime."

"I'd like very much to speak with you, Mrs. Fletcher, about the death on the *Glacial Queen*. I have a feeling you might have something to offer."

"I'd be happy to," I said. "Just name the time."

"Could we meet this afternoon?" he asked.

"Yes, that would work. Where?"

"Our offices are at 6255 Allaway Avenue. Say two o'clock?"

"We'll be there. And thank you."

We paid for our coffee and stepped out onto the busy sidewalk.

"I think it's time to see if we can find Maurice Quarlé," I said.

Kathy looked at her watch. It was eleven thirty. "I promised Bill we'd meet him back on the pier at noon," she said. "Besides, I'd feel more comfortable having him with us when we confront Mr. Quarlé. You know, in case there's some sort of violence."

"I certainly don't expect anything like that to happen," I said, "but if you would feel better having him with us, then that's what we'll do."

Bill Henderson was waiting at the kiosk when we arrived. He greeted us with a big smile, gave Kathy a kiss on the cheek, and insisted upon buying us lunch. "I got a recommendation from the cruise director for a restaurant. He suggests the Fiddlehead Restaurant and Bakery, on Willoughby Avenue. Not fancy, he says, but the food is good. They bake their own bread for sandwiches."

"Sounds perfect," I said. "I'm suddenly hungry."

The restaurant was attractive, with lots of knotty pine paneling and stained-glass windows, and the food was simple but fresh and attractively served. Over lunch, we filled Bill in on what we planned to do that afternoon—try to find the elusive Maurice Quarlé and meet with Trooper McQuesten.

"Kathy says she'd be more comfortable having you with us," I said.

Kathy placed her hand on his arm. "Especially since you worked out in the gym this morning," she said lightly.

"You make this Quarlé character sound like he's dangerous," Bill said.

"I'm sure he's not," I said, "but if it pleases Kathy, I'm all for you accompanying us."

Before we left the restaurant, Bill asked, "Do you really think that the fellow who went over the side of the ship was following you, Mrs. Fletcher?"

"Yes, I do."

"I wish I'd found him the day you slipped on the stairs."

"It wouldn't have made any difference, I'm sure," I said. "I'm hopeful that Trooper McQuesten will have the answers to some of my questions."

We walked from the restaurant to the base of the tramway.

"That's a long way up," Kathy said.

"Eighteen hundred feet," Bill said. "At least that's what I read."

"We could walk up there," Kathy said, not sounding as though she meant it.

"Not this lady," I said. "I love exercise, but this is too daunting. Come on. We'll take a ride. My treat."

We went to where tickets were being sold.

"Sure you don't want us to chip in?" Bill asked after seeing the sign on which the prices were listed. It was twenty-four dollars for each adult.

"Since I'm the one who doesn't want to walk, I think it only right that I pay. Besides, you bought lunch."

I paid the fare, and we climbed into the small car that would carry us to the top. We were joined by other tourists, and when every available seat was taken, the tram started its slow, undulating trip up to the top of Mount Roberts. The higher we climbed, the more spectacular the views. Juneau is a visual feast. It's shoehorned in between Mount Juneau and Mount Roberts, with the Gastineau Channel hemming it in from another direction. The mountains were snowcapped, as they are throughout the year. The channel and the pier, which became smaller and smaller as we ascended, were beehives of activity, with hundreds of tourists coming and going from their respective steamships, and dozens of smaller boats crisscrossing the channel. While everything below us diminished in size, the air became markedly colder, and I was glad I had dressed sensibly. Kathy also had on layered clothing and seemed comfortable. Bill, however, was dressed as though we were in the Bahamas. He wore a light-weight white shirt with long, billowing sleeves, a pair of chino pants, and sneakers sans socks.

"Aren't you cold?" I asked him when we were almost to the top.

He laughed and raised his arms to the sky. "Cold? Not at all. I must be warm-blooded."

Kathy laughed along with him. "You wouldn't say that in the winter back where we live, in Cabot Cove, Maine," she said.

"Don't be so sure," he said. "I just may visit you there and prove you wrong."

We stuttered to a stop at the top of the tram, and everyone exited the car.

"What a view," Bill said.

He was right. The vista from that vantage point was spectacular. But I was focusing on the hodgepodge of tiny houses that seemed to have been built haphazardly, many of them clinging to the side of the mountain. They were painted in a variety of colors, blues and greens, reds and yellows, and even an occasional purple or orange one. There weren't any streets as we know them in the East, which I knew would make it difficult to find the house in which Maurice Quarlé lived.

"Where do we begin?" Kathy asked.

Bill pointed to a cluster of houses a few hundred feet away. "We might as well start there," he said.

We reached the area he'd indicated and slowly went from house to house, looking for a sign that said SE-RENITY HOUSE. We got lucky. It was the second one we passed. A small front porch contained a variety of old, broken-down furniture, a mattress, the frame of a bicycle minus its wheels, and assorted other discarded items. I saw no sign of life and wondered whether we had made the trip for nothing. But I wasn't about to leave without ascertaining that for sure. I started up a rickety set of stairs, but Bill stopped me.

"I'll go," he said.

Kathy and I watched as he went up onto the porch and knocked. There was no reply. He looked back at us, shrugged, and knocked again, louder this time. He tried the door. It opened with a groan.

Kathy and I joined him on the porch and peered through the open door. Aside from minimal light coming through a window at the rear of the house, it was dark inside. Silhouetted against the window was what appeared to be large pieces of furniture.

Bill stepped inside, and we followed him tentatively. There was a musty smell that overrode other indefinable odors.

A narrow staircase was to our left. It occurred to me that the house didn't seem large enough to contain apartments for rent. Not only that, the chaos on the first floor made me wonder whether Maurice Quarlé—or anyone else, for that matter—actually lived there.

"Stay here," Bill said as he started up the stairs.

"I'm coming with you," said Kathy.

I fell in behind them.

When Bill reached a tiny landing at the top, he motioned with his hand for us to wait. We did as he asked, and he proceeded down a confined hallway covered with threadbare carpeting to a door at the far end. Now I could see that there was the possibility of apartments, although they would have to be very small ones. I counted four doors off the hall.

There was another hand signal from Bill for us not to come any farther. Kathy and I stayed where we were as Bill opened the door. If someone did live there, he or she was a trusting soul. Neither the front door nor the door Bill had just opened needed a key.

Bill disappeared through the open door. I started to join him, but he suddenly stepped back into the hall and said, "I don't think you'll want to see this, Mrs. Fletcher."

His statement only made me want to see what I'd been told not to see. I went to where Bill stood, just outside the room, and looked past him. A man, a very dead man, was sprawled in a large yellow upholstered wing chair. His arms were flung over the sides, and his legs were akimbo in front of him. His head had fallen to one side; his mouth was wide open, as were his eyes. He wore a pale blue T-shirt, through which a large amount of blood had seeped from his chest. The cause of the bleeding was evident. The handle of a knife protruded from his heart, once beating and circulating blood throughout his body.

Kathy now joined us. She uttered an anguished cry and shoved her fist to her mouth to muffle it. I entered the room and approached the body.

"Don't!" Kathy cried.

I ignored her and placed two fingertips against the side of the dead man's throat. It was an academic exercise. That he was dead was beyond debate. But I did it anyway, from force of habit.

I looked around the cramped room. There was a single bed in one corner and an armoire in another. There was no closet. A small desk beneath a window was encrusted with years of dirt. I went to the desk and looked down at items strewn about on it, including a wallet. I opened it. Peering back at me from beneath a plastic sleeve was an Alaska driver's license. The picture on it was of the dead man in the chair. The name on the license was MAURICE QUARLÉ.

# Chapter Nine

The natural instinct was to call 911, but since I had Trooper McQuesten's direct line, I dialed that on my cell phone instead. He answered on the first ring. I told him what we had discovered, and he said he would dispatch a team there immediately. He and two uniformed troopers arrived in less than ten minutes.

McQuesten greeted us on the porch, where we had congregated while waiting for his arrival. I judged him to be in his mid to late thirties. He was a big man, well over six feet tall. He wore a gray and black tweed jacket, wrinkled gray pants, and muddy ankle-high boots. His white shirt appeared to be too tight for his sizable neck; its collar points turned up. The tie he wore was maroon, in an old-fashioned knit style.

"Where's the body?" he asked.

"Upstairs," I replied. "The room at the end of the hall."

He dispatched his officers into the house, but he stayed on the porch to speak with us.

"What brought you here?" he asked.

I explained why Kathy and I had a particular interest in Maurice Quarlé.

"So you think he had something to do with your
sister's disappearance?" he said to Kathy.

"I'm the one who came to that conclusion," I said.

"Do you have any tangible evidence of that, Mrs.
Fletcher?"

"No, just a series of coincidences. He seemed to have
spent a great deal of time with Wilimena Copeland on
her cruise. Besides, another passenger who knew him
didn't speak very highly of his character."

McQuesten smiled. "Whoever that is," he said, "is a
pretty good judge of people. Mr. Quarlé was not what
you'd call one of Juneau's most sterling citizens."

"I take it he's no stranger to you," I said.

"Hardly. Maurice has been in and out of trouble
here in Juneau ever since he arrived four or five years
ago. Nothing violent, just a succession of scams, con-
ning people out of money, bad checks, a couple of
phony credit cards, things like that. But despite that
record, he had a legitimate side to him when it came
to steamship companies. He wangled jobs aboard
some ships teaching French to passengers, and he
made some money booking tour groups—got a commission, I suppose. He was a pleasant enough little
guy, talked a good game. But that's not surprising.
You can't be an effective con man unless you have the
gift of gab."

"I would imagine someone like that makes quite a
few enemies," I said.

"Sure. By the way, you haven't introduced me to
your friends."

"This is Wilimena Copeland's sister, Kathy Cope-land, and this is our friend Bill Henderson."

As McQuesten shook hands with them, one of his officers emerged from the house and asked whether McQuesten was coming up to the murder scene. He said he was, excused himself from us, and followed the uniformed trooper back inside.

"This is just beginning to set in on me," Bill Henderson said. "I never figured when I booked this cruise that I'd be coming across dead bodies."

"It's my fault," Kathy said. "If I hadn't asked you to accompany us here, you wouldn't have been subjected to this."

"Don't give it a second thought," he said, giving her a playful hug. "I lead a pretty dull life. I can use some excitement."

"Who could have done such a terrible thing?" Kathy asked no one in particular. "How can anyone take another person's life like that?"

"The world is full of bad people," Bill said. "Look what the cop had to say about the deceased. Can you imagine all the people he'd swindled who'd be glad to see him dead?"

"If that's the reason he was killed," I offered.

Kathy and Bill looked at me.

"I still can't help but believe that Mr. Quarlé had something to do with Wilimena's disappearance," I said.

"Are you saying that he might have been killed because of a connection with Willie?" Kathy asked.

"I don't know," I answered, "but it is a possibility."

I slipped into my what-if mode of thinking.

What if Quarlé had learned from Willie about the gold and had decided to befriend her in the hope of getting his hands on it? And what if he'd shared that aspiration with someone else? It wouldn't have been very smart of him to do that, but it wasn't smart of Willie to blab about it, either. According to what McQuesten had said about Quarlé, he was the sort of person who wouldn't be comfortable keeping things to himself. What if he had brought someone else into his confidence in the hope of getting money up front by promising a piece of the action? Had he gotten the money and reneged? Was that why he was killed?

Of course, this was all pure speculation on my part, my sometimes overworked imagination shifting into high gear. That's usually the way I come up with plots for my novels, playing the what-if game with myself. But I've also had good results applying it to real-life crime, and I saw no reason to put the brakes on where the murder of Maurice Quarlé was concerned.

It became evident to Kathy and Bill that I had drifted into a reverie of sorts, because they asked in unison, "Are you all right?"

"What? Oh, my mind was elsewhere. Don't mind me. It happens from time to time."

Trooper McQuesten came from the house, followed by another trooper. "We have a coroner on his way, and a crime scene technician," he said. "I'm leaving one of my men here until they arrive. In the meantime, I would appreciate it if you folks would come back to my office so I can take a formal statement about what happened here."

"Do we have to?" Kathy asked.

"This has been quite a shock for her, Officer," Bill said.

"Yes, I imagine it has been," the trooper said. "Tell you what. I'll have Trooper Jenkins take a statement from you here at the house. But I would like Mrs. Fletcher to come with me. I want to take her statement in a more formal setting, and I also want to discuss with her the death that occurred on the ship in Glacier Bay." He turned to me. "Is that all right with you, Mrs. Fletcher?"

"Yes, of course," I said, surprised at how easily he'd agreed to excuse Kathy and Bill.

"Will you be okay?" I asked Kathy.

"Sure," she said.

"Don't worry about her, Mrs. Fletcher," Bill said, pulling her close to him. "I'll make sure nothing happens to my favorite lady."

Kathy said she wasn't up for another trip on the tram, so Trooper McQuesten drove the three of us back down to the dock and dropped Kathy and Bill off there. We agreed to meet in the Crow's Nest, where Kathy was scheduled to be interviewed by David Johansen.

"Well," McQuesten said once we were settled in his small office in a building used by both the Juneau police and the Alaska State Troopers, "I didn't expect to end up meeting you at the scene of a murder."

"I'm as surprised as you are," I said. "Frankly, I prefer the fictitious murders in my books to real ones."

"I can't say that I blame you," he said. "I'll be candid, Mrs. Fletcher. I preferred that you come back here with me without your friends."

"Why is that?"

He pulled a photograph from a drawer and slid it across the desk.

If he meant to shock me, he succeeded. The color photograph was of a smiling Kathy Copeland.

"Where did you get this?" I asked.

"From a dead man's room."

"Mr. Quarlé?"

"No, from the cabin of the man who went over the side of the *Glacial Queen* yesterday."

I tried to formulate a question, but he saved me the trouble. "I have no idea why he had this photograph, Mrs. Fletcher, nor did I know the identity of the person in the picture until I saw your friend—Ms. Copeland."

"But why would that man have Kathy's picture?" I asked, despite knowing that he didn't have an answer.

"Maybe you have an idea about that, Mrs. Fletcher."

"I can certainly speculate," I said. "The fact that he had her photo confirms for me that he was, in some way, interested in her sister's disappearance. The question I have is why he seemed to be following me and not her."

"Maybe this will answer that," he said, retrieving something else from the drawer. It was the hardcover version of one of my earlier books; my photograph took up the entire back cover. A sticker indicated that it had come from the *Glacial Queen*'s library.

"Somehow," I said, "he didn't strike me as a man who enjoyed reading."

"I'm sure he wasn't. He wanted that picture of you, not the words you wrote."

"I should be disappointed."

"I sense that you aren't."

"You sense right. What else did you find in his cabin?"

A third item emerged from the desk drawer, a passport. I opened it and stared at the photo of the man. The name on it was John Smith.

"The passport is a phony, just like his name," McQuesten said.

"John Smith," I said absently. "Any idea what his real name is?"

McQuesten shook his head. "We're working on it. He evidently was from New York."

"So I understand. Would I be wrong in assuming that there's more in that desk drawer that might interest me?"

He smiled and rubbed his eyes. "I'm afraid that's all that's in my goody bag for the moment," he said.

"I'd say that's quite enough for one day. I think I'll head back to the ship. This has all been very fatiguing."

"I'll drive you."

"Thank you. I appreciate that. You will let me know if anything comes out of the Maurice Quarlé investigation that has bearing on Wilimena Copeland's disappearance?"

"Of course. By the way, I spoke with Detective Flowers this morning. He's in Ketchikan following up on possible leads."

My expression asked the obvious question.

"Nothing tangible so far," McQuesten said. "It's really strange that she's disappeared so completely without leaving a trace. It makes me think perhaps she doesn't want to be found."

Which, I knew, was a possibility with Willie Copeland. I didn't say it. I also knew that Alaska was a huge wilderness, with hundreds of thousands of untamed acres in which a body could disappear, never to be seen again. I didn't say that, either.

I followed him to his car, and we drove back to the pier. As I was about to get out, I saw the ship's security officer, Officer Kale, come onto the pier and head for the gangway leading up to the ship. He was dressed in civilian clothes—jeans, a blue sweater over a white shirt, and sneakers. He carried a small plastic shopping bag and was obviously in a rush. He ran past groups of passengers, dashed up the gangway, and vanished into the ship.

"That's Officer Kale," I told Trooper McQuesten. "He's the ship's security officer."

"Yes, I know Officer Kale," said McQuesten. "I've had the occasion to speak with him a few times."

"He's terribly concerned that Kathy and I not disturb other passengers while we look for an answer to Wilimena's disappearance."

"You can't blame him," McQuesten said. "He and the rest of the crew have an obligation to all those people enjoying themselves on their ship."

I agreed with him, of course, and said so, adding, "Has he been at all helpful in trying to find Kathy's sister?"

"I haven't had that much interaction with him about

that case, Mrs. Fletcher. Detective Flowers is the lead investigator. Have you found him uncooperative?"

"Oh, no, but not anxious to help, either. I was just wondering. Thank you for everything, including driving me back to the ship."

"My pleasure, Mrs. Fletcher. I assure you I'll stay in touch if I have any news of interest."

I went directly to my cabin, then kicked off my shoes, removed the outer layers of clothing I'd worn, wrapped myself in the terry-cloth robe provided by the cruise line, and went out onto the balcony. The sun had broken through the gunmetal gray sky, although its light was fleeting as fast-moving clouds came and went, obscuring it from view.

My goal of taking an idyllic cruise to relax and immerse myself in the wildlife of Alaska had certainly turned into something I hadn't bargained for. Of course, I'd known when I invited Kathy to accompany me that the cruise would take on a different dimension. Searching for a missing person didn't qualify as a relaxing pursuit.

But murder? Two violent deaths within a few days of each other, one definitely a murder, the other a distinct possibility of being murder.

I sat in the chair and allowed my eyes to close. I didn't need for them to be open for me to see, in vivid color, Maurice Quarlé sprawled in that yellow chair, his eyes and mouth open, a knife rammed into his chest. That vision sent a shudder through me, and I decided to go back inside. Once there, I had a sudden urge for a cup of steaming-hot tea. Call for room service? I decided instead to go to a public room. Somehow the spacious cabin now felt claustrophobic.

I knew from the daily newsletter that tea was served every afternoon in the Lower Vista dining room. As I walked in, I immediately spotted Gladys Montgomery sitting by herself at a window table. I didn't intend to disturb her—she seemed engrossed in a magazine—but she looked up, smiled, and waved for me to come to her table.

"I didn't expect to see you back on the ship so early," she said, placing the magazine on the table. It was the new issue of *Vanity Fair*.

"I see that you keep up with the latest publications," I said after taking the chair next to her.

"Maynard always sees to it that I have a selection of reading material," she said.

"He takes good care of you," I commented.

"He's a sweet young man. I've grown very fond of him. So, Jessica, tell me about your day in Juneau."

I was tempted to tell her about the murder of the man she'd met and for whom she had such disdain, Maurice Quarlé, but thought better of it. "Uneventful," I said. "Kathy and I and Mr. Henderson walked around a bit and had lunch at a very pleasant restaurant. Frankly, there doesn't seem to be much to see in Juneau, unless you're interested in buying jewelry."

She laughed. "I know exactly what you mean," she said. "I spent about an hour there the first time the ship visited, but I don't bother getting off anymore. I suppose there are interesting things to do, but I prefer to stay on board the ship."

A waiter brought my tea and a selection of finger sandwiches and pastries.

"Have you seen Kathy or Mr. Henderson?" I asked.

"No, I have not," she replied. "I have the feeling that your friend Ms. Copeland is smitten with the handsome Mr. Henderson."

"I have the same impression," I said, "although I haven't asked her about it. She seems very happy when she's with him. That's all that matters."

"I agree with you, considering the mental turmoil she must be going through, having lost a sister. I have lost a sister *and* a brother. It's always terribly sad when you lose a beloved sibling. Have you ever suffered such an event?"

"Not a sibling. My parents, of course, and my husband."

She drew a deep breath, and her lip trembled. "I finished your book," she said, without preamble. "I enjoyed it very much. You are a very elegant writer, unlike too many younger writers these days. I did identify the killer quite early in the story, however."

I chuckled. "I must be losing my touch. I always hope that readers can't figure out who did it until the very end."

"I didn't mean to offend you," she said.

"Oh, no, you haven't. This tea hits the spot."

"There is nothing more refreshing than a properly made pot of tea," she said. "Is there anything new about the unfortunate accident that occurred yesterday in Glacier Bay?"

There certainly was something new. The question was whether I should mention what I learned from

Trooper McQuesten. As with the murder of Maurice Quarlé, I decided it would be prudent not to tell her that John Smith's name was not John Smith, that he was traveling with a bogus passport, and that he had in his possession a photograph of Kathy and a copy of one of my earlier books, taken from the ship's library shelves.

"No, nothing new as far as I know," I said.

"Why do I have the feeling you aren't telling me the truth?" she asked, not at all confrontational.

Her hand, deeply veined and covered with brown age spots, rested on the arm of her chair. I placed my hand on top of it, gave it a little squeeze, and said, "I have no doubt, Gladys, that you very quickly solved the mystery in my novel. You're very astute."

"At my age, I have nothing but time to observe and be astute. You'll share with me what you wish at the appropriate time, I'm sure. But for now, it's time for my nap before dinner. Maynard will have turned down my bed and placed a small glass of Metaxa brandy at bedside. My husband was Greek, you know, and he loved his Metaxa. You will excuse me."

"Of course. Enjoy your nap. I'll see you at dinner."

"Salmon or duck on the menu tonight," she said, standing, using the chair's arm for support, and walking away somewhat unsteadily. The maître d' quickly came to her side and escorted her from the room.

*I really like you, Gladys Montgomery*, I thought. *You're one classy lady.*

I lingered over my tea and finger food, enjoying that moment of solace, as well as the sense of well-being provided by the nourishment. Gladys's mention of a nap before dinner sounded good. Although it had not been a physically strenuous day, it had been mentally challenging. Of course, I wouldn't have a snifter of Metaxa brandy. I could do without that.

I was about to leave when the maître d' who'd escorted Gladys came to me. "Mrs. Fletcher?" he asked.

"Yes?"

"There is a gentleman wishing to see you at the front office on the main deck."

"Who is it?" I asked.

"I don't know, ma'am."

I thanked him, left the room, and went down one deck. Standing there was Trooper McQuesten.

"I didn't expect to see you again so soon," I said.

"I didn't plan on it," he said, "but I came across something I wanted to share with you as soon as possible."

"I appreciate that," I said. "Why don't we find a place where we can be more comfortable? The Vista Lounge is on this deck, at the front of the ship."

We found a secluded table in the large lounge. "I just had tea," I said. "Would you like something?"

"A soft drink would be fine. I'm still on duty."

"And what do you enjoy when you're off duty?" I asked.

He grinned. "I'm partial to good single-barrel bourbon, Mrs. Fletcher, although I also enjoy some of our better microbreweries."

"I'll be happy to treat you to some of each whenever you're off duty. Now, what is this information you have that couldn't wait?"

"I had a chance to go through things we found in

Quarlé's room," he said. "Take a look at this." He withdrew some papers from his inside breast pocket and handed them to me. I motioned for a waiter, who took the trooper's order for a Coke, and unfolded the sheets of paper. There was a lot of writing on them, scribbling actually, and some of it was hard to read. But the message that came through from these random jottings wasn't difficult to understand.

> Gold! Gold! Gold!—crazy old whore got it from her boyfriend—left to Willie—crazy broad—has a sister—Maine???—someplace like that—a couple of hundred thou—maybe more—play it cool—romance the crazy bitch—maybe marry her if I have to—hell, been married how many times before?—go slow—see if Joey wants in—put up plenty of dough—can't trust him—trust nobody—gold, baby!!!—lots of gold!!!

"I was right," I said. "Quarlé was after Willie's gold."

"I would say that you were," McQuesten said.

I placed the scraps of papers I had been reading on the table and looked at a final sheet. On it was a series of names and numbers, some of which were followed by numbers preceded by a dollar sign.

"What do these mean?" I asked.

"I called Charlie Flowers in Ketchikan to see if he could make any sense out of it."

"And?"

"Those are the names of various floatplane operators in the Ketchikan area," McQuesten said. "I assume the numbers represent how much it would cost to hire one."

I sat back and chewed my cheek, as I sometimes do when trying to sort out my thoughts. "Why would he want to hire a floatplane?" I asked.

McQuesten shrugged his large shoulders. "That's something we'll have to find out, Mrs. Fletcher."

After silently trying to process what I had just read and learned, I asked, "Who is this Joey he mentions?"

"I can't be sure," McQuesten replied, "but it might be another local grifter like Quarlé. Joey Casone. I have my people out looking for him as we speak."

I shook my head and smiled.

"We're making progress, Mrs. Fletcher."

"Almost too much, too fast," I said.

"If you'd rather I—"

I sat up straight, came forward, and said, "No, I take that back. The more information, the better."

"All right," he said, draining his Coke in one long, continuous swallow. "I'd better get back."

I walked him to the ship's exit, and he showed his badge to the crew member on duty. "A word of advice?" he said.

"Please."

"Watch your step for the rest of the cruise."

He held me in a hard stare.

"I will," I said.

# Chapter Ten

Without the little man in shorts following me at every turn, the evening turned out to be considerably more relaxing than previous ones had been. I joined Kathy and Bill Henderson in the Crow's Nest, where she'd been telling David Johansen what she knew about Dolly Arthur and how she was related to the former brothel owner.

"This has been great," David said after he'd turned off his tiny digital recorder.

"I'm afraid I don't know much about my heritage," Kathy said, "at least that aspect of it."

"You remember more than you think," David said. "I always enjoy getting firsthand accounts. They fill in the gaps for me in the courses I teach. Of course, I loved the story about the pretzel lady and your father."

Johansen left to get ready for dinner, and I spirited Kathy away to a secluded corner, where I filled her in on what Trooper McQuesten had told me. She listened intently, her eyes wide, her head shaking back and forth in disbelief. When I'd finished, she said, "Something terrible has happened to Willie."

"Not necessarily," I said. "We mustn't give up hope."

"With such dreadful people involved, how can I think anything else, Jess?"

"The important thing," I said, "is to keep digging. I'm sure we'll have the answer eventually."

I wasn't sure I believed that, but I felt a need to boost her lagging spirits.

"I'm afraid of what the answer will be," she said. "The man who went over the side had my picture *and* your book?"

"Yes."

"I feel so—so violated," she said.

"I know what you mean. Look, let's enjoy the ship this evening, and in the morning when we arrive in Sitka, I'll call Trooper McQuesten and Detective Flowers, too. We'll stay on top of it."

"I'll give it my best," she replied.

Which she did during dinner, although I didn't harbor any illusions that it was because of my pep talk. The perpetually upbeat Bill Henderson was clearly responsible for Kathy's elevation of mood. He was unfailingly flattering and solicitous, and she responded appropriately, actually becoming girlish at times.

Gladys Montgomery was in an especially good mood as well. She laughed easily and was fully engaged in the conversation at the table.

"Do you ever tire of being on a ship?" Henderson asked her.

"Heavens, no. There's always something to do, a class to take, a lecture to attend, fascinating people to meet. I consider myself blessed to be living here. Are you happy living in Seattle?"

He seemed puzzled at the question.

"I ask," she said, "because I am a true believer in where we live determining how happy we will be. I assume that Mrs. Fletcher and Ms. Copeland are satisfied with being residents of their town in Maine."

"I wouldn't want to live anywhere else," Kathy said.

"Too much snow for me," Bill said.

"You get used to it," I said. "In fact, I actually look forward to it once winter has arrived. As long as it's going to be cold, there might as well be a white blanket on the ground to enjoy."

"Mr. Henderson," Gladys asked again, "are you happy living in Seattle?"

"Very."

"How long have you lived there?" I asked.

"A long time. Many years."

"I don't think I could stand all that rain," Kimberly Johansen said.

"Yeah, that is a problem," Bill said. "You never really do get used to it raining every other day."

"We had a wonderful dinner there before we left on the cruise," Kathy said. "A restaurant called Chanlis. It was beautiful."

"One of my favorite places," Bill said. "Chanlis is sort of like—well, like an event restaurant, you know, for special occasions."

"Every town and city has one of those," David Johansen said, and went on to describe his favorite restaurant in their hometown in Illinois.

The subject of the world's greatest restaurants dominated the remainder of the meal. Everyone had a list of favorites, and we took turns extolling the virtues of those places we particularly liked. The Johansens' taste favored seafood restaurants, while Gladys Montgomery's leaned toward French cuisine. My tastes were a little more eclectic; I realized I had so many favorite restaurants around the world that it was impossible for me to limit myself to a select list. Bill Henderson claimed to have a pedestrian palate, and admitted being partial to good steak houses, naming a couple of his favorites in New York City. We all agreed at the end of the discussion that an appreciation of good restaurants was an integral part of the joy of traveling. But Kathy ended the conversation with, "I enjoy eating out, but for me there is nothing like a home-cooked meal."

"Amen," Henderson said.

Following dinner, we again went our separate ways. I intended to join Gladys at the classical music concert, but Bill and Kathy persuaded me to go with them to the amateur talent show. They were right; it was funny and highly entertaining.

Once the show was over, and we joined hundreds of other passengers leaving the theater, Kathy and Bill tried to persuade me to extend the evening, but I demurred. "Thanks anyway," I said, "but I think I'll enjoy some quiet time in my cabin, maybe get a little reading done. I'd like to bone up on Sitka before we arrive there in the morning."

Henderson laughed. "You can be our tour guide tomorrow," he said.

"Fair enough," I said. "You two go on and enjoy yourselves. See you at breakfast."

I'd intended to go directly to my cabin, but found myself meandering around the ship. I went down one deck to the lower promenade and spent a few minutes in the art gallery perusing works of art that would be auctioned off the following day. From there, I continued past the coffee bar, the Windstar Café, and the Queen's Lounge until coming to the sports bar, adjacent to the casino. Despite the racket coming from the casino, and the chatter from multiple television sets in the sports bar, the more pleasant sound of a piano being played reached my ears. I followed it into the piano bar, where the rotund pianist I had briefly seen earlier in the trip sat at a piano built into a bar surrounded by a half dozen stools. He gave me a big smile as I entered and said, without missing a beat of the song he was play-ing, "Good evening. Come, sit, and join me. I'm just getting warmed up."

I debated for a moment, but decided to spend a few minutes listening to him play. When my deceased hus-band, Frank, and I traveled, we spent more than one enjoyable evening sitting in a piano bar and singing along with the performer.

"Anything special you would like to hear?" he asked.

"Do you know 'Laura'?" I asked. I always especially enjoyed that theme from one of my favorite movies.

The pianist laughed. "Of course I do," he said, seg-ueing immediately from the song he'd been playing into my request. "I know every song ever written."

I laughed along with him. "Do people enjoy chal-lenging that claim?" I asked.

"All the time," he said.

"Well," I said, "I assure you I won't be one of them."

I ordered an orange juice, closed my eyes, and let the beautiful melody wash over me. My eyes became misty as I thought of those lovely evenings spent with Frank, so pleasant and carefree, blending our voices with those of other amateurs and sounding a lot better to ourselves than to anyone else who might have been listening.

He finished playing. I opened my eyes and clapped. I looked around and saw that others who had been at the piano bar when I arrived were no longer there. I was alone.

"What's next?" he asked.

"You choose the next one," I said. "You play beautifully. Do you also sing?"

He responded by immediately starting "Hello, Dolly!" adding a rich baritone voice to his playing. It was a wonderfully spirited rendition, which attracted passersby, who filled the remaining stools around the piano bar.

He finished the tune, looked at me, and asked for another request. I hesitated. Frank and I had always had a favorite song, the beautiful Fischer/Laine tune, "We'll Be Together Again." I hesitated because every time I hear that song, I'm flooded with memories. But I requested it anyway, and this talented man who made his living entertaining passengers on steamships performed an especially poignant rendition. I kept my head lowered to avoid having others at the bar see that I'd welled up. When the pianist had finished, I quickly got up, thanked him, and said I'd be back another night.

The bittersweet mood that the song had engendered in me lasted after I'd returned to my cabin and had gotten ready for bed. Initially, it was a profound sadness that I felt. But that heaviness soon lifted, and I found myself smiling at the memory of Frank and me seated at other piano bars around the world, belting out lyrics to familiar tunes. As I often reminded myself, it was better to have those memories, happy or sad, than never to have experienced them at all.

# Chapter Eleven

I was wide awake the next morning as the ship eased into the Eastern Channel for its stop at Sitka, Alaska's first capital. I'd read about some of Sitka's history after having showered and dressed for the day.

It had been the ancestral home to the Tlingit Indian nation until the Russians arrived at the end of the eighteenth century. These new arrivals and the original inhabitants didn't get along, to the extent that the Russian settlers attacked the Indians in 1804 and drove them out (shades of the American experience). Russia eventually sold Alaska to the United States in 1867 for $7.2 million in gold, and the transfer of ownership was formalized in Sitka on October 18 of that year, with the American flag raised over Alaska for the first time. Sitka remained the capital until 1912, when the seat of government was transferred to Juneau. The Russian influence, according to what I'd read, was still pervasive in Sitka, and I looked forward to seeing what impact that culture had had on the town.

Unlike Juneau, Sitka's harbor wasn't sizable enough to handle the docking of the *Glacial Queen*; we would anchor in the channel and be shuttled to shore by the ship's tender boats, which also served as powered life rafts in the event of an emergency.

I was getting ready to go to the dining room when Kathy knocked on the door.

"Good morning," I said.

"Good morning, Jess. Mind if I come in for a minute?"

The serious expression on her face made it clear that she had something weighty to discuss.

"Not at all," I said. "Problem?"

She plopped down on the sofa and exhaled, as though to rid herself of thorny thoughts. "It's Bill," she said.

I joined her on the couch. "What happened?" I asked. "Did you two have an argument?"

"Sort of. No, I hate that kind of no-answer. We didn't have an argument."

"Then what's the problem?"

"He—he wanted to spend the night with me."

"Oh."

"I said no."

"Uh-huh. Was he angry?"

"Oh, no, no. He was a perfect gentleman. It's just that—"

"Yes?"

"I wanted to."

"But you didn't."

"I almost did."

"Almost doesn't count," I said.

"I think—"

"You think what, Kathy?"

"I think I'm in love with him."

"Why am I not surprised?"

"You're not?"

I laughed and patted her arm. "It's been obvious, not only to me but to Gladys Montgomery, too, that a pretty strong infatuation has developed between you two."

"Oh, God. It's been that evident?"

"Obvious—interesting—and pleasant. Have you told him how you feel?"

She shook her head emphatically.

"What about *him*? Has he said anything to indicate that he feels the same way about you?"

This time, her head went up and down rather than side to side.

"What did he say?" The moment I asked it, I held up my hand. "If you'd rather not share that, Kathy, I understand."

"Of course I want to share it with you, Jess. That's why I brought it up in the first place."

I waited.

"We went dancing again last night," she said. "They were giving dance instruction, and Bill insisted we join the group. Do you know what he said?"

"No."

"He said that he intended to dance with me for the rest of his life and didn't want it to be a lifetime of stepping on my toes."

"He said that out of the blue? No hint that it was coming?"

"No. He just said it. Like that."

"What did you say?"

"I was speechless. I don't think I said anything. We started the lesson—it was for jitterbugging, swing dancing—and we just—we just did that for the next hour."

"What happened after the lesson was finished?"

"We sat talking to some of the other passengers in the class. Bill is so comfortable talking with people he doesn't know. He listens to everything everyone says as though it's the most important thing in the world."

"Yes, I've noticed that he's a good listener. Too bad there aren't more of them in this world, including politicians."

My political comment brought a smile to her face. "*Especially* politicians," she added. "Anyway, Bill suggested we have a nightcap. We went to the main deck, that little circular bar down there."

"I know where you mean," I said. "I spoke with the bartender. He remembers Willie and Maurice Quarlé having late-night drinks there."

She shuddered. "Just thinking of Willie with that creep gives me the . . ."

"The willies?" I asked.

"Yes, the willies."

We both laughed.

She paused to gather her thoughts before continuing. "We sat at the bar and said nothing. Bill had fallen into what I suppose you could call a mood, very quiet, somber. I decided to ask about the comment he'd made about dancing together for life."

"Did you?"

"I did. That's when he told me he was falling in love with me. He said he'd dated only a few women since his wife died, and none of them interested him. He'd wondered whether he'd spend the rest of his life un-married, always searching for his soul mate. Until—until he found me."

She started to cry, and I gave her shoulder a squeeze.

"Sorry," she said. "Silly of me at my age."

"Not silly at all. I take it that that's when he asked to come back to your cabin and spend the night."

"Yes."

"What did you say?"

"I said I was flattered at what he'd said and that I'd found myself developing feelings about him, too. But we didn't know each other. I suggested we go slow and allow things to develop naturally, at their own pace."

"You were right," I offered.

"I know. Still . . ."

"No second-guessing," I said.

I was pleased, although not surprised, at how she'd handled it. On the one hand, I was delighted that Kathy had possibly found a man who loved her, and someone she could love back. On the other hand, ship-board romances were notorious for leaving one party heartbroken at the end of the cruise. I certainly didn't want to see that happen to this very special friend of mine. They had a lot of getting to know each other to do before any commitments were made.

"Tell you what," I said. "We have a busy day explor-ing Sitka. We're ashore for only a short time. The ship sails for Ketchikan at four. And we have some leads to follow up on while we're here. Did you bring Willie's receipts from Sitka?"

She pulled them from the pocket of her blue wind-breaker and handed them to me. I flipped through them. As in Juneau, they were mostly from stores where she'd picked up trinkets, probably to bring back home as gifts. There was also a stub from the Alaska Raptor Center, where rescued bald eagles, hawks, and owls are nursed back to health, hopefully to the extent that they can again be released into the wild. I'd learned of the organization a few years ago and started sending an annual donation to help defray the cost of operating this wonderfully worthwhile undertaking. Another slip of paper showed that Wilimena had opted for a three-hour whale-watching trip while in Sitka.

"I think we should take this whale-watching trip, too," I suggested. "Let's go down to the shore excursion desk and see if they have any vacancies."

We were in luck. There were two openings on the whale-watching boat, and we signed up. A bus that would take us to the appropriate dock was scheduled to leave at nine forty-five, which didn't allow us much time to follow up with the shops Willie had visited.

We joined Gladys for breakfast in the dining room.

"And what do you two ladies have planned for today?" she asked.

I told her about the whale-watching trip, and that we intended to visit the Raptor Center.

"Sounds like a full day," she said. To Kathy she added, "I see that Mr. Henderson isn't joining us this morning."

"I guess he slept in," Kathy said.

"You look as though you could use some extra sleep yourself," Gladys said.

She was right. There were dark circles beneath Kathy's eyes, and she wasn't as erect in her chair as she usually was. "Burning the candle at both ends," Kathy said.

"My husband and I used to do that," said Gladys, a wistful expression crossing her face. "He had insatiable energy and loved nightclubbing. My goodness, what a swath we used to cut in Paris and New York. London, too. But that's a young person's game, isn't it?"

I pictured Gladys as a beautiful young woman, exquisitely dressed and cavorting in posh nightspots around the globe with her wealthy husband, a pair of jet-setters living the high life. That vision brought a smile to my lips.

"A word of advice?" Gladys said to Kathy.

"Sure."

"Don't allow your candle to burn too low. It's difficult to relight once it's gone out."

"I'll remember that," Kathy said.

After Gladys had left the table, I asked Kathy if she knew why Bill hadn't come to breakfast. She didn't. "In fact," she said, "he said he'd see me here this morning."

"Must have overslept," I said. "Well, time for us to get moving."

We rode the tender to the main pier and took in the main street in downtown Sitka. As in Juneau, jewelry stores prevailed, one after the other. We stopped in one that Willie had visited, but no one remembered having waited on her.

"Just as well," I said after we left the shop and stood outside, constantly having to move to avoid knots of tourists walking three and four abreast and taking up the entire sidewalk. "Obviously, the answer to her whereabouts won't be found in the shops she visited. Let's find a quiet spot for coffee or tea where I can call Trooper McQuesten and Detective Flowers."

I first reached Flowers, who reported that there was no new progress in the search for Wilimena. He did say, however, that he would be in Ketchikan when the ship arrived, and he looked forward to spending time with us.

McQuesten had said he would be in Sitka when we arrived, and so he was.

"Where are you?" he asked.

"A coffee shop on Lake Street. Highliner Coffee."

"I know it well," he said. "Be there in a jiffy."

He walked through the door a few minutes later and joined us at a tiny table near two computer stations that patrons could rent by the half hour.

"How was your sail?" he asked.

"Uneventful," I said.

"For which you were grateful, I'm sure," he said.

I agreed with his assessment.

"Is there anything new?" Kathy asked.

"No," he replied. "Afraid not."

"Did you drive here overnight?" I asked.

"Drive? You can't reach Sitka by road. Only boats and floatplanes. One of our pilots flew me in this morning. I'll be going on to Ketchikan later today."

"I've never been on a floatplane," I said.

"Jessica has her pilot's license," Kathy said.

"Do you really?" McQuesten said, obviously impressed.

"It's a bit of a joke back in Cabot Cove," I said. "I don't drive, don't even have a driver's license, but I'm licensed to fly a single-engine plane."

"We pretty much use floatplanes for everything up here in Alaska," he said.

"So I've read. Maybe I'll have a chance to fly on one before we leave," I said, seriously doubting that I would.

"Hopefully, we'll find an answer to your sister's disappearance in Ketchikan," he told Kathy. "Retracing her steps on the cruise was a good idea, but Ketchikan is where she was last seen. I have a feeling that we'll do better once we're there."

"Are you working the case?" I asked. "I thought Detective Flowers was, and that you were only offering a hand as a friend. At least that's what Mort Metzger told me."

"That's the way it was," he answered, "but things have changed. The gentleman who was following you ends up very cold and dead in Glacier Bay, and Maurice Quarlé is a murder victim. There's now more to this case than just Ms. Copeland's disappearance. Flowers is still following up on the missing-person aspect. I've been assigned to investigate those deaths."

"I never thought Wilimena's disappearance would end up being linked to murder," I said.

"No one did," McQuesten said.

"Have you time for coffee?" I asked.

"Sorry, no, but thanks for the offer. I'm due at a meeting."

As we stood on the sidewalk in front of the coffee shop, he asked, "What's on your agenda today?"

"Whale watching," Kathy replied, "and a visit to the Raptor Center."

"Wish I could join you. They say the whales are plentiful this year, even orcas. Orcas don't usually show up for another couple of weeks."

"Wilimena took this same whale-watching excursion and went to the Raptor Center when she was in Sitka," I said.

He smiled. "Knowing your reputation, Mrs. Fletcher, I was sure you had more on your mind than simply playing tourist. Well, good luck. Hope you see plenty of whales. See you in Ketchikan."

We joined dozens of other passengers waiting for the bus to take us to where the whale-watching boat would depart. The expectation level was high. So often, going on a whale watch can be disappointing. You can spend hours on a boat and never see one of the magnificent creatures. In any case, Kathy and I had dressed appropriately: sneakers, jeans, sweaters and rain slickers, hats, gloves, and an extra sweater in case it was needed. Everyone else in the group was dressed similarly.

A large, modern bus pulled onto the pier, and we boarded. The ride to the embarkation point took longer than I had anticipated, considering Sitka's relatively small size. As Alaska's fourth-largest city, it has a permanent population of under nine thousand. But there are many who say it is Alaska's most beautiful seaport, rich with natural scenery, including lush and stately spruce forests that stretch all the way to the water's edge.

We pulled up next to a substantial-looking modern

vessel. A young man and woman directed the boarding, and Kathy and I found seats at the front of a spacious enclosed center section. There was also a sizable deck at the stern, from which we could indulge our desire to see whales and other wildlife—provided there were any to be seen. A narrow deck that ran along either side of the enclosed space also provided vantage points, although I wasn't sure I would want to be on it if the weather got rough.

We received a safety briefing from the captain over the PA, including an admonition to be especially careful when on the slippery decks. He also suggested that if we saw someone fall overboard, we should yell for help and keep our eye on the person in the water. He assured us that when the vessel approached wildlife, he would maneuver it to give us an optimal view and asked that if we were on the deck we move slowly and quietly to avoid startling the animals. He further asked that we close doors gently and speak in a low tone of voice. Flash attachments on cameras were to be turned off or covered with a tiny piece of tape that one of the crew members would supply. He ended his welcome by pointing out that there were snacks and soft drinks for sale and that a naturalist was on board to keep us informed over the PA of any sightings.

We were soon under way, slowly moving from the calm waters of the small harbor and picking up speed as we reached the open sea. It wasn't long before we began to enjoy the purpose of the trip. We passed a rocky formation on which hundreds of stellar sea lions lolled, rolling on their backs, splashing down into the water, and in general putting on a show for us. At one point, the captain brought the ship close to a shoreline as the naturalist pointed out a huge eagle's nest atop a clump of tall evergreens. "That nest," she said, "has been there for years. Eagles mate for life and return to the same nesting areas year after year. That particular nest, as you can see, is more than six feet across. Eagles build the largest nests in North America. They lay one to three eggs per year, and their hatchlings mature very quickly, just in time to feed on the salmon runs that occur late each summer. Interestingly enough, female eagles are larger than male eagles. We have approximately fifteen thousand bald eagles living in southeastern Alaska. We are really blessed to have so many of these magnificent creatures to enjoy."

We'd no sooner moved back into open water than the first whale sighting was announced over the PA. We headed in the direction of the "blow," a stream of water dozens of feet high exhaled by the whale. By the time we reached where it had last been seen, a whole pod of humpback whales suddenly was visible, displaying their flukes, or tails, before diving after having surfaced for air. There was palpable excitement as everyone spilled out onto the rear deck. Kathy and I, like everyone else, had brought binoculars and used them to get close-up views of the humpbacks as they cavorted only a hundred feet from the boat. A few children on the boat were giddy with glee, and their parents had to remind them of what the captain had said about keeping voices low.

Moments later, the naturalist announced that a pod of orcas—or killer whales—could be seen on the opposite side of the ship. "You can recognize the orca because of its prominent dorsal fins and distinctive black and white markings," she said. "Orcas have teeth and are very efficient hunters. They can bring down large prey, even gray whales. The humpbacks, on the other hand, feed by straining water through baleen, which acts like the teeth of a comb. The baleen traps krill and other small fish."

"I've never seen anything like it," one woman said excitedly to her husband. "There are dozens of them."

Her enthusiasm was shared by everyone.

The captain announced that it was time to turn around and head back to the dock, then asked if anyone wished to visit the bridge. Naturally, the children wanted to, and their parents obliged. I started a conversation with one of the young crew members, who'd made me a cup of tea. By this time, I'd reached the conclusion that showing Wilimena's photo around while in Sitka wouldn't accomplish anything. But I pulled it out of my shoulder bag anyway and showed it to the young man. "Do you recognize her from a previous whale watch?" I asked.

His response was totally unexpected. He laughed loudly.

"What's funny?" I asked.

"I think you'd better go up and talk to the captain about it, ma'am."

"I just may do that," I said, and headed for a flight of narrow iron stairs leading to the bridge. A family with children was just leaving, and I took their place alongside the captain, a strikingly handsome, bearded man who I judged was in his late forties or early fifties.

"Enjoying yourself so far?" he asked.

"It's been wonderful," I said. "I'm from Maine. I've been on whale watches there, but I've never seen anything like this."

"We always know we'll see some whales," he said. "In fact, we guarantee it. But this was a particularly successful run. The humpbacks and orcas are out in droves today."

"My friend and I are in Alaska looking for someone who has disappeared."

"Is that so? Disappeared? *Really* disappeared?"

"I'm afraid so," I said, reaching for Wilimena Copeland's photograph. "I showed this to the young man downstairs and he had an unusual reaction. He laughed and said I should show it to you."

He took the photo from me, turned, and said through a big smile, "So you know the gold digger, too."

"Gold digger?" I said.

"Just a nickname I gave her," he said, handing me back the picture. "No offense."

"None taken. Obviously, you got to know her."

"I guess I did, sort of. She's quite a character. I mean that in a nice way. After the trip she was on, I met up with her in town. We had a drink and a quick bite to eat before she got back on the ship. That's the last I saw of her. Say, did she ever get the gold she was going after? It was left to her by some distant relative."

"I don't know," I replied. "You see—"

"Hey, wait a minute. Is she the person you said was missing?"

"Yes."

"I'm sorry," he said.

"Her sister and I are trying to find her. Did she say anything to you that might help us accomplish that?"

"I don't think so. I mean, she told me about this aunt of hers who used to own a brothel in Ketchikan, Dolly Arthur. We all know about Dolly Arthur here in Alaska. She's our most famous and colorful madam. According to your friend, as I remember it, some boyfriend of Dolly's stashed a bunch of gold with her, took off, and never came back. Willie—that's the name she liked to be called—Willie said she had found out where Dolly hid the gold and was going to collect it."

"Did she indicate where that was?" I asked.

He answered with a knowing laugh. "I've never in my life met a person who talked as much as your friend," he said, "but she was smart enough not to share *that* information with me. For all she knew, I would've raced down to Ketchikan and grabbed the gold for myself. Not that I would, mind you. Let me ask you a question."

"Go ahead."

"Do you think she told a lot of people about this gold she claimed she was going to collect? If so, that might explain why she went missing."

That analysis certainly didn't elicit any disagreement from me.

"Did she come on the whale watch alone?" I asked.

Another laugh from him. "If she didn't, she sure dumped whoever was with her. I never saw her with anyone else. If I had, I wouldn't have asked her out."

"Well, Captain, I really appreciate your taking the time to talk to me. And thank you for a wonderful experience."

I recounted for Kathy the conversation I'd just had with the captain. "What is it about your sister that makes her so incredibly attractive to every man she meets?" I asked.

"Her attitude, I suppose," Kathy said. "Not that Willie isn't a beautiful woman. She's always worked hard on her looks and her figure. But it's more than that. She makes sure every man she meets knows that she's interested in him. Call it constant flirtation, I suppose."

"Well," I said, "whatever it is, she certainly has never wanted for male companionship. I just hope that need of hers didn't lead her into a situation that she couldn't find her way out of."

Kathy nodded. "I know," she said, turning to the large window splattered by the boat's spray.

She said nothing all the way back to the dock.

# Chapter Twelve

We got back to the ship barely in time for its four o'clock departure for Ketchikan. Security Officer Kale looked on disapprovingly as we ran up the gangway and handed our shipboard ID cards to the crew member scanning them into a computer.

"You just made it," Kale said.

"But we did make it," I said pleasantly. "We spent more time at the Raptor Center than we'd planned."

He walked with us to the elevator.

"I'd appreciate a few minutes of your time, Mrs. Fletcher," he said.

"Of course."

"Come to my office?"

"Now?"

"If you wouldn't mind."

"You go ahead," Kathy said. "I'll see if I can find Bill."

At his office, Kale closed the door and indicated the chair I should take.

"What's this about?" I asked.

"It's about Maurice Quarlé."

"What about him?"

"I understand that it was you who discovered his body."

"Where did you hear that?"

"It doesn't matter. What *does* matter is that since you came aboard in Seattle, there have been two violent deaths—the passenger who went overboard in Glacier Bay and now Maurice."

I almost laughed, but caught myself. "Are you saying that my being a passenger had anything to do with those deaths, Officer Kale?"

"Did you cause them? No, of course not."

"I've jinxed the ship?"

"No. But as I told you on your first day here, I don't want the other passengers to be disturbed or upset because of your—"

"Because of my *what*?"

"Because of your tendency to ask too many questions, and to be at the wrong place at the wrong time."

"My tendency to snoop. Isn't that what you were about to say?"

He ignored my question and went on. "Maurice— Mr. Quarlé—was well-known to everyone on the *Glacial Queen*. He taught French on some cruises and also booked groups. Word of his murder in Juneau has already spread throughout the crew, and that means passengers are learning of it, too."

"That can't be helped."

"They'll be asking you questions about it."

"That can't be helped, either."

"Since you were the one who found Mr. Quarlé's body, maybe you can fill me in on what the police are doing."

His abrupt change of topic caught me off guard for a moment. I said, "I really know nothing beyond having been unfortunate enough to, as you say, be at the wrong place at the wrong time."

Ordinarily, when speaking with someone in Officer Kale's position, I wouldn't have hesitated in sharing what I'd learned—that we had found evidence in Quarlé's room that he had, indeed, befriended Wilimena in order to get his hands on the gold, that John Smith had a photograph of Kathy and a copy of one of my books with my picture on it in his cabin, and that his passport was forged. But there was something about Kale's demeanor and attitude that was off-putting to me, and I found myself not offering any information. I did say, however, "You are aware, are you not, that Mr. Quarlé was not considered by the Juneau police to be an upstanding citizen? In fact," I continued, "he was considered a con man."

"I find that hard to believe," he said.

I found it hard to believe that Kale wasn't aware of that.

"Believe what you will, Officer Kale. I do want you to understand that I am conscious of your need to avoid having any of this intrude upon your passengers. I assure you that is not my intent. At the same time, you might keep in mind that there have been two deaths since this ship left Seattle, one an obvious murder, the other a possible homicide. On top of that, there is still a question of one of your passengers disappearing, namely Wilimena Copeland." I stood. "By the way, did you enjoy your time in Juneau? I saw that you had some time off there."

"Just a little shopping," he said. "Thanks for stopping in."

I left his office and decided to do a mile around the promenade deck. The first leg was downwind. The wind blew briskly, its velocity enhanced by the ship's movement, catching me in the back and threatening to propel me onto my face. The ship was under full steam toward Ketchikan, leaving a long, wide wake in its path. I reached the bow, crossed it, and started the upwind leg of my walk, the wind causing my rain slicker to billow out and my eyes to sting. There were only a few others out exercising at that moment, and an occasional passenger stood at the rail looking for whales and other sea life. I'd almost reached the stern of the ship when I saw Kathy and Bill leaning on the railing. I stopped not far from them and sensed that they were engaged in serious conversation. I considered turning around and retracing my steps so as not to disturb them, but decided to keep going. They were so engrossed in what they were talking about that they were oblivious to everything around them.

By the time I'd circumvented the deck once and was on my second trip, Kathy and Bill were gone. *What had they been talking about?* I wondered. I thought about what she'd shared with me earlier in the day and hoped that she'd meant what she'd said, to go slow and let things take their natural course. She barely knew Bill. I knew even less about him than she did, aside from the fact that he was handsome, polite, considerate, and a good listener. I had to smile. The adjectives I'd applied to him painted a very appealing picture.

By the time I was on my third trip around the deck—

which constituted a mile—my thoughts turned to the reason I was on that cruise.

Originally, the trip was to be purely for pleasure, aside from the book signing in Seattle. Then searching for Wilimena had taken center stage. And now two murders had entered the picture. Although I had nothing tangible to base my opinion on, I was certain that the man who called himself John Smith had not accidentally fallen from the ship. He, like Maurice Quarlé, had been murdered. There was one other thing now beyond debate: Their deaths were connected with Willie's disappearance.

I was happy to go to my cabin to take a hot shower and slip on my robe. It had been a long, physically active day, and a mentally fatiguing one, too. I considered a nap but decided against it, not wanting to wake up groggy before dinner. Instead, I sat at the desk and made notes of everything I had learned since coming aboard. Unlike Officer Kale, Trooper McQuesten was extremely forthcoming and willing to share with me what he knew. I was comfortable being around him and anticipated that once we met up again in Ketchikan, the mystery surrounding Willie's disappearance would become less mysterious. At least I hoped it would.

I thought of the piece of paper McQuesten had shown me on which Quarlé had made a list of float-plane operators in the Ketchikan area and the prices they charged. Ironic, I thought, that I might end up flying on a floatplane after all.

Despite my determination not to give in to fatigue, I was having trouble keeping my eyes open. I turned and looked at the bed. It was inviting, and I might have succumbed to the temptation to curl up on it had the phone not rung. It was Kathy.

"Hi, Jess. I didn't wake you, did I?"

"Another few minutes and you would have. What's up?"

"Join Bill and me for a drink? I'm dying to hear what Officer Kale wanted to talk to you about."

"Sure," I said.

"The Ocean Bar in fifteen," she said.

I dressed for dinner and joined them in a semicircle banquette, directly across from the bar. If the conversation I'd seen them having on the deck earlier had been as serious as it appeared to be, they had obviously resolved whatever issue was at the root of it. They were in a happy, expansive mood.

"We missed you today," I said to Bill.

"I was under the weather," he said. "It must've been something I ate. I decided to lay low and take it easy. I'm feeling better now."

"Glad to hear it," I said. A waitress took my order for a glass of white wine. "We had an interesting day," I said. "The whales put on quite a show for us, and the Raptor Center was fascinating. I've been donating money to it for the past few years and was happy to actually see it in operation. The birds they care for are magnificent, and the dedicated staff of young volunteers is inspirational. I'm glad we had a chance to see it."

"Yes, Kathy told me. Sorry I missed it. She also said you met with the cop. What's his name, McPherson?"

"McQuesten," I said. "Joseph McQuesten."

"Kathy said he didn't have much to say, and that there hasn't been any progress in finding her sister."

"I'm afraid that's true," I said.

"What did Officer Kale want to speak with you about?" Kathy asked me.

"He's anxious that we not bother other passengers on the ship while we try to get answers about Willie. I understand his concern."

"Kathy has told me about all the other stuff you've learned," Bill said. "It sounds like the fellow who went overboard and the French guy might have had something to do with Willie's disappearance."

I wasn't particularly pleased that Kathy had shared so much information with Bill, but I didn't express it. There probably was no harm in it, although my instincts told me that the fewer people who knew at this juncture, the better.

The conversation turned to less-serious subjects, and we chatted about myriad things until it was time to go to dinner.

"I understand you and Kathy had a dancing lesson last night," I said as we made our way to the dining room.

Bill and Kathy glanced at each other, tiny smiles on their faces. Bill said, "Yes, we cut quite a rug last night."

"I haven't heard that expression in a long time," I said.

"I'll bet you cut a few rugs in your day, Jessica," Bill said, laughing pleasantly.

"Come to think of it, I did," I said. "I'm sure Mrs. Montgomery did, too."

The Johansens didn't join us for dinner that night. They'd made reservations at the Bistro, a small, intimate restaurant that passengers could enjoy for an additional fee. The conversation among the four of us flowed easily and touched upon many subjects. Gladys, who seemed to have an unending wardrobe of elegant dinner dresses, regaled us with tales of when she and her husband had been globe-trotters. They'd been friends with many powerful business and political leaders, and their travels had taken them around the world many times. One thing was certain: She was not a woman who allowed life to pass her by.

As usual, we parted company just outside the restaurant. Gladys headed for her evening concert. To my surprise, Bill begged off on extending the evening with Kathy. "I thought I was over whatever bothered me today, but I'm still not feeling right," he said. "Maybe it was all that dancing last night." He laughed and gave Kathy a hug. "Not as young as I used to be. I hope you'll excuse me if I make it an early night. I want to feel tip-top tomorrow in Ketchikan."

"Bill is going to spend the day with us, Jess," Kathy said.

"That's—that's fine," I said. "But I'm afraid we're going to be spending it trying to find out what's happened to Kathy's sister. It won't be much fun."

"I'm not looking for fun, Jessica," Bill said. "Kathy has filled me in on everything, and I want to help in any way I can. Don't worry about me having fun. There'll be lots of time for fun when we celebrate with Willie."

"That would be wonderful," I said. "You enjoy an early night, Bill."

To Kathy I said, "I think you and I should have a nightcap."

We found a relatively empty lounge, and I ordered a club soda with lime, Kathy a snifter of cognac.

"Are you angry with me, Jess?" she asked after we'd been served.

"Of course not," I replied. "But I'm not especially happy that you've asked Bill to join us tomorrow."

"Why? It was nice having him with us in Juneau when we found the body. Having a man along makes me feel more secure."

"I can understand that," I said, "but it isn't as though we won't be with men. Trooper McQuesten is meeting us in Ketchikan, and Detective Flowers will be there, too."

Her expression told me she wasn't happy with my reaction, and I decided that I was probably making more of it than was warranted.

"All right," I said. "We'll have Bill join us."

"Thanks."

"Nothing to thank me for. What about you and Bill? I saw the two of you on the deck when I exercised this afternoon. It appeared to me that you were into a heavy-duty discussion."

"I guess we were," she said. "Bill wants to come back with us to Cabot Cove. He wants to move there."

My eyebrows went up. "Can he do that?" I asked. "I mean, doesn't he have a job in Seattle?"

"He said he can set up a one-man shop as a financial advisor just about anywhere."

I wasn't sure what to say, or ask, next.

"He's asked me to marry him."

"Oh, Kathy, that's—"

"I know, I know. It's all happening so fast."

"Did you accept?"

"No. I said I had to have a few days to think about it."

I breathed a surreptitious sigh of relief.

"Please don't be judgmental, Jess. I've always been happy and satisfied living alone. You know that. But at the same time I've wondered what my life would be like as a married woman, wondered whether I'd ever meet a man who was perfect for me. I think I've found that man."

"He certainly seems nice enough," I said, aware of how weak and noncommittal my comment sounded.

"Jess?"

"Yes?"

"Are you jealous of me?"

"Jealous?" I sputtered. "Of course not. Why would I be jealous?"

"I don't know," she said with a shrug of her shoulders. "It's just that you seem to have reservations about Bill."

"That's not true, Kathy. I don't know him. Maybe that's why I don't share your enthusiasm, at least not yet. You don't really know him, either."

"I know him enough to think I want to marry him."

I fell silent.

"What is it, Jess? What's bothering you?"

"I've never known an impetuous financial advisor," I said. "He says he's been a financial advisor in Seattle for a long time, yet he's willing to simply pull up stakes at the drop of a hat and move across the country. Doesn't that strike you as odd?"

"I hadn't thought of it that way," she said, a serious expression on her pretty face.

"When we were at dinner discussing favorite restaurants, you mispronounced the name of the restaurant we'd had dinner at in Seattle. Canlis."

She laughed. "So? I'd never been there before, never heard of it until you took me there."

"But Bill mispronounced it, too. You said 'Chanlis' and so did he. I would think that—"

"Jess, are you sure you aren't thinking more like a writer of murder mysteries, looking for clues to plug into your books?"

"Maybe I am," I said, smiling. "But he said something else that causes me to have questions about him."

Her raised eyebrows said loud and clear that she wasn't in the mood to hear more. I proceeded anyway. "He talked about it raining in Seattle every other day. But it doesn't rain as often as people from out of town think. Everyone I've ever known in Seattle is quick to point out that misconception."

"Well," said Kathy, "I know you care about me and want only the best for me, but I think you're grasping at straws to find something wrong with Bill."

My face brightened, and I nodded with conviction. "And you are absolutely right, Kathy. I'm delighted for you whatever you decide to do. I mean that."

"I know you are, Jess," she said, reaching over to give me a squeeze.

She spent the next half hour extolling Bill Henderson's virtues, his philosophy of life, his views on myriad subjects, and his aspirations for the future. This time, I restrained from playing devil's advocate. The more she talked, the better Bill sounded, and I became caught up in her schoolgirlish enthusiasm. I was sincerely happy for her, and we spoke of planning a wedding back home, where it would take place, the sort of reception that would be held—"Small," she said, "just my closest friends. You'll be my matron of honor, of course."

"You bet I will be," I said, aware that not including Wilimena in the plans spoke volumes about Kathy's expectations of finding her sister alive.

We eventually decided to emulate Bill and make it an early night. We agreed to meet at seven for breakfast and went to our respective cabins. I undressed for bed, turned on the TV, and flipped through the channels until coming upon an old black-and-white movie that looked interesting. The story and characters took my mind off what we might face tomorrow in Ketchikan. So far, we hadn't gotten any closer to finding Wilimena than we'd been back in Seattle. Hopefully, being where she was last seen would prove more fruitful.

The movie ended. I turned off the lights, climbed into bed, and closed my eyes. They didn't stay closed very long. Something—some thing—was rattling around in my brain. I couldn't identify what it was, was unable to pin it down no matter how hard I tried. Maybe it was the grim expectation that if we did find Wilimena, she wouldn't be alive. What had kept me going was her past history of disappearing now and then, sometimes for months at a time, and then happily resurfacing with a tale to tell. If that were the case now, we'd all be relieved—and lining up to give her a good spanking. If she was off on some adventure, she'd not only caused concern on the part of her loving sister, but she'd turned my pleasure cruise into a tense search for her, to say nothing of wasting countless hours on the part of law enforcement.

I gave up trying to sort out my jumbled thoughts and finally allowed sleep to overtake me. But whatever it was that had kept me awake obviously hadn't vanished. It must have been rattling around in my brain all night because I woke up groggy, out of sorts, and as the saying goes, loaded for bear.

# Chapter Thirteen

$K$athy, Bill, and I came off the ship and stood on Front Street, Ketchikan's main drag along the waterfront. As in our other ports of call, the *Glacial Queen* wasn't the only cruise ship docked at the huge pier, constructed to accommodate Ketchikan's thriving tourist industry. And, as with those other stops we'd made, Front Street was already clogged with tourists seeking bargains in the shops.

I was about to pull out my cell phone when I saw Trooper McQuesten approaching.

"I must've missed you when you disembarked," he said, his signature smile on his rugged face. "I ran a little late this morning."

"And we were earlier than usual," I said. "It's good to see you, Trooper McQuesten."

"I see you've brought along reinforcements," Mc-Questen said, referring to Bill Henderson.

"I'm afraid I'm no help," Henderson said. "I'm just along to provide moral support."

"You can never have too much moral support in a situation like this," McQuesten said. "I've arranged for us to meet up with Detective Flowers. He's already contacted the floatplane operators who were listed on that piece of paper we found with the murder victim in Juneau."

"Any luck?" I asked.

"Afraid not," McQuesten answered. "He showed Ms. Copeland's picture to all of them. Only one remembered her, but he said she'd never booked any of his planes. Still, I think it might be worthwhile to revisit that company. Sometimes a second go-round results in things being remembered that weren't the first time. Come on. My car is over there."

We drove in McQuesten's unmarked sedan to a series of small docks to which a variety of floatplanes were tethered. The trooper led us into an office where half a dozen pilots sat around drinking coffee and talking. A man behind a desk stood as we entered and warmly greeted McQuesten. He, in turn, introduced us to the man we were looking for, whose name was Gilroy. "Bob Gilroy owns this floatplane operation," McQuesten said.

"Pleased to have you visit us," Gilroy said. "Grab some chairs."

We formed a semicircle around the desk.

"Detective Flowers showed me the picture of the missing woman," Gilroy said. "I remember her coming in here asking about renting a floatplane and pilot. I don't know whether the price was too high, but she said she'd think about it and left. That's the last I saw her."

Gilroy looked up as the door opened. "Here's Detective Flowers now," he said.

The detective was a short, slight man wearing a

double-breasted blue blazer, gray slacks with a razor crease, a white shirt, and a regimental tie. If I'd been asked to pick out a detective from a lineup of men, he would have been the last one I would have chosen. Another round of introductions was made, and Flowers pulled up a chair and joined us.

"I was just telling these good folks about my brief encounter with the missing woman," Gilroy said to Flowers. "Wish I could be more help."

"Did she indicate why she wanted to rent a float-plane?" I asked.

Gilroy shook his head. At least she hadn't shared with him her quest for gold.

"None of the other floatplane operators remembers her at all," Flowers said.

"Are the other floatplane operators listed on that piece of paper the only ones in Ketchikan?" I asked.

Gilroy replied, "The only ones *licensed* to operate here. There are some independent operators who own planes and rent themselves out. They're not always reliable, and a few don't keep their equipment up the way we do."

"But they're allowed to take passengers?" Henderson asked.

"Sure," Gilroy replied. "When I say they're not licensed, what I mean is that they aren't licensed as businesses in Ketchikan, or registered with the steamship companies as official shore excursion operations. But they're okay as far as the FAA is concerned. They can legally take paying passengers."

"Maybe Willie decided to go with one of them," Kathy offered.

"How many of these independent operators would you say there are in Ketchikan?" I asked.

Gilroy shrugged. "Hard to say," he said. "A dozen, maybe."

"Would you have a list of them?" I asked.

"No, I don't. No need for me to keep such a list. I can give you the names of a couple off the top of my head."

"Please," I said.

He came up with three names, which I dutifully jotted down in my little notebook. He pulled a phone directory from a desk drawer, looked up the addresses and phone numbers of the names he'd given me, wrote them down, and handed the paper to me.

"Anything else I can do for you this morning?" he asked. "We've got a busy day ahead of us, every plane booked solid. It's tourist season, you know."

"You've been very helpful," I said. "Thank you for your time."

"I feel as though we've just hit a brick wall," Kathy said as we stood next to Trooper McQuesten's car.

"Don't talk that way," Bill Henderson said. "We're just getting started. Maybe one of those independent pilots Mr. Gilroy mentioned was hired by your sister. I say we visit every one of them."

I judged from the expression on Detective Flowers's face that his thinking was more in line with Kathy's than with Bill's. Had I been totally honest, I would have sided with the detective. There we were, in Ketchikan, Alaska, without a tangible bit of evidence to justify continuing our search for Wilimena. But I wasn't about to express my inner feelings. We'd come this far, and to throw up our hands and admit failure was the last thing Kathy needed. Yes, it was entirely possible—no, make that probable—that we would not find Willie before it was time to get back on the ship at the end of the day and leave for Vancouver, the final stop on the cruise before returning to Seattle. That would be an unfortunate conclusion, especially for Kathy. We had to use the day to at least follow up on every lead, and the list of names Mr. Gilroy had given us was a start.

There was also Dolly Arthur's former brothel to visit. It was now a tourist attraction, according to the guidebooks. Whether anything there would prove helpful was pure conjecture. But then again, everything at that moment was conjecture.

"I agree with Bill," I said. "Let's see if we can find out anything from these independent floatplane pilots."

Trooper McQuesten said, "That's probably a good idea. Now, Detective Flowers and I need to go to our barracks here in Ketchikan."

Flowers added, "We have a task force operating around the state, troopers looking for your sister, Ms. Copeland. They report in every morning at nine." He checked his watch. "Trooper McQuesten and I need to be there to coordinate their reports." He handed Kathy his business card. "Check in with us later this morning."

McQuesten slid behind the wheel, and Flowers headed for his car, parked a few feet away.

"There's one problem," Bill Henderson said.

Both officers looked at him.

"We don't have any way to get around," Bill said.

McQuesten laughed. "Yes, I'd say that *is* a problem."

"Will you drop us off at a car rental agency?" Bill asked.

McQuesten gladly accommodated us, and thirty minutes later we drove away from a car rental lot with Bill behind the wheel of a relatively new Subaru.

"Where to first?" he asked.

I consulted the list given us by Gilroy. "Might as well start here," I said, calling out the address. "His name is Borosky. Bob Borosky."

Kathy consulted a map of Ketchikan she'd brought with her from the ship. "Up that road," she said, pointing.

The road took us along a narrow strip of land that jutted into Tongass Narrows, the body of water on which Ketchikan is situated. As we pulled up in front of a small house in need of painting, a man who was fixing something on a floatplane looked up and scowled.

"Do somethin' for you?" he asked, wiping oil-stained hands on an oil-stained towel that was once white. He looked as though he'd just gotten out of bed. Thinning hair sprouted in multiple directions. He needed a shave, and the yellow T-shirt he wore hadn't benefited from a washing machine in a long time.

"Mr. Borosky?" I said.

"That's my name."

"My name is Jessica Fletcher," I said, "and these are my friends. We're in Alaska trying to find a woman who disappeared from a cruise a few weeks ago."

"That so? What's her name?"

"Wilimena Copeland."

He screwed up his weather-beaten face in exaggerated thought. "Nope, can't say that I ever heard of her."

"We think she hired a floatplane here in Ketchikan," I said.

"Well, if she did, she didn't hire me," he said. "Probably went with one a' the big boys, paid a fortune compared to what I charge. Don't make any sense to me. I'm FAA-certified, keep my plane in tip-top shape."

"Yes, I'm sure you do," I said. I turned to Kathy. "Show him Willie's picture."

She did. He shook his head. "Never seen her before." He broke into a toothy grin. "Wouldn't mind knowin' her, though," he said.

"Well," I said, "thanks for your time."

"How about you folks take a ride with me? Take you into the Misty Fjords. Make a good deal for the three of you."

"Love to take you up on it," Bill said, "but we're busy looking for the missing woman. Much obliged, though."

"Suit yourself. Good luck findin' her." He cackled. "You'll need it."

We got back in the car and tried to decide where to go next.

"This is a waste of time," Kathy said. "We don't know for certain that Willie took a floatplane anywhere. All we're basing it on is that piece of paper the Frenchman, Maurice, had in his room. If Willie *had* taken a floatplane, she would have chosen one of the bigger operators." She looked back to where the pilot had resumed work on his aircraft. "I wouldn't get in that plane with him for any kind of deal."

Bill laughed. "He is a little scruffy, but that doesn't mean he's not a good pilot."

"Tell you what," I said. "We can check out these other independent pilots later. Let's head for Dolly Arthur's house."

They agreed, and Bill drove us as close as we could park to Creek Street. I don't know of many other cities or towns in which a former brothel is a magnet for tourists, but then again Ketchikan isn't just any town.

They call it Alaska's "First City" because it's the first stop for most cruise ships plying the Inner Passage. Before that, in 1900, the U.S. Customs House was moved to Ketchikan from Mary Island, and all northbound vessels of any size were forced by regulation to stop there. Ketchikan boomed. It became a center for the smoking and canning of salmon, which are abundant, and it soon became an important trading community, serving gold miners who'd flocked to the area in search of their fortunes.

While stores proliferated, so did saloons and brothels. It was estimated that at one point, as much as two-thirds of the miners' money went to Ketchikan's prostitutes and barkeeps.

Shortly after Ketchikan was incorporated as a city in 1900, the town fathers decided that the girls from the brothels were becoming a public nuisance. Most of them were located in Newtown, and that area's residents petitioned to have the bawdy houses relocated to Indian Town, on the opposite side of a small creek. The Indians of Indian Town weren't happy with this arrangement and promptly moved out. That was when Creek Street became established as a legal red-light district, and it remained so until, remarkably, well into the 1950s.

There were ups and downs, of course. The Depression caused a slump in business, and many of the working girls, including Dolly Arthur, headed south for extended vacations. Business picked up again until World War II, when the military closed down the brothels. The girls took it in good humor, even holding a "Going Out of Business" sale, with themselves as the discounted merchandise. But once the war ended, prostitution thrived until the early 1950s, when a federal grand jury held hearings in Ketchikan (part of a sweeping national inquiry into official corruption) and identified the primary reason why prostitution had remained legal there for so long. Elected officials were impossibly corrupt. A married chief of police was in business with one of the bawdy houses. Another top-ranking cop was routinely drunk while on the job, and offered an out-of-town spread that he owned to the prostitutes for vacations. Virtually every elected official was fired or charged with myriad crimes, and the days of "legal" prostitution in Ketchikan, Alaska, were officially over, leaving the houses of ill repute on Creek Street as nothing more than relics of a colorful bygone era.

Although it's designated as a street, you can't drive on Creek Street. In reality, it's nothing more than a rickety wooden boardwalk built on stilts above the creek that runs below. It's said that when the salmon are coming upstream during spawning season, you can almost walk across the creek on the backs of the fish. That's how plentiful they are.

We parked in a lot close to Creek Street and went by foot to where it began. The ramshackle old wooden structures that line both sides of the boardwalk were once Ketchikan's infamous bawdy houses. Now they house an assortment of gift and curio shops. Business was already brisk. Men, women, and children moved from shop to shop, holding up T-shirts with amusing sayings to check their sizes, perusing arts and crafts created by local Native Americans, and chatting with shopkeepers, who were more than willing to share with their visitors the city's rich, albeit infamous, history.

The recorded music and the chatter coming from the shops as we passed were appealing, almost drawing us in. But we resisted until reaching our destination, number 24 Creek Street, the Dolly Arthur Museum, a small, modest house painted pale green with white trim.

The first thing I noticed was a plaque on the front of the house.

**Dolly's House**
**Circa 1905**
**Presented by**
**Ketchikan Historical Commission**

We were reading it when the door opened and a slender young blond woman came from the house. She wore a red dress with fringe hanging from the bodice and waist, and red high heels. Red-and-white feather boas were draped over her arms.

"Good morning," she said in a seductive voice, her attention on Bill Henderson. "Care to come in for a party?"

Bill seemed flustered. He looked at Kathy and me before replying, "Too early for a party."

"Never too early for a party," she said in the sexiest voice she could muster.

"You work here?" Kathy asked.

"I certainly do," she said.

With that, a second woman joined her from inside the house. She, too, was dressed in what was probably the style of Dolly's era, a tight black dress with lots of spangles, gaudy jewelry, and black spike heels.

"This is Pearl," the first woman said. "I'm Princess."

"Hello, Princess and Pearl," I said. "I take it the museum is open."

Princess batted long, dark eyelashes at Bill, placed a hand on his arm, and cooed, "It's always open for a handsome fella like you."

"We'd like to see the museum," I said.

"Be my guest," Pearl said. "Only five dollars."

I started to reach into my purse, but Bill waved me off. He handed her a twenty-dollar bill and said, "Keep the change."

"Thank you, kind sir. Enter."

We stepped through the door and immediately were faced with a narrow set of wooden stairs. Princess was our guide; Pearl remained outside to try and drum up business from passersby. We went up to the second floor.

"This is where Dolly lived until she died in 1975," Princess said. "She was eighty-seven and lived alone. Dolly was a very proud woman, wouldn't accept handouts or help from anyone. Toward the end, she had to climb up and down the stairs on her hands and knees."

"She left quite a legacy," I said.

Princess laughed. "She was a real character in Ketchikan—bigger than life, that's for sure."

We continued our guided tour of Dolly Arthur's house. I kept glancing at Kathy to see her reaction. This was, after all, where her aunt Dolly had spent most of her life, dispensing sexual favors to the miners and fishermen of the area and acting as madam for the women who worked for her.

The second-floor bedroom was surprisingly large for homes of that era. I mentioned it, and Princess explained that after the brothel closed and the house became Dolly's home, she had a wall removed, turning the upstairs into a larger bedroom where she spent most of her time until her death.

Princess opened a closet door and pointed to a nail protruding from the wall. "Behind that nail is a secret compartment where Dolly hid her supply of whiskey," she said. "The girls who worked for Dolly made more money from serving drinks than they did from serving up sexual favors."

"Mind if I look?" I asked.

"Sure. Go ahead," Princess replied.

I pulled on the nail, and a portion of the wall came with it. Inside was a large space with shelves. Did I believe that the secret to Wilimena's disappearance would be found in that cubbyhole where bottles of liquor were once stashed? No such clue emerged, of course, and I replaced the panel.

"How many visitors do you get every day?" Bill asked as he ran his hand over a pink chenille bedspread that covered a sizable bed. A lamp draped in red velvet was attached to the headboard.

"Depends on the day," Princess said. "Rainy days are good. People come in to get out of the rain. We get lots of rain here." She laughed. "Other places measure rain in inches. We measure it in hundreds of inches. But we don't get much snow. That's good."

"Could we see the downstairs?" I asked.

"Sure," Princess said, leading us from the bedroom and down the staircase.

Like the upstairs floor, the downstairs one was covered in linoleum.

"This was Dolly's bedroom when she was still in business," said Princess. "The girls used the upstairs rooms to entertain their male guests. Dolly did a lot of needlework. That's some of it on the table."

I examined what Princess had pointed to. Along with other attributes, Dolly had a deft hand with needle and yarn.

The kitchen contained a large stove and not much else. A small room off the kitchen was, Princess explained, another "parlor" where male guests were entertained. "Lots of married men came down to the house over the 'Married Men's Trail,'" she added, giggling. "Sort of a private way so nobody would see them, especially their wives. You can take a walk on it when you leave here."

As we prepared to leave, we stood in the entry hall and thanked Princess for the tour. I looked over at a rusted metal tank whose side had been cut away.

"What's that?" I asked.

"A urinal. Dolly always filled it with ice before the men arrived."

"Oh. And that?" I said, referring to a heavy piece

of furniture whose single drawer was secured with a formidable padlock.

"That's where Dolly kept her money," Princess explained, "locked up safe and sound."

"What's in it now?" Kathy asked.

"Nothing," Princess said. "Just some things Dolly's niece left."

It was as though a bomb had gone off in the small, confined space of the Dolly Arthur Museum.

"Her niece?" I said.

"Uh-huh," Princess confirmed. "She stopped by here a few weeks ago."

I didn't have to suggest to Kathy that she show Willie's photograph to our guide.

"That's her," Princess said.

"She was *here*?" Kathy said.

"Right. A nice gal. Kind of funny. Her name is Wilimena, only she calls herself Willie."

"What did she leave with you?" I asked.

"I don't know," Princess responded. "Pearl spent more time with her. Ask her."

Kathy and Bill stayed inside as I went out to the boardwalk, where Pearl was wooing tourists.

"Excuse me," I said. "Princess told us that Dolly Arthur's niece was here a few weeks ago."

Pearl, who'd been smoking a cigarette through an elegant holder, removed the butt and ground it out beneath her shoe. "That's right," she said. "Wilimena Copeland. That was Dolly's real name, you know. Copeland. Thelma Copeland."

"Yes, I know. I understand Wilimena left something with you."

Pearl nodded and made a pitch to a family that included two small daughters. "Come," the mother said, grabbing her children's hands and propelling them away from us. "It's a brothel," she hissed at her husband, who seemed interested in hearing more from Pearl.

"We're trying to find her," I said.

"Who?"

"Dolly Arthur's niece, Wilimena Copeland. She disappeared from Ketchikan."

"You're kidding!"

"No, I'm not. I'm with her sister, Kathy. We're from Maine, and we've come to Alaska in the hope that we can find out what happened to Wilimena."

"Wow! I'm really sorry to hear that."

"What did she leave with you?" I asked.

She lit another cigarette, placed it in the holder, and took a deep drag. "I don't think that it would be appropriate for me to tell you. I mean, she left it here for safekeeping, and we promised we'd look after it."

"I understand," I said. "It's just that—"

"You know," she said, "confidentiality and all, like lawyers and clients, or doctors and patients."

"I admire your loyalty," I said, "but there's more at stake here than that. We're working with the Alaska State Troopers. In fact, we just left two of them a little while ago. I'd hate to have to call them to bring along a warrant."

"No, don't do that."

"Well?"

"It's her sister, you say?"

"Right."

"I suppose that would make it all right. Maybe she could show me some identification."

"I'm sure she'd be happy to."

The second cigarette was extinguished, and we went inside, where Kathy obliged Pearl's need for identification. Pearl and Princess left us alone for a minute as they conferred in the kitchen. When they returned, Pearl said, "Okay, we'll let you see what she left with us."

We stood there like characters in a motion picture who after a lengthy and dangerous journey have finally come upon the object of their search, a long-lost ark containing a king's ransom. In this case, of course, the treasure would hopefully be a hint as to Wilimena's whereabouts.

Pearl had fetched a key while in the kitchen. She ceremoniously used it to open the padlock, removed it from its hasp, and slowly, deliberately slid the drawer open. Kathy, Bill, and I strained to look over her shoulder as the drawer's contents were revealed—a small, tan leather bag approximately eight inches long and four inches wide. A zipper ran the length of it. Pearl picked it up, held it in both hands for a moment, and handed it to Kathy.

"It's Willie's!" Kathy exclaimed. "She's had it for years. She never travels without it."

"Open it," Bill said.

Kathy looked at Pearl and Princess, who discreetly walked away. Kathy undid the zipper and removed the first item from the bag, placing it on the top of the piece of furniture.

"Look," she said. "It's the digital recorder Willie bought in Seattle."

It certainly looked like the Sony recorder the man in the electronics shop had shown us. I picked it up and examined it more closely. I was again surprised at its small size, only slightly larger than a cigarette lighter.

"What else is in there?" Bill asked.

"Just this," said Kathy, holding up an envelope.

"Open it," I said.

She did. Inside were the names and addresses of the *Glacial Queen*'s staff to whom Wilimena had promised gifts once she'd found the gold. Kathy shoved it into her jacket pocket.

"I suggest we listen to what's on that recorder," I said. I handed it to Bill. "Do you know how to work this thing?" I asked. "It has all these tiny buttons."

"Sure," he said. "It only looks complicated."

He pushed one of the buttons, but I stopped him. "Not here," I said. "Let's take it outside."

"Good suggestion," Kathy said.

As we started to leave the museum, Pearl called, "Hey, where are you going with that?"

"Outside," Bill said. "We want to listen to what's on the recorder."

"I don't know," Pearl said.

"Why don't you call police headquarters?" I suggested. "Ask for Trooper McQuesten. He'll vouch for us."

That seemed to satisfy her, at least for the moment. We left the building and walked to where a small section of the boardwalk jutted out, providing space for a bench. "Ready?" Bill asked once Kathy and I had taken seats on either side of him.

"Go ahead," I said.

He pushed a button or two. We waited.

"Hi, Kathy," the female voice said.

Kathy gasped. "It's Willie," she said.

Wilimena Copeland continued: "I bet you think it's funny, hearing me on this little recorder. You always kid me about never writing when I take a trip, not even a postcard, and I know that I should stay in touch when traveling. But I always did hate to write. Remember when we were in school, and I used to ask you to write my term papers? Maybe it's because I have such terrible handwriting. I should've been a doctor.

"So I decided the best thing was to get myself a little tape recorder and talk into it whenever I'm on a trip. I thought I'd get a recorder that had one of those little tiny tapes that I could send you, but the nice man in the store where I bought this recorder said tapes were old-fashioned, and you know that the last thing I ever want to be considered is old-fashioned." She giggled at this point, then went on.

"The salesman said I could hook this up to my computer, and that what I said into it would come up on the screen, just as though I'd written it. I know I'd never be able to figure something like that out, so maybe I'll just send this whole recorder to you and you can listen for yourself.

"Actually, Kathy, if this were just any other trip, I probably wouldn't have bothered buying a recorder. But this isn't an ordinary trip. Far from it. When I sent you that note about us becoming rich, I meant it. Remember when I lost those papers about Aunt Thelma? Well, your disorganized sister finally found them. Ta-da! It took me a while to figure out what was in the papers, but when I did, I almost had a heart attack. There were always those rumors about Aunt Thelma having been given a whole bunch of gold by that guy she used to go with, Lefty something or other. I never paid much attention, but lots of times I had little daydreams about finding that gold and becoming a rich woman. Not just me. You and me, Kathy. We would both be rich and travel the world like queens, with private jets and the best suites in the fanciest hotels, a couple of jet-setting sisters with all sorts of dashing, handsome men pursuing us. I know, I know, that's not the kind of life you've ever wanted. But I bet you could get used to it once you experienced it.

"Anyway, sis, I did figure out what was in those papers, and once I did, I made up my mind to see whether Aunt Thelma's gold really did exist. And you know what? I think it does exist, and I'm here in Ketchikan to go after it.

"It's been an interesting trip so far. Originally, I intended to come directly to Ketchikan, but I decided I might as well enjoy a cruise as part of the experience. If the gold didn't pan out—pardon the pun—I'd at least have had some fun. I must say that I did meet a lot of fascinating people on the ship, including a cute little Frenchman named Maurice. He was teaching passengers on the cruise how to speak French. He was kind of funny with his pencil-thin mustache and Continental ways. The problem was that I finally figured out that his interest in me had to do with the gold. I know, I know, I shouldn't have told anyone why I was on the trip. But you know me, Kathy. Keeping things to myself has never been part of my gene pool. I'm still worried about Maurice, and expect him to show up here in Ketchikan at any time. Just so you know, I'm sitting at this moment on a secluded little pier talking into this silly machine. God, I have never seen so many tourists in one place in my life, or so many jewelry stores." Another giggle. "I bought a cup of coffee and brought it with me to this quiet spot where I could dictate this note to you. I hope the recorder is working. I'd hate to do all this talking and have nothing come out.

"So where was I? Oh, right. Another person I met on the cruise was the ship's security officer. His name is Kale. When I told him someone had broken into my cabin—twice!—he just shrugged and said he couldn't find any evidence of it. Jerk! I *know* somebody was rummaging around the cabin, no matter what he says. I didn't like him one bit!"

Kathy slapped me on the arm. "Same as you, Jess," she said.

Willie continued: "I just looked at my watch and realized I'd better get on my horse. Here's why. I went to Aunt Thelma's house—I guess I should call her Aunt Dolly—and introduced myself to the women who work there. Can you imagine that our aunt used to run a brothel and that they've turned it into a museum? She's really famous in Alaska. I visited her grave. It's in a pretty little place called Bayview Cemetery. Her plot is number forty-nine forty-nine. People say that when she died, every newspaper up and down the West

Coast carried a big obituary about her. Imagine that, Kathy, a famous prostitute and madam in our family. Momma would turn over in her grave.

"Anyway, I went to the museum that used to be Aunt Dolly's house of ill repute and got friendly with the women who work there as guides. You should see what they wear. I guess that's the way prostitutes dressed in those days. They were really nice and let me hang around for a long time. I mean, once they knew who I was, I didn't even have to pay the entrance fee. They left me alone to just sort of soak up the atmosphere. That was what I wanted, to be left alone, so that I could find what I was looking for. According to the papers I lost and then found again, Dolly had a map that showed where the gold was hidden, and I figured that after all these years, anyone could've taken the map and grabbed the gold for themselves. Maybe if there had been only one map, that would've happened. At one point, when the guides were out front trying to drum up business, I found a key that opened a padlock that secured a drawer in a piece of furniture in the hallway. Dolly must've been pretty smart, besides being a good businesswoman. There were at least ten maps in the drawer, so if anyone did know that Dolly had a map leading to the gold, they wouldn't know which one it was. But I figured it out from the papers I went through. Sure enough, one of the maps had a little symbol on it that you really had to squint to see. It was the same symbol I picked up from the papers. Voilà! I was sure I had the right one.

"I just had a brilliant idea! I think I'll leave this recorder in the drawer where I found the maps. You know me, sis. I'm likely to drop it in the water, and that'd be that. I'll retrieve it when I get back and bring it with me to Cabot Cove along with the gold.

"I'd better wrap this up now. According to what I'd learned, Dolly was afraid to leave the gold in Ketchikan once her boyfriend, Lefty, never returned from a trip, so she took it to a cabin way out in the wilderness. I read that the state of Alaska built cabins in remote areas that hunters and fishermen can use, or people who get caught in a storm can use to survive. According to Aunt Dolly's map, the cabin she chose is in the Misty Fjords. I read about it in a guidebook. It's a national monument. It's really huge, Kathy, more than two million acres. From the pictures I've seen, it looks cold, even in summer. I'm sitting here shivering just thinking about it. At any rate, I'm about to fly there. Can you believe it? You know how much I hate to fly, even in a big jet plane. But I'm going in one of these little puddle-jumper planes with one propeller. I just hope I can trust the pilot. He's a sour old guy named Harold, but the price is right. I went to some of the big companies here in Ketchikan who rent out floatplanes, but they charge a fortune. You know me and what a cheapskate I can be." Giggle. "I know what you're thinking, Sis, that I live as though I were rich. I also know you don't approve of all the men I've had in my life. I guess I do take advantage of them. I can't think of the last time I paid for a meal. Men are always so willing to pick up the tab. But please don't think poorly of me, Kathy. Once we have Aunt Dolly's gold, I won't have to pretend I'm rich. I will be! And so will you!

"Well, big sister, I'm off. Harold looks like the kind of guy who doesn't like to be kept waiting. I'm not sure how I'll get back after I find the gold. I don't really trust this guy Harold. Funny, huh, me becoming paranoid? A couple of people I talked to here in Ketchikan say there's always a lot of fishermen coming in and out of Misty Fjords, so I figure I'll catch a ride with one of them, use my feminine charms. Ha! I don't know how long it'll take to actually find the gold once I'm there, but I'm hoping it won't be long. At any rate, sis, you'll be listening to this recording back in Cabot Cove in front of a warm fire, and with gold dust at our feet, as the song goes. As Momma used to say, 'If the good Lord's willing and the creeks don't rise,' I'll show up on your doorstep in Cabot Cove toting a great big bag of gold nuggets. What a party we'll have. Ciao! Adios! Lots of love!"

We sat there in the ensuing silence, deep in our respective thoughts. Kathy started to cry, and Bill put his arm around her shoulder.

I stood. "Let's go," I said. "At least we now know the name of the pilot who took her."

"What about the police?" Kathy said. "Shouldn't we go to them with what we've learned?"

"Not yet," Bill said. "Let's make sure what we have before bothering them."

We agreed, although I was not as enthusiastic as Kathy.

We returned to the Dolly Arthur Museum, where Pearl and Princess stood in front, batting their false eyelashes at passing tourists and touting the virtues of a tour.

"We're leaving," I said. "Thank you so much for all your help."

"What was on that recorder?" Princess asked.

"Oh, nothing much," Kathy said.

Pearl and Princess—I wondered what their real names were and what they did when they weren't acting as guides to Dolly's brothel—looked at each other.

"I guess it's okay for you to take it," Pearl said, "as long as you bring it back."

"That's a promise," Bill said. He reached into his pocket, pulled out a twenty-dollar bill, and handed it to Princess. "For being so understanding," he said.

Princess stuffed the bill into her cleavage, and they wished us a pleasant day in Ketchikan.

"That was so sweet," Kathy said to him as we walked to where we'd parked the car.

He smiled and said, "The least I could do."

Once in the car, I checked the names of independent floatplane operators given us by Mr. Gilroy. "No Harold," I said, "but there is a Hal. Hal Fitzgibbons. Could be him."

We consulted our map of Ketchikan and headed for his address, a small, well-cared-for house on a canal near Totem Bight State Historical Park. Ketchikan has, according to guidebooks, the world's largest collection of totem poles. I would have enjoyed visiting the various centers where they're displayed, but that wasn't in the cards.

Mr. Fitzgibbons's vintage floatplane sat at a crude dock, bobbing up and down in the water in the wake caused by small pleasure craft that passed by. We exited the car and approached the front door. Before we reached the porch that spanned the front of the house, the door opened and a woman faced us. "Can I help you?" she asked. She was dressed simply and nicely— a neatly pressed, clean housedress in a flowered pattern and white sneakers. She had a long, angular face and wore large, square glasses.

"We're looking for a Mr. Fitzgibbons," I said.

"That's my husband," she said.

"Harold Fitzgibbons?"

"That's what his mother named him. His friends call him Hal." She had a pleasant smile.

"My name is Jessica Fletcher," I said, "and these are my friends Kathy Copeland and Bill Henderson."

"Yes?"

"You see, my sister is missing," Kathy said, "and—"

"What does that have to do with us?" Mrs. Fitzgibbons asked.

Bill replied, "We've learned that she took a floatplane from Ketchikan to someplace in the Misty Fjords, and that her pilot was someone named Harold."

"I'm afraid that Hal isn't here at the moment," his wife said. "He's down in the Lower Forty-eight visiting a brother who's dying. Cancer. Two years younger than Hal."

"I'm sorry," I said.

"Quite a blow for Hal. He and his brother are very close."

Kathy asked whether the woman in the doorway might know anything about her husband having had a passenger named Wilimena a few weeks earlier. She pulled Willie's photograph from her pocket and started up onto the porch to show it to her. But Mrs. Fitzgibbons stopped her with, "I think I know who you're talking about. Please come in. I just put on a pot of coffee. I make it the way Hal taught me. I add an egg to the grounds."

# Chapter Fourteen

The inside of the Fitzgibbons house was as pristine as its exterior. Nothing was out of place. The windows sparkled, and the floor looked as though you could safely eat off it. An old black Lab that had been sleeping in a fancy dog bed when we entered struggled to its feet, gave us a cursory sniff, and went back to bed.

"That's Beaver," Mrs. Fitzgibbons said.

"Looks more like a dog to me," Bill said jokingly.

The woman of the house smiled and said, "Hal's floatplane is a DeHavilland Beaver. He named the dog after the plane. The plane is his pride and joy. So's the dog."

She invited us to join her at the kitchen table, where she placed empty coffee mugs in front of us, along with a pitcher of cream and a sugar bowl.

"Is this your first trip to Alaska?" she asked. "By the way, my name is Flo."

"My second visit, Flo," I said, "although I didn't see very much of it the first time. I was only here for a day."

"Jessica is a writer," Kathy said.

Flo scrutinized me through narrowed eyes. "Yes, of course. Murder mysteries. Jessica Fletcher. I get your books from the library."

"I'm pleased that you read them," I said, looking up at a wall clock. As much as I enjoyed being in this woman's company and sharing a cup of coffee with her, I knew that we were pressed for time. "You indicated you knew the woman we're looking for."

"Yes, I do," Flo replied. "Hal flew her into Misty Fjords."

"When was that?" I asked.

"I can get you the exact date."

She left the table and returned with a printed form with handwriting filling in the blanks. "Here's the trip ticket," she said. "We keep very good records."

I didn't doubt that for a moment. But as I quickly scanned the form, I saw that the passenger's name was listed as Wanda Walters.

"According to this," I said, "the passenger isn't the person we're looking for."

"I can't account for that," she said. "But the picture you showed me is certainly the woman who booked Hal. Considering her reason for making the flight, I'm not surprised that she used an alias."

We looked at each other before Kathy asked, "Why is that?"

"Well," she said, "I don't have much patience with spouses who cheat on each other."

"Willie—Willie was cheating on a husband?" Kathy asked incredulously.

"Willie?"

"That's her real name," Kathy explained. "Her nick-name. Short for Wilimena."

"Let me explain," said Flo. "When she originally came here, she said she was meeting some friends in a cabin in Misty Fjords. They were going to spend time 'roughing it,' as she put it. I have to admit that I wasn't especially keen on Hal flying her. She was an attractive woman, even beautiful, and Hal is a handsome man. But he's flown beautiful women before." She laughed ruefully. "Jealous me."

"Go on," I said.

"She didn't appear to me to be the sort of woman who would enjoy roughing it," Flo said. "But who am I to judge? More coffee?"

We all declined the offer.

"Well," she continued, "Hal agreed to take her. She didn't have much with her, just a small suitcase. At least she wore a flannel shirt and sensible footwear. They left in the early afternoon—you can see the flight log on the bottom of that form—and Hal returned just before sunset. He was, to put it mildly, not happy."

"Why?" I asked.

"She told him during the flight that she'd lied about why she was going to Misty Fjords. It wasn't to spend a week with friends in a cabin. It was to have a rendez-vous with her lover. She's a married woman."

Kathy gulped. "She told your husband that?" she said.

"Yes. She confided in Hal the real reason for her trip, and swore him to secrecy."

"But he told *you*," Bill said.

"Telling your wife is different," she said, slightly defensive.

"Of course," Bill said.

"What else did your husband tell you?" I asked.

"He said she appeared to be very nervous. I suppose that can be explained, considering why she was going there. Hal said she seemed to be a distrustful person. She kept asking him to promise he wouldn't tell anyone that he took her into Misty Fjords."

"Did your husband plan to pick her up after her—well, I guess you could call it her tryst—after it was over?" Bill asked.

"No, and that was what was really strange about the whole thing," Flo replied. "Hal asked whether she wanted to arrange a date and time for him to bring her back to Ketchikan."

"And?" I said.

"She said no, she didn't want to do that. Naturally, he asked how she planned to return. She told him that the man she was seeing had arranged for them to return by boat. That didn't make any sense to me. After all, if she was so concerned about people not knowing about her trip there, why would she be willing to arrive back here in a boat with her lover?"

"A good point," I said.

Kathy sat mum at the table, obviously trying to make sense out of what Mrs. Fitzgibbons was saying. I couldn't blame her. Why, after being so willing to tell the world about her quest for gold, would Wilimena suddenly turn secretive and paranoid, making up a name and weaving a tale about being married and meeting a lover? The distrust she'd expressed on the recorder about Maurice Quarlé might have had something to do with it. Maybe she got smart and realized that by sharing with others the purpose of her Alaskan trip, she was placing the gold, as well as herself, in jeopardy.

Flo poured herself a fresh cup of coffee, and gave every indication that she would be pleased if we stayed for the day.

Kathy came out of her fugue and asked, "When is your husband due back?"

"Two or three days," his wife answered.

"We don't have that much time," I said.

"Are you saying that she never came back?" Flo asked.

"Exactly," Bill said.

"Are you sure? Maybe she returned with her lover and they quietly slipped away to somewhere else," Flo offered.

"I don't think so," said Kathy.

"Mrs. Fitzgibbons," I said, "can you recommend a pilot who could take us to where your husband delivered Wilimena?"

She laughed and blew a stream of air at an imaginary wisp of hair on her forehead. "It's tourist season," she said. "Everyone is booked solid. That's why it's a difficult time for Hal to be away. We live all year on what he makes these few months. Of course, there are fishing groups and hunters looking to go into the backcountry, but it's the tourists who provide the most business."

"I can certainly understand," I said.

"You might try Bobby Borosky," Flo said.

Kathy looked at me and grimaced.

"We met him earlier," I said.

Another laugh from Flo. "I take it you weren't impressed."

"You might say that," Bill said.

"Bobby's not what you'd call a people person," Flo said, "but he's an excellent pilot. He's been flying the bush since he was a teenager, knows Misty Fjords like the back of his hand. The problem is he seldom takes tourists. He likes flying mail and medicine runs better than flying people."

"Can you think of anyone else?" I asked.

She shook her head. "Not anyone who won't be tied up. Want me to call Bobby for you? He's really a big pussycat. I know he doesn't come off that way at first, but he's a real decent guy."

"If you say so," I said.

Flo took a cordless phone from the wall and dialed a number. "Bobby, it's Flo Fitzgibbons—just fine, thank you—you?—that's good to hear—Bobby, I have some very nice people sitting here in my kitchen. Remember that woman Hal told you about, the one heading into Misty Fjords to meet up with her lover?"

*So much for preserving the secret,* I thought.

"It seems she never surfaced—that's right, never showed up—so these good folks need to fly to where Hal dropped her off at that cabin in Walker Cove—that's right, they want to go this afternoon—I just thought you might have some time and—what's that, Bobby?—I'm sure they're willing to pay what you ask."

She glanced at us, and we all nodded like bobble-heads on an automobile's dashboard.

"That's right, Bobby—they said they'd met you earlier today—what?—you will?—that's wonderful—I'll send them right over."

"Trust me," she said after rejoining us at the table, "Bobby Borosky is a fine pilot. The reason he and Hal don't fly for the big floatplane operators is that they prefer to pick and choose their passengers. You don't get to do that with the big boys."

"Had your husband alerted the authorities about his passenger and her destination?" I asked. "You said she didn't seem like the sort of woman who would enjoy roughing it."

"He intended to," Flo said, "but then his brother's wife called and he left and forgot about it. We can't always be responsible for someone else's foolish decisions, can we?"

"I suppose not," I said, not sure that philosophy applied in this case.

As we got up to leave, the wail of sirens could be heard in the distance.

"Always something," Flo said, "especially with so many tourists."

"Could I use your bathroom before we go?" I asked.

"Of course," Flo said. "You all should. You won't find a lavatory on a floatplane."

"We'd better call Trooper McQuesten and Detective Flowers," I said, pulling my cell phone from my handbag.

"You go ahead to the john," Bill said. "What's his number?"

I handed him the phone and recited the number for

Ketchikan's police headquarters. He started to dial as I left the room, and even with the door to the small bathroom closed, I heard him say, "Trooper McQuesten, this is Bill Henderson. I'm with Jessica Fletcher and Kathy Copeland. I think we know where Kathy's sister, Wilimena, went. It's a place called Walker Cove in Misty Fjords. We're flying there with—what's his name, Mrs. Fitzgibbons?" Flo answered. "Borosky. Bob Borosky. Right—Walker Cove—we're leaving for Mr. Borosky's place now—what's that?—fine. Thank you, sir."

Kathy took my place in the bathroom.

"What did McQuesten say?" I asked Bill as he handed me back my phone.

"He and the detective are tied up with a homicide that just happened. I guess that's what those sirens were all about. He said that if they can't get to us before we leave, he'd dispatch a police plane to Walker Cove and meet us there."

Flo wished us the best of luck as we left her home and headed for Bob Borosky's house. When we arrived, he'd put on a beat-up tan leather jacket over his T-shirt and donned a Seattle Mariners baseball cap. "I figured I'd see you again," he growled as we approached where he stood next to his floatplane.

"We appreciate you agreeing to take us, Mr. Borosky," I said.

"Long as you've got the money," he said. "And hell, let's not be so formal. Name's Bobby."

"All right, Bobby," I said. Between the three of us we had just enough cash and traveler's checks to pay Mr. Borosky's eight-hundred-dollar fee.

"Let's go," he said.

I looked back along the road we'd taken to his house, hoping to see an approaching police car. There wasn't one.

"I'd like to wait until Trooper McQuesten arrives," I announced.

"He said he didn't think he'd make it in time," Bill Henderson said. "Remember?"

"Still—"

"If you folks want to go to Walker Cove," Borosky said, "we'd better get to it. There's a front comin' through later this afternoon, and I don't intend to get caught in it. We go now or we don't go."

Bill started for the plane, which was secured to the dock with ropes. He turned and said, "Come on. You heard the man."

"We'd better," Kathy said, her voice lacking conviction.

"I suppose so," I said. "But I'd feel better if the police were with us."

Because the plane was parked against the side of the dock, you could enter only from the left side, the pilot's side.

"Why don't you sit up front with him?" Kathy suggested. She said to Borosky: "She's a pilot."

"Is that so?" Borosky said, laughing. "Looks like I can sit back and let you do the flyin'. "

"I hardly think so," I said.

Borosky opened the door for me on the left-hand side and told me to get in. I could see that it wouldn't be easy. It meant scrambling over his seat and wedging myself into the one on the right-hand side of the plane.

Thank goodness I'd decided to wear slacks and not a skirt that morning.

Once I was settled, Borosky pulled his seat back forward to allow Kathy and Bill to climb into seats behind me. A bench to the rear of them provided additional space for passengers, although in our case it wasn't needed. Borosky squeezed his large frame into the seat next to me. "Get those seat belts on," he said. "If you get a little queasy and think you're going to toss your cookies, there's bags in the pockets behind the seats. Don't bother looking for parachutes. There ain't any."

The control panel and dual yokes looked primitive to me compared to the fairly new Cessna that I'd been flying back in Cabot Cove. In fact, the whole aircraft looked like something from another age.

"How old is this plane?" I asked, trying to sound simply interested and not concerned.

"Damn near sixty years," Borosky said as he went through a preflight ritual that he'd undoubtedly performed thousands of times. "Came off the assembly line up in Canada in 1950. Cost damn near fifty thousand bucks back then. If I wanted to sell it today—and I'm not saying that I do—it could fetch almost five hundred thousand. At least that's what they tell me."

We were all duly impressed.

"Everybody ready?" Borosky yelled over the roar of the engine, which he had coaxed to life.

We confirmed that we were. He had disconnected the ropes holding the plane against the dock before coming on board. Now, with his door open, he pushed away with his foot and we drifted out into the open water of the canal. He slammed his door shut, increased the rpm, and guided us into the middle of the channel. A small boat with a lone fisherman saw us coming and quickly moved out of the way.

We reached Tongass Narrows. Borosky pointed the DeHavilland Beaver into the wind, advanced the throttle to achieve maximum power, and we started our bumpy trip across the Narrows' chop. It seemed an eternity, but then I suddenly felt the aircraft becoming lighter as its pontoons began to plane on the water. Borosky pulled back on the yoke, and we were airborne.

Ending up on the sixty-year-old plane had happened so fast that there hadn't been time to think.

Once we had learned where Wilimena had gone, a sense of irrational elation had set in. Now my mind began to process what was happening. I'd wanted a ride on a floatplane, but was convinced that there wouldn't be time. But here I was, sitting in the right-hand seat next to a grisly, but not entirely unpleasant, veteran pilot. Of course, I was as excited as Bill and Kathy about the possibility of finally finding Wilimena Copeland. After all, that had been the purpose of the trip.

But more somber thoughts replaced the excitement as we left the Ketchikan shoreline and headed into that magical place known as Misty Fjords. What would we actually find once we arrived? It had been weeks since Willie's disappearance. Was it possible that she'd spent those weeks in a remote cabin? Had she actually found the gold? If she had been in that cabin for two weeks, how had she survived? My mind raced. Why had she told her pilot, Hal Fitzgibbons, that she would be returning by boat? What boat? Had she made some prearrangement to be picked up by someone else? The encounter we'd had with Mrs. Fitzgibbons suggest that her husband was a man Willie could have trusted. What had caused Wilimena, who had been so open with everyone about her reason for coming to Alaska, to suddenly develop a severe case of paranoia?

Had Wilimena's disappearance been covered in the local Ketchikan newspaper? If so, why hadn't it prompted the Fitzgibbonses to report her missing? Being called to his ailing brother's bedside would explain Hal's lack of action, and it was entirely possible that Flo Fitzgibbons didn't read the local paper. But surely there had been talk in town of a missing woman. The police would have questioned at least a few Ketchikan citizens.

I forced these thoughts from my mind. They represented the past. What was important was that we deal with the present and find out once and for all what had happened to Kathy's sister.

Civilization was behind us now as we banked left and went up what Borosky said was the Behm Canal. There was a set of headphones for everyone on the plane. Once we had them on, we could hear his comments above the steady growl of the old Beaver's Pratt and Whitney 450-horsepower radial engine. His pride in his aircraft was heartening. He said he could fly as far as 700 miles without refueling, and that he could get up to a cruising speed of more than 150 miles per hour. It wasn't an easy aircraft to fly. He was constantly busy adjusting the trim to take the pressure off the control yoke and repeatedly working the fuel mixture lever to keep the engine humming at peak performance without wasting fuel. He took special pains to point out to me various features of the cockpit, including the fact that because so much of his flying was done in extremely cold weather, the oil reservoir filling spout was located in the cockpit itself, where warm oil could be added to the engine. Despite all the uncertainty about what we would find once we reached Walker Cove, I had to admit that I was enjoying this impromptu flying lesson.

"Everyone all right back there?" I asked, turning to Kathy and Bill.

Kathy nodded, although the expression on her face said something else. She was leaning into Bill, which reminded me that aside from finding Willie, there was a budding romance to consider. That brought a smile to my lips. Would there be a wedding back in Cabot Cove? It was entirely possible. My hope was that Kathy's sister would be there to celebrate with her.

The farther we progressed into Misty Fjords, the more desolate and rugged the terrain became. Low clouds had settled over the area, and sheer granite cliffs, their tops obscured, seemed to hurtle down from the heavens, hemming us in. Majestic waterfalls poured down the face of the cliffs, nature's force a thing of beauty yet also ominous.

"I don't like those clouds," I said.

"I've seen a lot worse," said Borosky. "It'll get bad later tonight. There won't be much flyin' tomorrow, I can tell you that."

We flew over New Eddystone Rock, which rose more than two hundred feet above the water, the last vestige of a once active volcano. Borosky pointed out that it was named by an explorer of the region, Captain George Vancouver, after a lighthouse on Eddystone Rock in the English Channel. His occasional commentary was interesting, although sightseeing wasn't high on our list of priorities.

The closer we got to Walker Cove, the narrower the Behm Canal became. The sheer walls on either side seemed to be closing in on us. They were higher than the plane, creating the impression that we were flying inside a box. Winds swept down off the canyon walls, buffeting the aircraft, each jolt a reminder that being up in the air wasn't a natural act for man.

Borosky banked the plane hard right.

"Walker Cove," he announced.

If it had seemed that we were closeted by encroaching walls while flying up Behm Canal, that sensation was now magnified. The granite cliffs seemed only a few feet from the Beaver's wingtips, and I worried that a sudden strong gust of wind could slam us up against them. Borosky seemed calm and confident, although he now worked even harder to control the plane.

"Do many people come here?" I yelled.

His reply came through my headset: "Not many. Every once in a while I bring a fishing party here, but there's lots better places to fish, that's for sure."

"Is there a camp of some sort?" I asked, again having to raise my voice over the Pratt and Whitney's masculine roar.

"Nope. There's a cabin at the end of the cove, back in the woods. Built by the state, but I don't know anybody who uses it. Used to be a little dock, just pieces of wood nailed together and floating on empty oil cans. Don't even know if it's still there."

I had noticed since entering Walker Cove that Borosky had begun losing altitude, deliberately, of course, and we were now only a few hundred feet above the slate gray water.

"Over there," Borosky announced, pointing ahead to the shoreline on the right, where towering evergreens came down to the water's edge.

"What's there?" I asked.

"Where that dock and cabin used to be."

He banked right; being so close to the water gave the impression that the right wingtip might dip into it. He leveled off and cut power. Now, through mist and wisps of fog, I saw what he'd pointed to. A tiny dock bobbed in the water. Behind it was what appeared to be an overgrown path leading into the woods.

"That's it?" I asked.

"That's it."

He cut power completely, and we settled down onto the water. He maneuvered the plane until his side was within a few feet of the dock, opened his door, stepped out onto one of the floats, grabbed a strut, and waited for the natural momentum of the plane to nuzzle it up against the dock. He hopped onto the dock and continued to hold the Beaver's strut to keep it from drifting away.

"Toss me that rope," he ordered. "It's on the floor under your seat."

I did as instructed, and he used it to secure the plane to the dock.

"Come on, come on," he said. "I got you here. Get out and do what you have to do."

I reversed the difficult task of exiting the plane, followed by Kathy and Bill.

"There's nothing here," Kathy said. "It's so desolate."

"You say there's a cabin in the woods?" I asked Borosky.

"Used to be."

"Let's go," I said, taking steps toward the path.

"Maybe we shouldn't," Kathy said. "I'm—I'm scared."

"We've come this far," Bill said. "Nothing to be scared of."

Borosky remained with his plane as we started up the path. Bill led the way, with Kathy and me only a few steps behind. It was eerily still and quiet as we left the shoreline and were immediately surrounded by the dense forest, the only sound our footsteps on the densely packed trail. It crossed my mind that Alaska wasn't known as bear country for nothing. I tried to remember what I'd once read about how to thwart a bear attack, but came up blank. Lie down in a fetal position or run? Remain quiet or scream like a banshee? The only advice I could come up with was to avoid going where bears were likely to be found—useless information at this juncture.

We'd gone perhaps three or four hundred feet when Bill stopped. "Look," he said.

Kathy and I peered beyond him. Fifty feet ahead, a small cabin stood in a clearing that wasn't much bigger than the cabin itself.

"Oh, my God!" Kathy said. She ran past Bill, reached the cabin, and threw open its door. "Willie!" she shouted.

Bill and I looked at each other. He smiled and nodded in satisfaction. I started for the cabin, got halfway there, and turned to see him still standing where I'd left him.

"Coming?" I asked.

"You go ahead," he said.

I reached the cabin and poked my head through the open door. Kathy was on the floor in a corner of the single room, sobbing, her arms wrapped around Wilimena. I wasn't certain whether Willie was dead or alive, but then I saw her move.

"She's alive," Kathy managed. "She's alive!"

I went to where they were huddled and looked down at Wilimena, who was wrapped in a heavy wool blanket. Kathy was right; her sister was, indeed, alive, but only barely so far as I could see. She was skin and bones. Her hair was a matted mess, her face smeared with dirt.

"We have to get her out of here," I said. "I'll send Bill back to get Mr. Borosky. We can carry her and—"

Willie mumbled something through parched lips that were swollen to twice their normal size.

"What?" Kathy asked.

Willie said it again, and this time both Kathy and I understood.

"I found it!"

"The gold?" Kathy said.

"Uh-huh. We're rich, Kathy. We're rich."

Wilimena struggled free of her sister's grasp and

dragged a filthy canvas bag from behind her, where she'd had it wedged.

"That's it?" Kathy said.

Willie managed a feeble nod.

I looked around the cabin in search of something that might be used to transport Willie to the plane. There was nothing. As the sisters continued to talk, I went to the rough-hewn cabinets and opened them. Inside were cans of food, mostly beans and vegetables. Open cans sat on a crude counter next to a can opener, along with the stun gun and canister of Mace that Willie'd purchased in Seattle. A plastic jug of water was half consumed; a full one was in a cabinet next to the canned goods. Thank God that food and water were there, I thought, left by previous occupants to help those who would follow. She couldn't have survived without it. I also realized how fortunate she was that the open cans hadn't attracted local wildlife, particularly bears or wolves.

I looked down and saw where a section of the floor had been removed, exposing a fairly large open space beneath it, probably where Wilimena had found the sack of gold.

I returned to them.

"Can you stand?" I asked Willie.

She shook her head. "My leg is broken. I fell the first day I was here."

All I could visualize was what the bones in her leg must look like after weeks of not having been set. The pain must have been excruciating. Still, she'd managed to get around enough to open the cans of food. Amazing what we're capable of doing when the chips are down.

"We're taking you home, Willie," I said. "You and Kathy stay here. I'll be back with help in a few minutes."

I turned to fetch Bill Henderson and Borosky to help move her. Bill was standing in the open doorway.

"She's in bad shape," I said. "She has a broken leg, and she's wasting away. We have to get her to the plane and to a hospital."

"Did she find the gold?" he asked.

"Yes. She—"

He walked past me, went to where Kathy and Wilimena were still wrapped around each other, and looked down.

"Hello, Willie," Bill said.

She looked up, blinking as she tried to bring him into focus. When she succeeded, she gasped. "What are *you* doing here?"

# Chapter Fifteen

Kathy and I looked at each other, then at Bill Henderson.

"You know her?" I asked.

He grinned and said, "Yeah, you might say that. I mean, I never really did get to know her, but then again, we weren't married very long."

This time when Kathy and I looked at each other, it was with our jaws hanging open.

"You and Willie were married?" Kathy managed.

"Right. You and I talked a while back when I called. That's when you told me that Willie was missing and that you intended to take the same cruise and look for the gold."

"You said you were Howard."

"Right again. That's me, former husband of your wacko sister."

Wilimena struggled to get to her feet. She stood on her good leg and leaned against the wall. "How did you end up with *them*?" she asked, indicating Kathy and me.

"Took a little bit of ingenuity," Bill—or Howard—

said. "But I was never as dumb as you made me out to be, Willie. Let's just say I decided to treat myself for putting up with you for a year."

Kathy faced him, her face a mask of rage and hurt and every other conceivable emotion generated by the situation. "You lied to me," she said, thrusting her jaw at him. "You told me you loved me. You said you wanted to marry me. You—you—you bastard!"

She swung at him, but he brushed her hand away.

"What did you think, Kathy?" he said. "That I'd fall for a dolt like you?" He guffawed. "If I had to hear one more time about how you love baking pies and taking hikes in the woods and—God, you are the most boring woman I've ever known."

This time she attacked him with both hands, her fists pummeling the arms he held out in front of him. She started to cry, desperate sobs of the hurt he'd inflicted upon her, the betrayal, the lies, the callous manipulation. Finally, as though drained of all energy and emotion, she slumped to her knees, her arms wrapped about herself, and gasped for air.

"Enough of the theatrics," Howard said, reaching beneath his jacket and pulling out a small handgun, which he pointed at me. "Everything worked out just fine," he said. "You're all alive, and I've got what I came for." He picked up the canvas bag containing the gold and backed toward the door, the weapon still aimed squarely at me. I didn't want him to leave. I leaned against the counter on which the stun gun and Mace rested, and slowly moved my hand to cover the gun.

"What's your real last name?" I asked.

He laughed. "That's no concern of yours."

"You're very smug," I said, "and smooth. You had a lot of us fooled."

"Thanks for the compliment."

"It wasn't meant as one. Actually, I had a few doubts about you."

"Did you really?"

"Yes, I did. I wondered whether you actually did live in Seattle."

"Oh?"

"You talked about it raining there every other day, but that isn't true. Seattle has less rainfall than any East Coast city. And there was your mispronunciation of the restaurant, Canlis. Kathy called it Chanlis, and you did the same."

"Maybe I didn't want to hurt her feelings by correcting her."

"I doubt if you care about anyone's feelings," I said. "I also wondered why we so quickly found the house in which Maurice Quarlé lived. You led us right to it, and didn't hesitate to choose which of the four upstairs doors was his."

"You're a regular Sherlock Holmes, aren't you, Mrs. Fletcher?"

I ignored his sarcasm and said, "So, here you are. You have the gold you came after, using Kathy to get to it. Now what will you do? Shoot us all?"

"Why would I do that? The three of you can enjoy a few days of solitude in this dump. By the time you get out of here, I'll be long gone to a place where no one would ever think to look for me."

"Where *are* you from?" I asked. "New York? You seemed to know a lot about New York steak houses." I

was still trying to prolong his exit to give me more time
to think the situation through. I hoped the police plane
that Trooper McQuesten had said he would dispatch
would be arriving soon.

"Yup, the Big Apple. That's where Little Mary Sun-
shine and I met and lived until I decided to dump
her."

"The man who went overboard was from New York,
too," I said. "A friend of yours?"

"A friend? That little creep? I figured I needed someone along with me, so I hired him. He was a punk I met
in a bar. I dangled a free cruise in front of him and he
salivated. My mistake for getting involved with him.
He was a bumbler. When I realized that you were traveling with Kathy, I grabbed one of your books off the
ship's library shelf and gave it to him so he'd know
what you look like." He guffawed. "He almost screwed
up everything—and I sure as hell wasn't about to let
that happen."

"So over the side he went," I said.

Howard, aka Bill Henderson, said nothing.

"And what about Mr. Quarlé?" I asked, working to
keep my voice steady. Up until that moment, I knew I
was faced with a slick con man, a handsome guy whose
morals and ethics were in the gutter. But I now knew
that he'd pushed the little man in the blue shorts over
the side of the *Glacial Queen* into Glacier Bay. He was
more than a con man. He was a cold-blooded killer.

"You ask too damn many questions, Mrs. Fletcher,"
he said. "Remember, curiosity killed the cat."

"You weren't with us the morning Quarlé was
killed," I said. "You told Kathy that you worked out

in the gym. I think you got a different form of exercise that morning." I had nothing to base that on, but it was a reasonable possibility.

His reply was nonresponsive. "Look," he said, "let's all be grown-ups about this. You and your buddy there on the floor got a nice cruise out of it. Her flaky sister is alive. All you've lost is a million bucks' worth of gold. None of you need it, but I do. I'll give a little to some charity, if that'll make you feel better."

I started to ask another question, but he cut me off.

"Hey, by the way, don't hold your breath waiting for that dumb trooper to arrive. I didn't talk to him on your phone. I talked to myself. Not bad, huh? Really had you fooled."

No doubt about it—he certainly had fooled me. He'd fooled everyone. He was as effective a con man as he was a despicable human being.

"Howard!"

He turned his attention to Willie, who struggled to remain standing. Kathy was at her side, helping to prop her up.

"Howard, don't do this to me," Willie said, extending a hand in a gesture of pleading. "You can take half the gold. I won't care. But leave some for me. Please."

"Hey, Willie, you don't need gold. There'll always be some sap out there ready to marry an over-the-hill gimpy broad like you. Ciao, baby."

He turned toward the door. As he did, Bobby suddenly appeared. "Thought I'd come see what was—" He spotted the handgun in Howard's hand. "What the hell is goin' on?"

"Get out of my way," Howard told him.

"He's a murderer," Willie said. "He's stealing my gold."

"Move," Howard commanded Borosky, and went to push past him. Borosky shoved his hand against Howard's chest, causing him to stagger back a few feet. I, too, retreated. Kathy came from where she'd been comforting Willie and moved toward the countertop and cabinets.

The sound of the weapon being discharged reverberated throughout the small cabin, causing everyone to flinch. Borosky stood ramrod straight and stared at Howard as though nothing had happened. But then blood the color of cardinals seeped through the shirt at his right shoulder. The leather jacket, which he'd removed and carried in his left hand, slipped from his fingers and landed at his feet. His mouth opened as though to protest what he was feeling. His left hand went to his injured shoulder and blood oozed through his fingers, coming faster now and dripping to the floor. He tried to raise his right hand, but appeared unable to move it, and he groaned against the pain before sinking to his knees.

Kathy, Willie, and I could only gape at the scene playing out before us. Would Howard turn the gun on us now and eliminate us along with the pilot?

Willie was in no physical condition to do anything, and I felt as though my shoes were nailed to the floor. I decided to take a chance and try to disable him with the stun gun. But before I could act, Kathy picked up an unopened can from the counter and flung it at him. Her aim was true. It struck him on the side of the head and knocked him to the floor, the handgun flying from his fingers and coming to rest against a wall. Kathy was a woman possessed. She leapt on top of him, her fists flailing against his face and head, a string of four-letter words erupting from her mouth. She continued to beat him until her knuckles were bloodied and she'd run out of breath. Finally, she picked up the can she'd thrown at him and brought it down on his skull. His body jerked a few times, then became still.

I went to Borosky and knelt next to him. "You'll be all right," I said. "We'll get you to a hospital."

"You'd better get that madman tied up before he goes and shoots somebody else," the pilot growled.

Various rope and leather straps hung from a peg on the wall. With Kathy's help, I secured Howard's hands behind his·back and strapped his ankles tightly together. For good measure, Kathy wrapped a piece of rope around his neck and tied its other end to the restraint on his ankles. Confident that he would be immobile when he came to, she went to the fallen Borosky and used the overblouse she'd worn that day to stem the flow of blood from his shoulder.

"It's broke," he said. "I can't move it."

"You'll be okay," Kathy said. She stood and said to me, "Well, Jessica, what do we do now?"

"From what I've just seen, we can all pile on your back and you can swim us back to Ketchikan."

"I was mad."

"And for good reason. You heard what he said, that he didn't call the police to send a plane. We're going to have to figure out how to get out of here."

"Can't we just radio for help?" Kathy asked. "The plane has a radio."

"Won't work down here on the ground and in these canyons. You've got to have some altitude before you can use it."

"Are you okay to fly?" Kathy asked Borosky, who'd managed to sit up.

He shook his head. "Not with this busted shoulder. No way."

"But *you* can fly the plane, Jess," Kathy said.

We turned to see Wilimena crawling across the floor in the direction of the bag of gold that Howard had dropped. I picked it up and handed it to her; she cradled it to her bosom.

"I'm not sure the gold was worth it, Wilimena," I said.

"What about it?" Kathy asked me. "You can fly us back to Ketchikan."

I turned to Borosky. "Are you well enough to ride in the right seat and tell me what to do?" My concern, of course, was that with his loss of blood, he'd lose consciousness once we were up in the air and leave me without his guidance.

"I think so," he said, grimacing.

"Then that's what we'll do," I said. "I hadn't planned to learn to fly a floatplane so soon, but it looks like my lesson is about to begin."

*And our survival would depend upon it.*

# Chapter Sixteen

Before even thinking about my flying us back to Ketchikan, there was the problem of moving Willie, Howard, and Bob Borosky from the cabin to the plane. Howard had awoken from his can-of-beans-induced sleep and verbally assaulted everyone until Kathy shoved a rag into his mouth and told him that if he tried to say one word, he could count on another can coming his way.

Borosky was capable of walking if he had someone to lean against. His loss of blood had weakened him considerably, and I didn't like his color. His face was ashen, his eyes sunken.

And, of course, there was Wilimena's emaciated condition and her broken leg.

Borosky, who'd collapsed into a rustic chair constructed of tree limbs, called me to his side. "Look, Mrs. Fletcher," he rasped, "we've got a big problem. That front I mentioned is comin' fast. Flying these canyons in the fjords is tough enough in good weather and visibility, but that ain't what we've got. Maybe we'd better sit it out here and wait for morning."

I processed his suggestion. He was right, of course, from a pilot's perspective. But as I looked at him, I seriously doubted that he would last until morning. As hard as we'd tried to control his bleeding, we'd been only partially successful. I also wondered where the bullet was in his body someplace. It hadn't exited; at least I hadn't found it anywhere in the cabin. The weapon was a small-caliber one. That sort of bullet could tumble around internally and travel to one of his vital organs.

"I agree with what you say," I told him, "but I don't think we can wait that long. Kathy's sister needs medical attention—fast. So do you. We'll make it as long as you're able to tell me what to do."

"How many hours have you got in a plane?" he asked.

"Fifty-seven."

"That ain't much."

"It's enough," I assured him.

I turned to where Kathy was sitting on the floor with Willie. "We've got to get moving," I said. "We'll take Willie first and get her settled in the rearmost seat. Then we'll take Mr. Nice and put him where you and he were on the trip here. You can keep an eye on him that way."

Kathy picked up a can of chili and waved it in front of Howard, who for additional security had been tied to the leg of a heavy table. "This comes with me, you creep," she said. His eyes opened wide and he focused on the can. "Got it?"

He nodded. I smiled, and almost applauded. My docile, peaceful friend from Cabot Cove was showing an entirely different side.

"Then," I continued, "we get Mr. Borosky into his right-hand seat. Okay?"

"Let's do it," Kathy said.

We fashioned a crude splint from a board taken from the top of the table and used it to stabilize Willie's mangled leg, which was grotesque to look at—twisted, displaced, and colored in myriad shades of black and purple. We gave Howard's weapon to Borosky to use if Howard tried anything, which was highly unlikely considering the way we'd trussed him up, but better safe than sorry. Between us, Kathy and I successfully got Willie, who held on to her sack of gold, to the plane. Squeezing her into the rear seat while trying to minimize her pain was an almost impossible chore, but we finally succeeded and returned to the cabin to transport Howard back along the same route. Carrying him was a torturous task that left us breathless. After wedging him into his seat and further tying him down, we sat on the dock to regain our energy.

"Why don't you go back and get Mr. Borosky?" I suggested. "I want to get in the plane and acclimate myself."

Kathy looked up into the heavy gray clouds that threatened to engulf us. She grabbed my hand. "Do you really think we'll make it?" she asked.

Had I answered honestly, I would have said, "I don't know." But this was no time for pessimism. I said instead, "Of course we will. Flying this old Beaver can't be that much different from the plane I fly back home. Besides, we have Superwoman with us."

"Superwoman?"

"You." I gave her hand a reassuring squeeze. "And

Mr. Borosky is an old hand at flying in these conditions. Between us, we'll do just fine." I stood and pulled her to her feet. "Go on, now, get him. Every minute counts."

There was a moment right after Borosky had been settled in the right-hand seat when I thought he was about to pass out. But when I asked how he felt, he smiled and said, "Don't you worry about me, lady. You just do what I say and get us home."

"Yes, sir," I said, and gave him a snappy salute.

I did not get off to an auspicious start. I followed his instructions about how to start the engine. That went fine. But then he said, "Might be a good idea if you untie us from the dock before you drag the whole damn thing behind us."

I opened my door, got out, and did as instructed. I remembered the way he'd pushed off with his leg in Ketchikan, and I did the same, but my legs were shorter than his and I had to fairly hang out of the plane to accomplish it.

"Okay," he said, "here's where flyin' a float and a landplane are different. On land, the plane'll sit still unless you make it go. Out on the water, the current and wind'll take it where you don't want to go. Give it some juice."

I advanced the throttle and we began to taxi slowly toward the center of the cove. "That's it," he said. "Pull that yoke back into your gut, lady, and hold it there. That'll keep the nose up. Less spray on the prop."

When we reached the middle of the cove, Borosky told me to position the aircraft facing into the wind. I would have done that even without his advice, knowing from my previous flying experience that you always try to take off and land into the wind.

"Okay," he said, "let's go down the CARS list." He didn't give me a chance to ask what that meant, and started ticking off a list of pre-takeoff procedures—carburetor heat control off, checking the area ahead to make sure it was clear, water rudders up, and the control yoke held back against my stomach: CARS—carb heat, area clear, rudders up, stick back. Borosky had to show me where things were. A floatplane, I quickly learned, had two sets of rudders, one on the rear of the floats for use in the water, and the other on the tail, just as in any airplane.

"You ready to roll, lady?" Borosky asked.

"I'd better be," I said, trying to keep a rapidly developing set of nerves out of my voice.

"All right," Borosky said, "here's what you do. Give her full throttle, hold back that stick, and keep holding it back until you feel that it's stabilized. Then you can relax the yoke and let it go to the neutral position, or maybe even a little forward. You'll feel us start to plane. When you've got enough speed to lift off, I'll tell you."

I have to admit that at that moment, I considered canceling, turning around, heading back to the dock, and huddling in the cabin until we got lucky and someone came upon us—a fisherman or a hunter, or maybe the police once they realized we were gone. But I reminded myself that there was too much at stake. I didn't think Borosky would last through the night, and I had my doubts about Wilimena, too. And, of course, there was the matter of our bound-and-gagged passenger in the seat behind me.

I closed my eyes for a moment, opened them, and advanced the throttle as far as it would go. The idling engine responded immediately and roared to life. As it did, the Beaver started its takeoff run down the length of Walker Cove, picking up speed, but not as quickly as I'd assumed it would. The spray from the front of the floats cascaded over the windshield, making it almost impossible to see. I remembered what I'd been taught when taking flying lessons in Cabot Cove: to use a light touch on the controls and to let the airplane fly itself. Once I did that, I could feel what Borosky had said would happen—the nose of the plane stabilized, followed by the sensation of the floats skimming over the water. The aircraft was becoming lighter.

"That's it," Borosky said into the microphone attached to his headset. "Take her up."

I pulled back on the yoke, just a bit, enough to cause the floats to lift off the water.

We were airborne!

Kathy let out a gleeful yelp, and I exhaled a breath I'd been holding since starting the takeoff roll. Borosky was instrument rated, of course, which meant we could have flown in the clouds had he been at the controls. Because he wasn't, we had to stay beneath the base of the clouds, which were only a thousand feet above us. Altitude, as every pilot knows, can be your best ally in the event of an emergency such as engine failure. I was uncomfortable maintaining our low altitude, but as the flight progressed I became less tense. I had the feel of the plane now, although it took a lot more work to keep it in straight-and-level flight than it did in my trusty rented Cessna back home.

Borosky used his left hand to operate one of the Beaver's radios and reported to the appropriate en route air-traffic-control people. "We've got us some medical emergencies," he barked into his microphone. "A woman who looks like death warmed over and whose leg is pretty badly busted up, and yours truly. Got shot in the shoulder, and it ain't worth much at the moment. Oh, one other thing. We've got us a criminal all wrapped up in the backseat. Request the law be at the dock in Ketchikan when we arrive."

"Trooper McQuesten," I said. "And Detective Flowers."

Borosky added those names to his radioed request.

As we exited the Behm Canal and made a right turn in the direction of Ketchikan, I sensed that Borosky was breathing heavily, actually gasping at times. I glanced over to see him leaning against his door, opening and closing his eyes, and slowly shaking his head.

"You okay?" I asked.

Kathy leaned forward and placed her hand on his neck. "He's getting cold and clammy," she said.

"Great," I muttered under my breath. "Don't fade out on me now, Mr. Borosky."

The radio crackled to life, asking for an update on our position and condition. I pressed the microphone button on the yoke and responded, explaining what was happening in the aircraft and telling them of my limited flying experience. I was told to continue in the direction we were heading and to await further instructions. A few minutes later, a different male voice came through my headset.

"This is Roy Mann," he said. "I'm a floatplane pilot. Sounds like you're doing just fine."

"I was," I replied, "but the injured pilot to my right has started to fade in and out of consciousness. He's been talking me through it up to now. I've never landed a floatplane and—"

Mann interrupted me. "Not to worry. I'll get you down safely. Sounds like Bobby's not doing too good."

"He needs to get to a hospital quickly. So does the female passenger."

"We have two ambulances on the way as we speak. Now, here's what I want you to do—"

Mann's soothing, unflustered voice calmed me, and he guided me every step of the way. I followed his instructions to the letter, leading us down to a smooth landing I didn't think I had any possibility of making. It was difficult controlling the plane because of the current and the winds, but I managed, and soon the Beaver nudged gently against one of many docks in the downtown Ketchikan area. I looked through my window. There must have been a hundred people standing there. Ambulances and police cars, their red emergency lights flashing, created a multicolored kaleidoscope.

I killed the engine, opened my door, and got out on shaky legs, grabbing the wing for support. Kathy followed. A man tied the plane to the dock. Applause broke out. Trooper McQuesten and Detective Flowers, followed by a cadre of uniformed officers, came over to us.

"I have never been so happy to see anyone in my life," I said to McQuesten.

"That goes double for me," Kathy added.

McQuesten looked inside the plane at Howard. "Him?" he said.

"Yes, *him*," I said. "He's a murderer. On top of that, he tried to steal Wilimena Copeland's gold."

McQuesten shook his head. "You'll have to sort this out for me," he said.

"Happy to," I said, "but over a good dinner. I am absolutely starving."

"It'll be my treat," McQuesten said.

Some of his officers removed Howard from the plane and carried him to one of their vehicles. Once that had been accomplished, emergency medical technicians went to work extracting Willie and Borosky from the Beaver and rushing them into the waiting ambulances. Wilimena still clutched the bag of gold, but Kathy gently took it from her as the stretcher passed. "It'll be safer with me," she told her sister, who didn't argue.

Bush pilot Roy Mann joined us.

"We all owe you a large debt of thanks," I said.

"It was my pleasure," he said, laughing. "I felt like I was in one of those Doris Day movies talking down a stewardess flying a 747 after the pilots were killed. Hey, you did great flying Bobby's Beaver. Anytime you want a job flying the bush, give me a call."

"Thanks for the compliment," I said, "but I think I'll stick to writing about murders. It's a lot safer."

I looked over the crowd and saw Gladys Montgomery standing with the Johansens.

"Well, it seems you've been on quite an adventure today," Gladys said in her controlled, patrician voice.

"I'm surprised to see you out here," I said. "You said you seldom leave the ship."

"I wouldn't have missed your arrival for the world," she said. "Word spread so quickly. But I think I will get back on board. I've arranged a special dinner for you and your friend Ms. Copeland. The ship leaves in two hours."

"That's thoughtful of you, Gladys, but I think Kathy and I won't be taking the ship to Vancouver. She'll want to be with her sister at the hospital, and I promised these gentlemen we'd have dinner together on terra firma."

"I understand," she said. "You will stay in touch."

"Of course. How do I reach you?"

"By e-mail, of course. Here's my address. My, how my husband would have enjoyed all this excitement. I certainly have."

I watched her walk away, erect, stately, a woman in command of her surroundings—and of her life. She could count on hearing from me.

The ship's security chief, First Officer Kale, suddenly appeared from out of the crowd.

"Glad to see that you and Ms. Copeland are all right," he said, his face set in its usual somber, weight-of-the-world-on-his-shoulders expression.

"Yes, we're fine," I said. "Ms. Copeland and I won't be sailing with you tonight, though, and we will need assistance getting our belongings off the ship."

"That's awfully short notice," he said. "I don't think that—"

"Officer Kale," I said, "I think you'll be able to manage it just fine. Look at it this way. You won't have us snooping around your ship and disturbing other passengers."

His face brightened.

"Have their luggage taken to police headquarters," Trooper McQuesten told Kale in a tone that left little room for debate. "You'll see that it's done right, I'm sure."

"Yes, of course," Kale said. "I'll have the cabin steward pack everything up and deliver it all to police headquarters."

"Good," said McQuesten.

"And might I offer a word of advice, Officer Kale?" I said.

He stared blankly at me.

"I know that you have your passengers' best interests at heart, but you really should try and be a little more—how shall I say it—?"

"Loosen up," Kathy provided.

"Yes," I said. "Loosen up. Yes, that's it precisely. You should try to loosen up."

Kale walked away. McQuesten said, "Come on. I'll take you to the hospital, get that bag of gold put in a safe place, and find you a nice place to stay." He turned to Kathy. "By the way, Ms. Copeland, do you always walk around with a can of chili in your hand?"

Kathy looked at the can she'd clutched during the entire flight. She blushed, laughed, and handed it to McQuesten. "I'll bet it's pretty good," she said. "Enjoy!"

"Any preferences for dinner?" McQuesten asked. "Aside from chili?"

Kathy and I shook our heads.

"Like moose meat?"

We shook our heads again.

"I didn't think so. I'll make a reservation at Bar Harbor. Best food in Ketchikan as far as I'm concerned. Really fresh seafood."

"Sounds good to me," said Kathy.

I started to laugh.

"What's funny?" Kathy asked.

"I just realized that we can *all* loosen up now. It's over! We found your sister."

"And Aunt Dolly's gold."

"Yes, that, too. Aunt Dolly's gold."

# Chapter Seventeen

Wilimena and Kathy Copeland stood side by side at the entrance to the newly renovated Cabot Cove senior citizen center. Mayor Jim Shevlin and a few other local politicians joined a hundred townspeople at the dedication. The sun shone brightly, and the air was ripe with the first hints of spring.

It had been a year since my Alaskan adventure. While the passage of time had put distance between me and those tumultuous days, the memories were never far from my consciousness.

Kathy had stayed in Ketchikan for six weeks while her sister healed. After two operations on her leg, Willie was cleared to leave the hospital and fly with Kathy back to the East Coast, where she went through months of difficult rehabilitation at a physical therapy center just outside of Cabot Cove. Although the doctors in Alaska and the therapists in Maine had done a splendid job, she would walk with a limp for the rest of her life, and often used a cane. I'm not sure she really needed it, but it gave her a modicum of confidence whenever she ventured out—like on this day in early May.

I'd kept in touch with Trooper McQuesten by phone and through e-mails. Howard Winslow, aka Bill Henderson, had been indicted for the murder of the man who'd gone overboard, whom we knew as John Smith (his real name was Jerry Quincy). He'd also been charged in the murder of Maurice Quarlé, although McQuesten told me that the evidence in that case was weak. And, of course, there was an indictment for attempted armed robbery of Wilimena's gold. A trial was set to begin any day in Juneau.

I'd also had communication with Bobby Borosky, our crusty pilot who'd been wounded by Howard Winslow. A doctor told me that it had been touch and go for a couple of days. Borosky had lost a considerable amount of blood and had gone into shock; they'd twice given him last rites. But he'd eventually pulled through. However, the damage to his right shoulder was extensive, and the best he could hope for was minimal use of it—not a good thing for a bush pilot. Wilimena had used a portion of the money generated by the gold to pay all his medical expenses and to set up a fund to supplement the disability payments he would draw for the rest of his life. I had nothing but fond memories of the man, and of my impromptu flying lesson in his vintage DeHavilland Beaver.

Speaking of fond memories—I corresponded with Gladys Montgomery for the first three months after I'd returned to Cabot Cove. Her e-mails were witty and profound. Although I doubted whether we would ever see each other again, I felt close to her and was greatly saddened when, after not hearing from her for a month, I received an e-mail from a daughter informing me that her mother had succumbed to a massive heart attack while on the *Glacial Queen*. I was glad it had happened aboard the ship. It was what she would have wanted.

"Ready?" Mayor Shevlin asked Wilimena.

"I think so," she said.

"Then go ahead and cut it!"

Wilimena used an oversized ceremonial pair of scissors to cut the yellow ribbon stretched across the senior center's doorway. As the two ends of the ribbon fluttered to the ground, a loud, sustained round of applause erupted, causing Willie to wave a hand back and forth. "No, no," she said, grabbing her sister's hand and raising it into the air like a prizefighter who'd just defeated an opponent in the ring. "If it wasn't for my courageous big sister," she shouted to the crowd, "none of this would have been possible."

I stood to the side with Seth Hazlitt, Mort Metzger and his wife, the mayor's wife, Susan, and Kathy's attorney, Michael Cunniff.

"It's a wonderful thing Wilimena and Kathy have done," Mort said.

"Very generous," said Seth. "Sets a good example for our youngsters."

"And benefits our seniors," Susan said.

Wilimena's gold had been converted into a sizable amount of cash, almost a million dollars. She'd followed through on her promises to some of the *Glacial Queen*'s crew members to send them gifts once she'd found the gold. While undergoing rehab for her leg, she'd asked me what Kathy and she might do to benefit the community. She'd decided to settle in Cabot

Cove to be near her sister and had purchased a small condominium in a new complex that had been built on Lake Cabot.

"I think just having you two live here is good enough," I said.

"No," she said. "We want to do something tangible for Cabot Cove. What's needed? We have all this money and—well, frankly, I won't be needing most of my half. My globe-trotting days are over. I've lived a fool's life for far too long. All I want to do is settle down here and be—what should I say?—settle down here and be *normal*."

A week later, I brought up her question at a meeting of the town planning commission. Its members suggested that an abandoned office building be renovated and converted into a much-needed new senior center, and that's what was done, thanks to Wilimena and Kathy's generosity. The Copeland Senior Center was now open for business.

Following the opening ceremony, a luncheon was held to celebrate the new addition to our growing town.

"Maybe it should have been named Aunt Dolly's Senior Center," Willie quipped to those at the head table.

"I still say it should have had your name on it," Kathy said.

"It does," Willie said. "Copeland. You and me, Kathy." She gave her older sister a hug. "I've been such a fool."

"No, you haven't," Kathy said. "You've lived your life the way you wanted to live it. I admire that. Don't you, Jessica?"

I had to laugh. "I admire the fact that you survived it," I said. "I had my doubts about that until we found you in that cabin."

We all went our separate ways after lunch. Seth drove me home. I pulled the day's mail out of my mailbox and went inside to peruse it. One envelope caught my eye. It was from my publisher in New York City. Inside was a smaller envelope that had been addressed to Buckley House. It was handwritten, with a Seattle, Washington, postmark. I opened it and removed a note written in neat, precise handwriting.

*Dear Mrs. Fletcher: I hope you get this. I write from a psychiatric hospital outside of Seattle. You may remember me. I was the one who accused you of stealing my book idea and attacked you at the Seattle Mystery Bookshop. They gave me permission to write this note to you because they thought it should be part of my treatment, acknowledging my behavior and asking forgiveness. I am doing well, and hope you are, too. I use my time here to write a novel of my own. When I finish, I would like to send it to you. I am sorry for what I did.*

*Sincerely,*
*Walter Munro*

It was good of him to write, I thought as I sat in a recliner, extended my legs, and closed my eyes. Mr. Munro's note reminded me that I was due to submit an outline for my next novel to Vaughan Buckley, my publisher. Maybe I could use a historical setting in Alaska. Maybe it could take place at Dolly Arthur's bordello.

Maybe I could pattern a character after Bobby Borosky and use Trooper McQuesten as inspiration for my cop hero. Maybe . . . maybe . . .

My final thought before drifting off was—*it's good to be home.*

Read on for an exciting sneak
peek at the next
*Murder, She Wrote* original mystery,

## Murder on Parade

Available now from Obsidian

"By the Old Lord Harry, it seems to get hotter every day, and no relief in sight."

Seth Hazlitt wasn't exaggerating. A front had stalled just off the coast, trapping a flow of hot, humid air coming from the southwest and turning Cabot Cove into a sticky, steamy mess. The temperature had broken records from as far back as they'd been kept, and the forecast for the next several days was more of the same. You couldn't help but notice a discernible rise in tempers as people slowly moved through their days, perspiration dripping down their necks, eyes stinging from the polluted, stagnant, greenish air, seeking out any place that had a high-efficiency air conditioner. Fortunately, Mara's Luncheonette, where I sat with Seth and Sheriff Mort Metzger, had an AC that kept up with the heat.

I'd met them for breakfast that morning to discuss the upcoming Fourth of July weekend celebration. As a physician, Seth was concerned with the well-being of citizens who might overdo things in the heat. "Folks don't realize how heatstroke can sneak up on you," he said, motioning for Mara to refill his coffee cup. "Too many damn fools go runnin' around in this weather, and before they know it, they're in the emergency room bein' treated."

Mort agreed. "The mayor's got us putting up notices around town warning people to take it easy until this heat wave breaks, but it doesn't look like it will until after the Fourth."

"I've heard people suggest we cancel some of the events," I offered.

"Hard to do that, Mrs. F," said Mort. "You know how folks around here feel about Independence Day. They take it real serious."

"Like the rest of the nation," I said, "and rightly so."

Mara brought a pot of coffee to the table and filled Mort's and Seth's cups. "More tea, Jessica?" she asked me.

"I don't have time," I said, "but thanks, anyway."

"What's your rush, Mrs. F?" Mort asked.

"Errands, and some correspondence to catch up on. I've been like everyone else these past few days, moving in slow motion."

"Best way to be," Seth advised.

"But not much gets done," I said.

I reached for my purse, but Seth waved me off. "My treat, Jessica," he said.

"Well, thank you, sir," I said, and prepared to leave. But Mort stopped me with, "Look who's here."

Coming through the door was Amos Tupper, Cabot Cove's former sheriff. After Amos retired, he moved to Kentucky to be near family. Mort, who'd been a police officer in New York City, replaced Amos and took up residence in Cabot Cove with his wife. I loved Amos, and still do, but I had to admit—not for public consumption, though—that the efficiency of our police department had improved since Mort arrived, bringing with him his New York street smarts. Cabot Cove had grown considerably, and with that growth had come a predictable increase in crime. Nothing major for the most part, thank goodness, but challenging enough to warrant a more—how shall I say it?—a more energetic approach to the job of keeping the town's citizens safe and happy.

"Hello, there, Amos," Seth said, struggling to get up from his chair, which was wedged against the wall.

"No need to get up for me," Amos said, coming to our table and shaking everyone's hand. He plopped down in the vacant seat next to me.

"We heard you were coming," said Seth. "Just wish you'd brought better weather with you."

"It is hot," Amos confirmed, wiping his brow with a handkerchief. "You must be breaking all sorts a' records."

"Ayuh," Seth said. "That we are."

"How are things with you, Mort?" Amos asked.

"Not bad, Amos. Got things pretty much under control. Getting ready for the Fourth."

Amos ordered a short stack of Mara's signature blueberry pancakes and coffee. "I had trouble finding a place to stay," he said to no one in particular. "Looks like Cabot Cove's Fourth of July celebration is attracting more people than ever."

Seth, Mort, and I looked at each other.

Amos was right. While our annual Fourth of July weekend was always a major event in Cabot Cove, this year promised to be the biggest yet. But not everyone was pleased with that. Past celebrations had always been festive but manageable in size and scope. This year was decidedly different, thanks to Joseph Lennon and his corporation, Lennon-Diversified, Ltd.

Lennon had moved his corporate headquarters from Massachusetts to Cabot Cove a year ago, wooed in part by a generous tax incentive designed to entice companies to relocate to Maine. He'd purchased the area's biggest building in our largest industrial park and expanded it to a size that had become a source of consternation for many citizens. The park itself was situated on a prime parcel of waterfront land. Originally, the property was to be turned into a multiuse area, with light industry and residential units coexisting side by side. But Lennon and his battery of lawyers managed to get the zoning law changed, allowing Lennon to conscript a large portion of the land directly on the water for his expansion plans. The rear of his building sloped down to the water's edge, where he added a promenade and dock for his employees' enjoyment. It was off-limits to others. Next to the building was a spacious grassy area that also went down to the water. Lennon designated it as a public park, which took the edge off his land grab at the rear of his building.

He hadn't created as many new jobs as had been expected. That was bad. On the other hand, he'd lowered the tax base. That was good. And he was a generous contributor to the town's various social and civic organizations, another plus for him and his company.

But there was a cost for his generosity. He'd injected himself into every aspect of our lives, using his clout as a major taxpayer, and his wealth, to influence countless decisions that otherwise would have been made by town leaders. Our Fourth of July celebration was a prime example of Lennon's looming presence and overbearing personality and tactics.

In previous years, we'd been perfectly content to have a small fireworks display, provided by a company in Bangor. Nothing special, but just right for a town the size of Cabot Cove. This year Lennon had persuaded our town leaders that we should set an example for the rest of Maine by presenting a pyrotechnics display to rival the famed New York and Washington spectaculars. Any arguments against it fell by the wayside when Lennon agreed to foot the bill and to make all the arrangements. He contacted Grucci, the world's most famous fireworks display company, and booked a twenty-five-minute show that cost seventy-five thousand dollars. Grucci had provided fireworks displays for many presidential inaugurations and for myriad Olympics. "Grucci is the best," Lennon announced in a press release after the deal had been made. "It's time Cabot Cove awoke from its slumber and joined the big time."

Lennon hadn't stopped with the elaborate fireworks display. Because he was the major tenant in the industrial park, he'd co-opted it for the Fourth as a site for a rock-and-roll concert to take place before the fireworks. And he'd used his influence with state officials to arrange for a flyover of F-16s from the Maine Air National Guard base. No doubt about it. The man thought big.

But Cabot Cove in "the big time?"

That didn't sit well with a number of people in town, although there was another contingent that welcomed this infusion of energy backed by big money. Seth Hazlitt was firmly in the camp taking the position that Cabot Cove should preserve its roots as a smaller community whose growth was steady and controlled. Mort seemed ambivalent, which reflected his position as the sheriff, who wasn't supposed to take sides in such debates. As for me, I accepted Mr. Lennon's right to spend his money any way he wished, as long as it wasn't used for negative purposes. What *did* bother me was a series of rumors about the man's personal life and business activities that were less than complimentary. But I kept in mind that they were, after all, just rumors.

"How's the family?" Mort asked Amos.

"Doin' well, Mort. I like it down there. Got a bunch of hobbies. It's nice to come back to Cabot Cove, though. Can't believe how much the town has grown." He waved to Barney Longshoot, who was sitting at the counter.

"Well," Seth said, "time for me to be going. I've got a full day of seein' patients."

After promising to catch up with Amos later in the day, Seth and I walked toward the door. We'd almost reached it when it opened and in walked Dr. Warren Boyle.

"Good morning, Doctor," Seth said as the handsome young physician stepped aside to allow us to leave.

"Good morning, Doc," Boyle said. "Mrs. Fletcher."

"Hello, Dr. Boyle."

"I think I lost a few pounds just walking over here," Boyle said, flashing a boyish grin. "I thought Maine wasn't supposed to ever get this hot."

"You shouldn't believe everything you read," Seth said, the edge to his voice telling me that he wasn't making small talk.

"Good advice, Doc," said Boyle. "You tell your patients that?"

"Most of them know it without me having to tell them. Have a good day, sir."

"You, too," Boyle replied. "Stay cool, Mrs. Fletcher."

Seth and I stepped outside into what felt like a sauna.

"Arrogant young fella, isn't he?" Seth muttered.

"More self-assured than arrogant," I suggested.

"All the same to me. Drive you someplace?"

"Home, if you don't mind."

Like many residents of Maine, I had never considered air-conditioning a necessity. Sure, there were bound to be some days during the summer that became uncomfortably hot, but strategically placed fans usually did the trick. We'd had an unusually warm summer a few years ago, though, which prompted me to purchase two window air conditioners for my home on Candlewood Lane, one for the kitchen, the other for my study, where I do my writing. I wouldn't have bothered had I not been a writer and someone who enjoys cooking. I function just fine in hot weather as long as what I'm doing doesn't involve thinking. But my kitchen and my writing room had become uncomfortable that summer, and I found myself focusing more on how hot I was than on the dishes I was creating or the words I was putting on the page.

As Seth drove up Main Street from the harbor, the air coming in the open windows of the car thickened. Away from the waterfront breezes, it gathered heat from the buildings and pavement and pressed down upon us like a flatiron. Seth switched on the air-conditioning and in tandem we closed our windows, eager to escape the blistering temperature. Cocooned in the cooling space, I thought about what had transpired at Mara's that morning.

It was good to see Amos Tupper again, and I was glad he would be in Cabot Cove through the Fourth of July weekend. He and Mort Metzger seemed to get along nicely, although there was bound to be some tension between them. I think Amos was envious of Mort's more modern approach to solving crimes, and Mort probably wished he was viewed as warmly as Amos had always been. No matter. They were both good men, and I counted my friendship with them among my blessings.

The growth of Cabot Cove had taken many directions, including an influx of new physicians, some of them Maine natives looking to set up practice, others emigrating from larger cities in search of a less stressful lifestyle. It wasn't long ago that Cabot Cove's citizens had to travel to larger cities like Boston, Bangor, and New York when in need of a specialist. That certainly had changed. We now had a good representation of specialists in our area, and they were welcomed by everyone, including old-time doctors like Seth Hazlitt.

Seth pulled up in front of my house, turned the ignition to off, and faced me. I patted his hand. "Thanks for the lift. Don't forget dinner at my house tonight."

"Wouldn't miss it, Jessica, not with lobster salad on the menu."

Seth turned his car around, and I waved as he drove away. I felt a certain sadness. *Oh, well,* I thought as I pulled mail from my mailbox and carried it inside. The first piece I opened was a mailing from the Boyle Medical Center announcing that a dermatologist from Boston would soon be joining the practice, offering a full array of beauty treatments, including Botox injections and skin abrasion "for a lovelier you."

I sighed and tossed the mailing in a wastebasket. Yes, Cabot Cove was growing. No doubt about that. The question was whether everything connected with that growth was for the better.

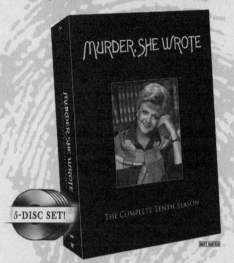

# MURDER, SHE WROTE:
## *Murder on Parade*

by Jessica Fletcher & Donald Bain
Based on the Universal television series
Created by Peter S. Fischer,
Richard Levinson & William Link

Every Fourth of July, the town of Cabot Cove
hosts an elaborate celebration—and no one is
more enthusiastic than the town's newest
resident, corporate mogul Joseph Lennon.
He's desperate to give the town an unwanted
21st-century makeover, including financing a
fireworks extravaganza to rival New York City's.

But when Lennon's lifeless body is found
floating in the water outside his office,
Jessica Fletcher has no choice but to investigate
her fellow Cabot Cove citizens to find out if
one of them is capable of murder...

# FROM THE MYSTERY SERIES
# MURDER,
# SHE WROTE
## by Jessica Fletcher & Donald Bain

Based on the Universal television series
Created by Peter S. Fischer, Richard Levinson & William Link

Available wherever books are sold or at
penguin.com